A ROOF OVER THEIR HEADS

CARMEN KLASSEN

ETA Publishing Ltd

CONTENTS

ALSO BY CARMEN KLASSEN

SUCCESS ON HER TERMS SERIES

Book 1: Sweet, Smart, and Struggling

Book 2: The Cost of Caring

Book 3: Life Upcycled

Book 4: Heartwarming Designs

Book 5: A Roof Over Their Heads

Success on Her Terms: Boxed Set 1 to 3

———

NON-FICTION TITLES

Love Your Clutter Away

Before Your Parents Move In

CHAPTER ONE

Carrie

Carrie sat at the table in her friend's house, her cup of coffee forgotten in front of her.

"So... let me try to get this straight." She looked at Jaz who was practically bouncing in her chair. "Your business is doing so good you have extra money." Jaz nodded, beaming.

"And you," she turned to Maria in her wheelchair, "you have some friends who need a different place to live..."

"Lovely people—and not only a different place, but a safe and affordable place," Maria added.

Carrie turned to Lisa, "And you've done the math, and think this is possible?"

"Well, we've got monthly costs covered for a large house, yes. An apartment would be a bigger challenge. Not impossible though," she quickly added.

"I just can't... I mean, I'm all for helping people, you know that. But what you're suggesting is so..."

"Don't say impossible!" Jaz warned. "You'll get Lisa going all over again if you use that word!"

"What other word is there?"

"I like bizarre. Ridiculous is good too. And definitely use amazing—that works perfectly," Maria offered with a grin.

Carrie looked at the three women around the table. It was Lisa's house, but her mom Maria lived with her, as well as Jaz and her baby Alex who was now making happy noises from his blanket on the floor nearby. Had it been just nine months since she had dropped off a shy, pregnant Jaz to live with her quiet, hard-working friend and her mother? She laughed, "What *happened* to you people?"

"It's not fair that people are trapped living somewhere they're super unhappy, because they don't have a better, affordable solution for housing," Jaz explained earnestly. "We know people that need a solution right now. And since we *can* do something about it, we should."

"I don't disagree with you. But what you're suggesting is so *big*. You want to buy a property—somehow—fix it up to suit your tenants, and then fill it with people. And you don't want to go through a charity or set up your own charity to do this, right?"

"Right. There are some great charities out there already. But we want to make whatever decision is the right one on our own, without a board of directors or anything. And besides, some people use charities to make themselves look good when they donate, and they don't actually care about the charity at all! That's why we want to do it ourselves. We can help a lot of people this way!"

"But Jaz, you've got your baby to think of, and your future with him. That's going to cost more and more money. And you're raising him on your own without another income. How can you take care of him and set yourself up for a secure future if you're giving away all your money?"

Looking at the other ladies, Carrie realized she was raising her voice. She tried to change her tone.

"It's a wonderful thing you want to do. But all of you have had so much hardship for the last few years. Those needs will always be there, and you need to meet your own needs first."

"Mom and I went to Mexico for Christmas two years ago," Lisa reminded her. "That was definitely us taking care of ourselves! And now that I don't have my nine-to-five job, I have a lot more time— maybe too much time. Even with doing the bookkeeping for the Jazzy Clothing Company and my freelance clients!"

"And I *am* taking care of Alex. He'll always be the best dressed boy in town," Jaz giggled. "Not that that's the most important. Plus, I'm getting together with your friend Jenny next week. She's going to help me with some financial planning so I don't miss anything. I've added a new line of clothing for the Jazzy Clothing Company that's doing *really* well. And it's time for me to do for someone else what you've done for me!"

Carrie didn't have an answer to that. Jaz had literally ended up on her doorstep last July, pregnant and terrified after her parents kicked her out of their house. Taking her in turned out to be good for everyone. Jaz was inspired by Carrie's own business upcycling frames and art and started to upcycle clothes she bought from thrift stores.

With Jaz's confidence growing, she moved from Carrie's place to live with Lisa and Maria—a daughter and mother team with their own story of healing and transformation. Thanks to Maria's unconditional love and support and Lisa's bookkeeping expertise, Jaz quickly grew her clothing business into a successful enterprise with other women doing much of the sewing for her on contracts.

The birth of her son Alex in February transformed her into a happy, driven new mom. Recently, her parents had come back into her life and she was rebuilding a relationship with them after almost a year apart.

Carrie wished all three of them would enjoy their good fortune and their happy lives without trying to do anything more or challenge themselves further. It was the end of her first week of practicum after graduating with her master's in counseling psychology and she was worn out and discouraged. There were so many people with overwhelming problems out there. All she wanted right now was to relax with people who were doing OK and didn't want a fresh new challenge.

"Oh my goodness!" Maria's voice jostled Carrie's thoughts. "We didn't even ask how your first week went! We've been so excited to talk to you about this we jumped right in. How has it been!"

Carrie blinked for a few seconds. It was like Maria was reading her thoughts. She took a deep breath and forced herself to smile, "Oh, it's been quite, uh, interesting. Lots of opportunities to work through everything I've tried to learn in the last few years."

"All those people are so lucky to have you working with them!" Jaz added enthusiastically. "I mean, you're the best, right? So you'll have them all happy and on their way in no time!"

Carrie smiled at Jaz, "Thanks! Oh, and thanks again for the new clothes you made for the party." Now her smile turned genuine. "I'm so glad I was wearing that dress when Jonathan proposed! My mom sent me some pictures she printed from that night, and we all looked good thanks to you!"

"Any word on a date for the wedding?"

"We're thinking of right after my practicum ends. Probably early November."

Jaz sighed, "It was such a romantic thing to do. Get your parents to come, get Jenny's parents to come, have us all there..."

"It's a good thing I was so busy with school at the end or I would've clued in that he was up to something. He even had Matthew in on it! I missed all the planning!"

"You did get the important bit!" Lisa reminded her.

Carrie smiled her acknowledgment. "So Lisa, how are you enjoying your new self-employed world?"

"It's only been a few weeks, but I'm loving it. Doing the books for Jaz's company involves a lot more time with people which is a nice change from sitting at a desk in front of a computer all day. And I'm taking on some really interesting new freelance clients. It's nice to get up in the morning and look forward to working again!"

"And Maria, how's your health?" Maria was diagnosed with rheumatoid arthritis two years ago, but had probably been living with it for much longer. Her late husband had kept her strictly under his control, and only after his sudden death was she able to get proper medical care.

"Well, I have good days and bad days. It helps to have Jaz and Lisa at home right now so I don't have to go out and pick up Becky from the bus stop." She looked down at her foot, which was in a cast. "I still feel so silly for thinking I didn't need my walker that day I fell and broke my ankle. But at least it turned out for the best!"

In a beautiful turn of events, Maria had met Jaz's mom at the hospital when she went for x-rays. She convinced her to give Jaz another chance, and slowly Jaz's parents were coming to accept not only their grandson, but also that their daughter was choosing her own path in life.

"Things are going OK with your parents then Jaz?"

"Well," Jaz hesitated, "it's not perfect. They're having a hard time believing I can make a living sewing and that I won't be going to university. But whenever they start getting upset about it, I shove Alex at one of them. It's hard to tell me I'm doing the wrong thing when he's smiling at them!"

Just then the door to the downstairs suite opened, and Carrie's children Matthew and Katie came in, followed by their friend Becky who lived downstairs with her parents. Carrie smiled. Matthew had worked hard to befriend Becky, and even though she didn't talk, she clearly considered him a friend now. And enthusiastic Katie was happy for any new experience or friend. They had gone downstairs to the suite Becky shared with her parents as soon as they arrived. Carrie guessed that

Carla, Becky's mom would be up shortly. All three kids made a beeline for baby Alex, who was working hard to roll over on the playmat in the living room that opened to the kitchen.

Becky came over after a minute to stand beside Maria. She gently touched the cast before touching Maria's face. "Yes, yes. I hurt myself. But I'll be OK. You go play with your friends." Maria said gently. Becky responded by putting her fingers to her mouth. "No honey, no cookies." With a sigh, she turned and went back to her friends.

Carrie was surprised. "Is the sign language new?"

"They've been working on it with her for a while, and she's starting to catch on. It's been quite exciting!"

Becky's mom Carla knocked on the door from the basement and came in. "Hello ladies! Sorry I'm late to join you. I got stuck on the phone." She came and sat at the table. "So what did I miss?"

"Well, I think we took Carrie entirely by surprise with our idea!" Maria seemed to be the most vocal spokeswoman for the group.

"Chris is totally on board," Carla added. "We both are. Whatever you need as far as renovations and adaptations. And he can be on call for any maintenance issues. Our new business will be official in a few weeks, and it's a great chance for us to be a part of something bigger right at the start!"

Chris and Carla were in the process of re-starting the home renovation business they had closed during the downturn.

Carrie tried again to change the topic, "Jonathan says you bought a fixer-upper?"

"Yep! It is literally the worst house for miles around! We're super excited to be back to renovating! Hopefully, by September we'll be ready to move in, and the house will be a great advertisement for what we can do. And we totally have your Jonathan to thank for going in with Chris on the house flips those guys did. I mean, that bumped our plan forward by years!"

"I'm so happy for you guys!" She turned to Lisa. "So that will mean new tenants for you downstairs?"

"Yes and no. Jaz suggested she could move down there, but we're not sure we want Alex to be so far away from us!"

Jaz rolled her eyes in true teenage fashion. She had grown up quickly in the past year, but she *was* still only nineteen. "Please. You'll be happy not to have my stuff all over the place! Oh! That reminds me! I can return your sewing machine, Carrie. My parents brought over ma ma's machine last week, so I'm using that now."

Jaz had spent years learning from her grandma who was a seamstress. Carrie knew it was a big deal for her to continue that legacy. "Aw, that's wonderful. And I may even have time to do some sewing myself soon! But speaking of sewing... any chance you could come up with something for me to wear to get married in?"

"What?!" Jaz's mouth dropped open. "No way! You want *me* to make your wedding dress?"

"Definitely. You are the only person for the job. And I want it upcycled from whatever you find."

"Oh!" she resumed her bouncing in the chair. "I'm so excited! Yes! Definitely! I'd love to make your dress!"

Carrie got up and hugged her. "Thank you! And on that happy note, it's time to get going. Matthew, Katie, say your goodbyes please."

Driving home Carrie thought about the ladies' ideas for creating housing. Not that it was a bad idea—it was a great idea. But the one thing Carrie had learned in her first week of practicum as a counseling psychologist was that people were really hard to help. She sighed deeply, and Matthew leaned forward from the back seat.

"Mom? Are you OK?"

Tears pricked the back of her eyes. Trust her 12-year-old to pick up on her worries. "Of course, bud!" She put back on the false smile that she had used all week.

CHAPTER TWO

Maria

"Well, what do you think about becoming a wedding dress designer?"

Jaz beamed. "It's so exciting! I'm already getting ideas. She needs something magical. You know, her first wedding dress wasn't at all what she wanted, she just went for something her parents could afford. *And* her first marriage was a train wreck with that jerk." She shuddered, remembering the one time she had encountered Carrie's ex-husband when he got out of jail. "So now that she's got a super-nice, super-hot husband-to-be, the dress needs to go all out."

Maria smiled. "Maybe it's the start of more weddings?"

Jaz and Lisa looked at each other. "Not a chance!" they responded in unison.

"Ah well, a mom can always try! I'm going to lay down for a bit. I'll be back out before supper." The broken ankle seemed to cause all of her joints to ache more than usual, but Maria kept that to herself. Nobody needed to hear bad news.

She wheeled past the kitchen and into her bedroom located just off the front entrance. Lisa had done a perfect job of renovating the house to be wheelchair accessible. Maria could go anywhere on the main floor with ease, and she had her own bathroom that she could use independently most of the time. She went there now, knowing that it would be difficult to get up again for a few hours.

After transferring herself onto the toilet, and then back to the wheelchair, and then over to her bed, Maria was exhausted and in agony. She set a timer on her phone for 45 minutes, took some pain pills, put her wrist splints on, and lay back with a sigh of relief.

Thank goodness for Jaz, she thought. Before the very pregnant teenager joined their household, Maria had been struggling to stay cheerful. Although her afternoons were full for a few hours with watching Becky until her dad came home from work, the rest of the day dragged on painfully. Without being able to do things like cook, clean, or go out and get groceries, she spent most of her time watching TV or looking out the window waiting for Lisa to come home. Being in constant pain at the same time made the seconds feel like hours.

Now Maria still experienced pain and exhaustion but her days had a purpose. Her official title was Executive Assistant to Jasmine Lee, owner of the Jazzy Clothing Company Inc. But Maria secretly thought of herself as the company Mom. She loved taking care of all the little things so her girls could lead happy, fulfilling lives. Granted, Jaz was only her daughter in spirit, but oh what a spirit that girl had!

Her mind wandered back to her own transition into adulthood. A much younger Maria had gone from high school to six months working as a secretary at the factory in town, to being married. Although her family cautioned her against marrying so young—and so quickly—Maria naively believed she was in love and everything would be perfect.

Robert quickly quashed all those ideas, insisting she quit her job, cutting her off from friends and family, and tightly controlling her life. Baby Lisa's arrival was a blessing and a curse. It was a dream to finally have someone to fill her days with, but when Robert thought Lisa was becoming too attached to Maria, he threatened to take her away.

Maria lived in daily fear of losing the one thing she loved more than anything. She withdrew from Lisa to appease Robert and by the time their only daughter was old enough to leave home, she ran from her family and never looked back. Fortunately, Lisa made sure her mom still knew how to get in contact with her.

When Robert suddenly died, Maria called the only person left in her life—Lisa. For reasons she would never understand, Lisa came home, sorted out a lifetime of lies from her dad that left her mom penniless and homeless, and brought Maria back to the city to live with her.

Now they lived in a beautiful home, they spent every day talking to each other, and Lisa's hard work and careful financial management ensured that Maria would never go without anything they needed. But Maria had continued to long for something more. She wanted to do something meaningful, not just sit around and wait for Lisa to come home from work.

When Chris, Carla, and Becky moved into the downstairs suite, Maria had jumped at the chance to help. Getting paid to watch Becky after school gave her the first chance in almost 25 years to earn some money. Then she also took over handling the Airbnb bookings for the upstairs bedroom that Lisa rented out. It gave her another small chance to connect with other people, and Lisa shared the Airbnb profits with her. But after Maria learned how to manage the bookings, the challenge passed.

Jaz claimed that Lisa and Maria had done *her* the favor of giving her a home where she could raise Alex and grow her business. But Maria knew she was the biggest beneficiary. With help from Jaz, she learned how to respond to all the messages from people wanting to try on the clothes that Jaz created along with her team of seamstresses. Jaz's unique brand of upcycled clothes that came from thrift stores was taking the city by storm, and her one-of-a-kind pieces were incredibly popular.

Maria spent hours every day messaging interested clients, setting up appointments for them, managing Jaz's Instagram page where most of her business came from, and coordinating the five ladies who did the bulk of the sewing. When she was feeling up to it, she also watched Alex so Jaz could do her own sewing.

Every day was interesting, different, and filled with people coming and going from the house, and Maria was in her glory. Thanks to Lisa always taking care of meals and Carla doing the housecleaning, Maria could 'save' her hands for the work she did for Jaz at her computer. She typed slowly and was careful not to do too much without a little break, but she could still take care of it all herself—at least for now.

When the timer went, she adjusted the pillows to support sitting up, and then pulled over the hospital-style bedside tray she kept close. On it was her laptop, a novel, and her water bottle. The essentials for someone who spent a lot of time resting in bed.

Logging into Jaz's account she was pleased to see how well the online ordering was going. Tomorrow morning Jaz would bring down the items for shipping and Maria would take care of printing out all the labels. In the evening Carla packed everything up and then dropped it off at the post office the next day. It was a system where they all got to take pleasure in seeing the business succeed—and get paid for doing it!

Maria responded to the requests for in-person visits to see Jaz's clothes and began to fill in the appointment calendar as responses came back in. She loved meeting all the different ladies who came to try on Jaz's clothes. There was even a husband who came after seeing his wife's Instagram feed, and he left with three stylish maternity outfits to surprise her with.

And now Jaz was pushing them to do the next great thing. She was making more than enough money to support herself and four-month-old Alex and she wanted to use the excess to help others. Jaz grew up in a privileged, sheltered home with parents who long ago decided what their only daughter would do with her life. An unexpected pregnancy changed everything, and they kicked her out.

In less than a year Jaz learned to stand on her own feet, pay attention to the real world around her, follow her dream of designing clothes, and even begin to forgive her parents. Now Jaz wanted to make sure that everyone who needed to leave a bad home situation could do so. But this new plan of hers left Maria secretly wondering if she was taking on too much.

One of her seamstresses was a 60-something-year-old woman named Susan who had to move in with her daughter and son-in-law when her husband left her. Susan had been trying to move out since January but her kids weren't willing to give up their free cook, cleaner, and child-minder. Jaz was certain that if Susan had a safe, affordable option she'd be able to leave and start a new life.

Maria knew that leaving a bad relationship wasn't always as easy as Jaz seemed to think it was, but she wanted to believe that with Carrie helping them, they really could make a difference for people.

Carrie was like a human relations magician in Maria's eyes. Her ability to understand where people were coming from and empower them to find and follow their own paths was nothing short of amazing. Whatever reservations Maria might have about Jaz's plans, she knew Carrie could fix them.

Her tasks done for the time being, Maria adjusted her pillows again and laid back against them. It seemed like each month it got a little harder to do everything. She tried not to imagine what the future might be like if she had to go back to a life of sitting and waiting for things to happen.

CHAPTER THREE

Jaz

After saying goodbye to Carrie and the kids, Jaz sat on the floor beside Alex. He grunted and pulled up his shoulder and leg, trying to reach towards her. Other moms told her to enjoy the time while he couldn't go anywhere other than where she put him, but Jaz couldn't wait for him to cross his next milestone. Now that her parents were slowly coming back into her life she loved sharing everything about Alex with them.

"Hey little man! How about some Mommy time before you need a nap?"

Alex looked up at her with bright eyes and smiled. Jaz put his favorite toy just out of reach and watched him work to roll over. After a few tries, she moved it close enough for him to grab and he squealed in delight over his accomplishment. Today Jaz had dressed him in a short-sleeve navy onesie that she had added a little blue and white checkered bow tie and mock suspenders to. She paired it with plaid shorts, white socks, and little brown slippers that looked like leather loafers. Every day was dress up with him, and she loved it.

Jaz's personal style was much more understated than her son's. She stuck to black and white outfits and only added color with bright earrings. All her trips to thrift stores had yielded a unique collection of earrings, most of them vintage.

Her white t-shirt had one of her new designs—the Chinese characters for 'success' cut-out with a black backing. There was a huge demand for the ethnic-themed t-shirts, and Jaz had already done ones with Greek, Arabic, and Chinese words that sold out every time she listed another one. It had also gained her a more international following, and they were selling almost double the online orders that they had two months ago.

Lisa and Jaz worked together to determine the best price to sell the t-shirts, and even though Lisa's suggested price of $55 seemed high to Jaz, they were still selling. She was so grateful Lisa was available to help with the business every day. It was overwhelming to suddenly be the owner of a business that was clearing thousands of dollars a month, and Jaz counted on Lisa to help her make the best decisions.

When Alex started to fuss, she picked him up and brought him upstairs. Laying him down in his crib she rubbed his tummy and talked to him quietly. "I'm the luckiest mommy in the world, aren't I? Who knew something so good could happen from one silly night, hey? And when you're older I'm gonna be happy as long as you're happy, aren't I?"

As she spoke, she watched his eyelids flutter, and stay closed for longer and longer until his breathing softened and he was fast asleep. She knew she was lucky. Her friend Lauren's daughter Brittany still screamed herself to sleep every night. She stayed to watch him sleep for a few minutes.

With every passing week, his features seemed to become a tiny bit more like the guy she had slept with. It was only a matter of time before her parents realized he looked just like their best friend's son Ellison. She wondered what they'd do then. Part of her tried not to care. After all, she'd done pretty well on her own. But she still didn't want them judging her. She squared her shoulders and quietly left the room, closing the door behind her.

Her favorite room in the house was the sewing room that Lisa had included in her rent offer last fall. It had changed a bit from the folding table and single mirror that were in it originally. Although the folding table was still there underneath a big window that faced the front yard, Jaz's late grandma's sewing machine now took pride of place. In front of it was a rolling stool which Jaz found gave her the best mobility as she moved from sewing, to hanging items in the closet, to her computer.

Behind the table was a three-way mirror that folded flat against the wall, with a black-and-white checkered armchair beside it. Beside the chair was a dressmaker's form that she found on eBay. It wasn't quite the same as the one her ma ma used, but it still reminded her of all the years she spent watching her sewing. On the walls were large empty frames painted a glossy black that Jaz had secretly ordered from Carrie's website when she saw them go up for sale. She knew Carrie would try to give them to her, and she wanted to support the single mom in her business of upcycling frames. Jaz almost laughed. Carrie hadn't been up to her sewing room since she helped Jaz move in last September. One day she'd find out!

Inside each frame was a solid black hook that Jaz used to hang up additional clothes for sale when she had clients coming over. It was her best strategy for upselling. Maria always told her in advance which item a client was interested in, and Jaz would gather other items in the same size and hang them on display. She had an ongoing contest with herself to see how well she could predict which clothes any one client would like, and how many of them she sold in one visit. It was something she learned from her grandma—always offer something more when clients come to you.

Jaz's latest project was a line of clothes marketed to people in their teens and early twenties. She spent enough years with girls who would pay anything for the 'right' clothes to know what a lucrative market it was, and she was determined to become one of the must-have brands.

The ethnic t-shirts were a big hit. Since every one was made with materials Jaz bought from the thrifts stores or online, it ensured that each one was a little different. And it seemed like people were willing to pay top dollar once word started to spread.

She was also doing well with little sporty skirts made from extra-large men's sweatpants. It wasn't hard to convert them into skirts and then add two strips of ribbon or seam binding down each side. Jaz had spent hours browsing online for a small patch or logo to sew onto the corner of each skirt until she finally discovered a case of vintage iron-on labels for a long-expired kids' club that someone sold to her for a little more than the cost of shipping.

Jaz had successfully used something similar for a line of baby bib bandanas. Now, the labels set the clothes apart as unique to the Jazzy Clothing Company, but were all a little different, leading clients to buy two or three skirts at a time.

There was a quiet knock at the door, interrupting Jaz's thoughts. She opened it and invited Lisa in, who made herself at home in the armchair. Now that Lisa didn't work a nine-to-five job she liked to visit with Jaz while she was working. It was nice, and since Lisa was the closest to her age of the people she spent time with, she was enjoying getting to know her better.

"So, there's an Airbnb guest coming tonight for three nights," Lisa began.

"Another businesswoman?"

"Yep. Some sort of conference going on. I wonder if they enjoy it. They always seem so tired—the ones who come for conferences."

"Why don't they stay at the hotel? Aren't those things always at hotels?"

"I think so. One lady said it was safer to stay in a house with a female host. Someone else said she preferred to get away from it all in the evenings."

"Did you ever go to conferences?"

"I went to a training seminar in Florida when I got promoted." Lisa smiled at the memory. "I had never traveled anywhere before so it was a pretty big deal for me. Thank goodness I had Janet to call and ask what to do and what to bring. She even lent me a suitcase because I didn't have one!"

"Who's Janet again?"

"The lady who got me into bookkeeping. I hardly see her anymore though. She's got her own bookkeeping company, and she takes care of her dad so she doesn't really have any free time."

"Speaking of parents, how do you think your mom's doing?" Unknown to Maria, Jaz and Lisa often talked about her health and did their best to make her life easier. They knew she tried to minimize her symptoms and probably felt worse than she let on.

"I think she's doing pretty good right now. She's wearing those new wrist splints every night, and they're helping. The bloodwork from her last rheumatologist visit came in yesterday, and nothing's changed so that's a good thing. I still get so mad that my dad didn't get her the right care. If she would have been on immunosuppressants years ago, maybe she'd be a bit better now." She paused, and Jaz gave her a sympathetic look. "Hey, how's the new line going?"

"Really good. I just need to put together some more things that aren't too expensive to make and are easy to find supplies for."

"Summer's coming. Does that open up any more options?" Lisa had only spent one summer being a carefree teenager before taking on two jobs to pay her way through college. She often admitted she was clueless about trends but had still developed her own classic, colorful style.

"Yeah, I think it does. I want to turn some of those really tacky men's Hawaiian shirts into girl's wrap-around beach cover-ups. The whole wrap style is perfect because it can fit so many different body shapes, and each one will be dramatic enough to catch everyone's attention. Plus, since they're bathing suit cover-ups it doesn't matter if they're short. With the wrap dresses I do for my maternity clothes I'm always looking for men's shirts that are long enough."

"And what about labor costs?"

"I still have to figure it out exactly, but we can do them for around $5 each—they really don't need a lot of work, just removing the button panels and adding a slit up each side. If I can get the shirts for under $5 each and sell them for $40, then we can easily hit our target. Look, I'm bidding on this lot of six online and it's only at $10 including shipping!" Jaz giggled as she pulled up the listing to show Lisa. The heading was 'I Hate These Shirts!'. Not the best advertising slogan and they looked pretty horrendous in the photo, but they'd be amazing when she was done with them.

"I don't see it. How can these shirts be anything but hideous?"

"So, first we take off the button and buttonhole panels and finish the raw edges. Then we cut and finish a slit in each side. And finally add a piece of coordinating seam binding onto the waist area here," she pointed to a spot about half-way down the shirt, "and another inside the shirt here on the opposite side to tie it. Then we finish it with a narrow scarf or something the same color as the seam binding to tie it at the waist. And ta-da! You have a swimsuit cover-up!"

"Well, as long as your clients love it... hey, who exactly will model these for you?"

"Oh, that's the best part! Sherry!"

"Sherry, the girl that pretends to be your friend now, but really wants first dibs at all your clothes?"

"That's the one! I know she's dying to model for me, and honestly, she can pull off a bathing suit. So this will be a breeze for her. And then I'll give her a cover-up in payment. She'll spread the posts to the ends of the earth if she's in them, so it's kind of a no brainer from a promotions perspective."

"Gee Jaz, you are one savvy cookie! Um, if you come across a shirt in a less… eye straining pattern, will you make me one too? I do like the idea of having something cute to throw on over my swimsuit."

"What color's your swimsuit?"

"It's a dark green."

"Got it!"

"OK, well, I'll leave you to it then. Don't forget to eat!"

Jaz rolled her eyes but made a mental note to watch the time. It was easy to get caught up in what she was doing and miss meals—especially lunch if Alex was sleeping—but as a breastfeeding mom, she really couldn't afford to go for long hours without eating.

CHAPTER FOUR

Lisa

Lisa quietly closed the door to Jaz's sewing room and went to check that the Airbnb room was ready. Carla took care of cleaning in between each guest, but Lisa always double checked. Not that there was ever anything out of place.

The room was carefully decorated to appeal to women. The bedspread was lilac with white flowers across it, and the eyelet lace white curtains added a soft touch in front of the white roller blinds that blocked out any light. Lisa wanted to do everything possible to give her guests the perfect night's sleep

A white bedside table held a silver lamp and a vase with flowers, and the towels were lilac. Since Alex's birth, Lisa made sure the listing was clear that an infant was part of the household and might make noise at night, but he was such a good baby most guests hardly noticed. The shared bathroom between the guest room and Jaz's room was sparkling clean and ready for the next guest.

She had worked hard to build a five star rating, and with her mom managing all the bookings and communications, it didn't add much work to her days. For the time being, the income was being directly applied to her mortgage every month. As of last month, she owed just under $160,000 on her mortgage, and her house was valued at $405,000.

The Airbnb income, along with her rental income from the upstairs rooms and the downstairs suite had allowed her to pay down her mortgage faster than expected. Until six months ago, her goal was to pay off her mortgage as soon as possible. But thanks to Jaz she was getting other ideas.

The story of her parent's terrible marriage still haunted her. As a teenager, she was so focused on avoiding her dad's verbal abuse and making enough money to leave home after graduation that she missed how miserable—and trapped—her mom was. Now, seeing what a transformation it made for her mom to live in a safe place and have control of her own life, she wanted to help other people in the same position.

Jaz's passionate insistence that they do something *now* had lit a fire under Lisa. Tonight she'd arranged to meet with two of the people who helped her get this house: her mortgage broker and her realtor. Both of them had worked alongside her to get the best deal possible, and now she hoped they'd help them all find a way to create a housing solution.

Lisa smirked. And it wouldn't hurt Sandra and Frank to spend some time together. Sandra was also her best friend Amy's mom. Amy lived about an hour away with her new husband Jesse, but she kept in regular contact with Lisa. Her mom and Frank hit it off at Lisa's housewarming party two years ago, but neither one of them seemed willing to take the plunge into a relationship. Lisa thought a project together might help things along.

After cleaning up supper Lisa was off to meet Sandra and Frank. She wasn't sure her idea would work, so she didn't tell Jaz or her mom about her plans. Now that she had time to take care of her freelance clients during the daytime, her evenings were free—something Lisa hadn't experienced in six years. She wondered if this was what retirement felt like. It was as if she *should* be busy, but really there was nothing to do. When Lisa turned 16, a high school teacher helped her find a job at a local café. Without her parents knowing, she spent the next two years either working or struggling to pass all her classes. The day of her high school graduation she left home without looking back.

For the next two years, Lisa worked as a waitress during the day and a janitor at night while taking classes towards her bookkeeping certificate. Her only day off was Sunday, and she spent it either studying, catching up on sleep, or at the laundromat.

When Lisa got a job as a bookkeeper, she kept her janitor job for as long as possible—always working for her dream of buying her first house. Then, overnight she became a caregiver for her mom while still trying to buy her first home. Nothing had come easy for Lisa, but a busy schedule had always given her a sense of purpose. This new life where she had free time felt weird and unsettling.

Frank was already waiting at the coffee shop when Lisa arrived, so she ordered a coffee and went to join him. "How's the house treating you?" he asked.

"Fantastic! Right now I've got Chris and Carla still living in the downstairs suite, although they're moving out in a few months. And upstairs I still have one room I rent out on Airbnb and the other rooms I rent out to my friend Jaz and her baby Alex."

"How's that working out?"

"Again, fantastic! Jaz started an upcycled clothing business last year, which is doing really well. She's hired mom as her Executive Assistant, and I'm the new CFO of the business as of last week."

"Chief Financial Officer, huh?"

"Yeah, well, it's not a million dollar business yet, but she's definitely headed that way."

"And how old is she?"

"Nineteen. Makes me feel like an underachiever!"

"Well, you're certainly not that. Oh look, there's Sandra." He waved to her until he caught her eye, and she dropped her bag off at the empty chair before going to grab a drink.

"So," she said as she sat down with her cup of tea, "to what do I owe the pleasure, Lisa? You were a bit cryptic on the phone."

"I'm hoping for your help. Both of you." Lisa took a sip of her latte and tried to calm herself. She so desperately wanted to hear that her plan would work, *and* she wanted Frank and Sandra to fall in love, get married, and live happily ever after. *One thing at a time,* she reminded herself.

"I was just telling Frank about Jaz, who's living with us now."

"Ah, the one who took Amy's room!"

"That's the one." Lisa smiled. Sandra had always been extra protective of her daughters. "So Jaz came to us last fall as a pregnant teenager. She had an idea to start a clothing company selling upcycled clothes— things she bought at the thrift store and styled into new outfits or really trendy things. And her company is doing *really* well."

"I could go on and on about her success, but the most important thing to know is that her business is very secure and growing every month." She paused and took another drink. Frank and Sandra were looking at her patiently. "One thing Jaz had to do to scale up the business was hire some outside help to keep up with demand. Naturally, Mom already knew some women who were available and knew how to sew, and the company now has five women doing contract work."

"Wow! That's a lot bigger than I imagined when I pictured a home-based business."

"Yeah, we all knew Jaz was good at sewing, but her ability to grow the business still leaves us shocked at times. It's the reason I quit working at Golden Lion Investments actually, because she offered me a part-time position with her company."

"I didn't know you quit," Sandra chastised her. "You didn't say anything."

"Well, I wanted to wait until I switched over to working from home. But that's not why I wanted to talk to you two."

"Go on," Frank encouraged.

"OK. One of our seamstresses is a lady named Susan. I'll spare you the details, but she's basically trapped living with her adult daughter's family because she can't afford a place herself. They're using her as slave labor, and every time she tries to leave they make up another reason why she can't. Mom and Jaz see her every week because she does as much sewing on the side as she can to try to save for moving out."

Lisa smiled at the sympathetic murmurings and continued, "It was the first time Jaz was introduced to the fact that people can be trapped in bad living situations because of lack of finances, and it really lit a fire underneath her. She's making more than enough money from her company to support herself and her son. And she wants to use the rest of it to set up affordable housing."

"You mean a charity?"

"No, that's the thing. She wants to do it privately. Aside from the tax benefits a charity might offer, this makes sense. Everything can be done quickly and without needing board approval or anything like that."

Now Lisa knew she had their full attention. "Jaz, Mom, and I have been talking about this idea for a few months. Today we met with Carrie—that's my friend who just finished her master's in counseling. We're hoping Carrie will help us with the counseling aspects of helping people transition to safe housing. Like I said, Jaz's company can cover the cost for a mortgage on a large house. What I'm wondering is if I can use the equity in my house as a down payment, and if you both can help us get a property to use for housing people like Susan."

Frank and Sandra exchanged glances, but neither one of them spoke for a minute. Finally, Sandra asked, "Who would own the house?"

"I'm not sure. Maybe Jaz, my Mom, and I? Or just myself? Or more than the three of us? This is where my expertise ends, and where I need both of you."

Frank leaned back and blew out a big breath, "I'm not sure whether to be impressed or worried. I absolutely agree that safe, affordable housing is a huge need in our city. But this idea of yours seems rather... ambitious."

"I was thinking of the word crazy, but I suppose I could settle for ambitious."

"Thanks Sandra—I think! My mortgage balance is about $160,000 and my tax assessment was $405,000. Can I use $100,000 in equity as a down payment for another house? Or can that go further, like for a small apartment complex?"

"Well, people do use the equity in one building to purchase another all the time. But whoever buys the house will still have to qualify for a mortgage. And buying an apartment building will have a different list of requirements than a house."

"But it's possible?" Lisa pressed.

"Possible and doable are two different things. If you can tick the right boxes, anything's possible. But I can't imagine... nothing like this has been done before."

"And there's a lot of logistics involved in renting out something like an apartment," Frank added.

"Well, my years at Golden Lion have set me up pretty well for that aspect," Lisa reminded him. "And I've already proved that grit and blind determination work out pretty well!"

He laughed, causing Sandra to smile too. "Yes, my dear. You have definitely proven you can accomplish big things. And if this Jaz girl is anything like you I suspect you'll be unstoppable. What does your mom think of all this?"

"It's pretty close to her heart, actually. For years she felt trapped in her home because my dad controlled all the finances. So helping someone else escape a bad situation is something she's willing to fight for. She has another friend she met at the library who spends his days there, hiding from his family, so he's not a 'burden'. It's not right, when people work their whole lives so they can retire and enjoy life, and then they can't even afford a nice little place of their own."

"And then there are girls like Jaz, whose parents kicked her out of the house when they found out she was pregnant. She was lucky to end up at Carrie's before she moved in with us, but things might have turned out much differently—much, much worse!"

"I think we can do it," She continued, "but we need your help. Both of you. Sandra, this might be the most untraditional mortgage application you've ever dealt with. And Frank, you know real estate and this city far better than any of us. And I trust you both. So, will you help?"

Sandra reached over and put her hand over Lisa's, "I still think you're crazy. But yes. If there's any way I can help you, I will. When I think about where Charity might have ended up if she didn't have me to come to when *she* got pregnant, I shudder."

Frank put his hand over Sandra's, "Well, I guess it's one for all and all for one then!"

Lisa beamed. "I can't wait to tell the others! They'll be so excited!"

"Well, there's still a long way to go," Frank cautioned as he moved his hand away, "but we'll do what we can, right Sandra?"

"Right."

"Great! Now for my next request!" Lisa smiled at both of them. Sandra looked dismayed, and Frank had a strange half-smile. "Don't worry, It's not that bad. Can you two check out some properties so we know what we might work with? It would be with $100,000 down and total costs of about $5,000 per month."

Sandra's shocked face was priceless. "She's *clearing* $5,000 a month?"

"Yes, on top of paying mom and I, all of her supplies, and the contractors. Not bad, huh?"

"So you got us to agree to help you, and then you dropped the money bombshell?" Frank was chuckling again. "Well played!"

"You know," Sandra said slowly, "there's maybe more of a need than I've realized. You heard Amy's working a few hours a week as a care aide while she takes her nursing training?"

Lisa nodded. Amy often talked about the clients she visited every week. Their stories of poor health and poor housing were sad, but Lisa hadn't really connected it with anything she could do to help.

"Well," Sandra continued, "*they* need safe, affordable housing too. I don't even like to think of Amy going into those places to care for them. Can you imagine what it's like to live in one?"

"Why don't you and I drive down there sometime this week and see the situation for ourselves?" Frank suggested. "Could Amy work things out for us to visit?"

Lisa worked to keep a straight face, but inside she was shouting a huge *YES!* and doing a fist pump. The plan to get Frank and Sandra together just might work out!

"That's a good idea," Sandra agreed. "And perhaps look at some properties too?" She turned to Lisa, "you may have more success with a bigger building outside the city."

"That's a great idea. Thank you both *so* much! Now, I know this part is further down the road, but Chris and Carla are starting a home renovation company again, and they've already offered their services to fix up a place. And Chris did a great job making our place and Jonathan's place wheelchair accessible. That's another thing we need to look at. Accessibility."

"Well, Frank and I will look at some properties and get back to you," Sandra said with finality.

"This will be fun!" he agreed. "Nice to have a new challenge on my plate."

CHAPTER FIVE

Carrie

Carrie had started her first week of practicum excited to finally put all her schooling to good use and help people. But after two hours, she knew was in way over her head. Her first day was at a charity that provided a variety of services to vulnerable women. The director introduced Carrie to the psychologist who would supervise Carrie's work for the next six months, and then left the room.

"First of all," the psychologist started, "don't expect too much. These girls are lifers. They're in and out of here on a regular basis. Any change they promise you is temporary, and they'll either end up back in abusive relationships, or back to beating their own kids."

Carrie was so shocked at his callous attitude that she couldn't speak. "Second," he continued, "they don't pay enough to hire good staff here. They can only afford me for one full day every other week, and that's not enough to get anywhere with these girls. Now that you're here, that's my time committed—and more. I'll sit in on a group session every week and check your summaries of each session, but other than that you're on your own."

He looked at his watch. "We should have started by now, but they're always late. I guess we'll go." He got up and left without waiting to see if Carrie would follow. After a moment's hesitation she followed, but the slight nerves she had when she started the day were quickly growing into full-on panic.

"Everyone!" he said as he walked into a room where half a dozen women were sitting in a circle. "This is Carrie. She's the intern here and will be running the group." He turned to Carrie, "They're all yours. Good luck."

Carrie looked at the suspicious gazes of the two women who were watching her. The others all had phones in their hands and didn't bother looking up. She turned back to the psychologist, but he had taken a chair to the back corner of the room and was already pulling out a laptop. She took the seat closest to her in the circle and sat down.

"Um, hi. Like Dr. Bradley said, my name's Carrie. Um, maybe do you want to tell me a bit about yourselves?"

The silence stretched on, only broken up by the sound of a girl smacking her chewing gum loudly. Carrie guessed the ages to range from sixteen to mid-thirties. She could feel the hostility pouring off them towards her.

"Fine!" A woman who looked older than the others sighed loudly. "We have to be here or we don't get a bed to sleep in tonight. It's one of lots of very *stupid* rules. We don't need someone fresh out of university to come in here thinking she's going to fix us and make everything better, either."

The girl with the chewing gum snorted loudly. "Shut up brat!" the lady said before turning back to Carrie. "We're stuck sharing rooms with *kids* who are too stubborn to swallow their pride and go back to mommy and daddy."

"Hey!" the girl protested.

But the lady brushed her off with a hand and continued. "There is *nothing* you can do to fix the shit we've lived through so don't bother trying. At the end of the day you'll go back to your prissy little life and we'll go back to hell."

"Wow." Carrie breathed. Her heart was pounding so hard she wondered if anyone could hear it. "Um, can I know your name?"

This whole session felt out of control and they were only a few minutes in.

"Name's Julia," the older woman offered reluctantly. "Miss smacky mouth there is Char, beside her is Liz, then Sandra, Ashley, Kim, and Nancy."

"OK, well, I'd thank you for coming, but I guess that rings hollow when you have to be here..." Carrie could have smacked her forehead. *Rings hollow?* When did she start using phrases like that? "Does anyone have a topic they want to discuss?"

This got the attention of one girl with her head down in her phone. "Yeah, how about why my asshole boyfriend is still a free man after stealing all my shit?"

Carrie opened her mouth but had nothing to say. Instead, she let out a long, "Uhhhh..." before managing to stop herself. The entire session dragged on, with the women either turning to each other and talking or scrolling through their phones.

"Well, another productive session I see." Dr. Bradley said suddenly before standing up and walking out.

"Um, I guess that's it?" Carrie had no idea what to do next.

"You need to walk us to the office and sign off our names so we can stay here tonight."

"Thanks, Julia." She followed everyone out and did what she was told at the office. The six women all left without another word to her, leaving Carrie standing beside a woman at a computer who seemed to be doing her best to ignore her.

"Um, do you know where the director is?"

"Next door on the left," she answered without looking up.

Carrie walked out and found the director's office. She could see through the window that she was on the phone, and stood there awkwardly until the director looked up and waved her in. Then she sat on the edge of a worn chair, trying not to eavesdrop until the conversation was over.

She tried to smile, "So, the morning group session is over... what else can I do Donna?" When she first approached the charity Carrie had spent over two hours talking with the lady she was facing now. She seemed pleased that Carrie wanted to do part of her practicum with them, and assured her that their clients would benefit from the two days a week Carrie would spend there.

"What did Dr. Bradley say?"

"Oh, I think he left already. I, um, I was the last to leave the room and he was gone when we got to the office."

"You signed off the girls? How many?"

"Yes, six of them. Is that the usual number?"

"It varies. We have twelve beds in total."

"So... the other programs you talked to me about. Um, the cooking class, and the computer class...?" She felt like the director was simply tolerating her until she left.

"Cooking instructor's away. Computers aren't working."

"Oh, is it something that can be fixed? My fiancé's a computer guy. He could look at them!" She loved being able to say she had a fiancé and felt her first genuine smile of the day begin.

The director sighed, "Nobody really went to the class anyway. Listen, I've got to work on this grant application. Why don't you wait in the front office with Pamela? Sometimes we get walk-ins that want to talk to someone."

"OK... where would I meet with them?"

"In the front office. That and my office are the only places with a panic alarm."

"So, just there with the other lady? Sorry, I didn't get her name."

"Her name's Pamela. Don't worry. I doubt you see anyone."

Carrie spent the rest of the day reading through the brochures available in the front office and watching the minutes tick by on the clock. Pamela left a few times and came back smelling like cigarette smoke.

The next day nobody showed up for group sessions or anything else—including the psychologist who was supposed to be supervising her. At least Carrie was prepared, and brought a counseling textbook to re-read. She was ignored by Pamela, thanked by Donna (*for what?* she wondered), and left the center counting the days until her practicum was over.

The other part of her practicum was one day of counseling a week at the clinic where her friend Kara worked as a Physician's Assistant. Simply seeing a friendly face when she walked in the door made her feel better.

"Hey! It's my favorite psychologist!"

"Well, if I pass my practicum," Carrie cautioned, "Until then I'm just an intern, apparently."

"Not here you're not," Kara assured her. "Come on. Dr. Henshaw's already here. You'll like him."

At least in Dr. Henshaw Carrie found a supportive mentor. He talked with Carrie for a few minutes about the various issues she was likely to face in her work at the clinic and asked her if she had any questions. Desperate to ask him about what to do at her *other* practicum, Carrie forced herself to smile and shake her head no. *Nobody likes a complainer,* she reminded herself.

The day flew by, and Carrie quickly went over time. By the end of the day, she was almost an hour behind, but Dr. Henshaw assured her she would get better at managing her time. He sat with her through every session and by the afternoon left her to handle each visit with him sitting quietly beside her.

She was grateful for his support, especially with referring patients on to a psychiatrist. Although she had studied every aspect of mental health and counseling in grad school, actually facing people dealing with challenges was entirely different.

When she got home she thanked the babysitter, closed the door behind her and fell into her sofa. Katie came up right away and cuddled into her.

"I *missed* you today Mommy!"

"Really?" She looked at her sideways, "I thought you couldn't wait to have a real babysitter!"

"Well, I like her, but why can't you pick me up from school like you're supposed to?"

"Katie, we talked about this. On the days when I go to work, I can't stop and come get you from school! Remember how we watched Magnus and his brothers when their dad used to work? And we got them from school? It's the same thing."

"No it's not," Katie said with finality.

At least Jonathan would be back next week and would pick Katie and maybe Matthew up at school. In the meantime, Carrie felt lucky to have found a high schooler who lived on the same street as them and was good with the kids. She didn't get off school early enough to pick up the kids, but at twelve years old Matthew was old enough to pick up his seven-year-old sister and walk her home where the babysitter met them.

Carrie had planned to make a stir-fry for supper, but she was too tired —and this was after only three full days of work! She had no idea how women like Kara managed full-time jobs and busy families.

She went online and ordered Chinese delivery. Tomorrow she'd have the time and energy to cook supper again.

"All right, I've ordered Chinese for supper. Katie, let's get your home reading done before it comes and then we can relax for the rest of the night."

"I have guitar lessons at seven," Matthew reminded her from the table where he was already doing his homework.

"Oh, right. OK, we'll relax *and* take Matthew to guitar." She wished she could have kept the after school slot for lessons, but there was no way she was asking a teenager to drive her kids to lessons, and Jonathan wouldn't always be around to help out. She rolled her eyes at herself. A year ago she was doing everything herself. There was no reason to get all whiny just because her fiancé was away once in a while now!

As soon as Matthew went to bed, Carrie went to her bed with a novel. She was exhausted, but her mind was still spinning with everything she had encountered in her first week of practicum.

By the time Carrie brought the kids to visit Lisa, Maria, and Jaz on Saturday, she was looking forward to a happy conversation, and celebrating Jaz's growing relationships with her parents. The idea of including her in some larger-than-life scheme to house the city's residents made her want to burst into tears. At least she hadn't let on how hard it had been to the others.

But when Jonathan came in the door Sunday night looking delicious and carrying a beautiful bouquet of flowers, she couldn't hold it all in anymore. After he popped up to see the kids that Carrie had just finished sending up to bed, he joined her in the kitchen where she was putting away some pre-made meals for the beginning of the week. He was wearing a pair of dark jeans with a grey Jazzy Clothing original short-sleeved dress shirt that had a paisley fabric on the collar and pocket.

"Here," he started, pulling a bottle of wine out of a gift bag, "I got this at the airport duty free shop. Thought it might be nice to try together."

Carrie closed the fridge and got out the corkscrew to hand to him before grabbing two wine glasses. "Where were you with this on Monday night? Oh, and Tuesday night and Wednesday night?"

He came around the counter and turned Carrie around to face him. Wrapping his arms around her waist he kissed her slowly, and long enough for her to forget about her practicum. "Sounds like you had a rough week."

"Hmmm? I seem to have forgotten. Keep doing what you're doing and I'll forget to complain to you about it all."

He kissed her again before stopping to pour them each a glass of wine. They walked over to the sofa and cuddled up. Carrie's vintage, bright orange sofa was well-known to everyone who visited her. They first mentioned the vivid color, but as soon as people sank into the plush, buttery soft cushions they stopped teasing her about her choice.

Carrie quietly told him about her first three days.

"Wow. Sounds like you've been dropped into the deep end. I'm sorry I wasn't here to support you."

"No, this contract of yours is important. And we managed OK. Although I have a hard time remembering how I survived all the time without you before we met."

"And that's the way we should keep it. At least I'll only have to head out for one week a month. The rest of the time I'll be here for you."

She smiled, "Thanks. Katie was quite unimpressed with not having me to pick her up from school. Hopefully, she doesn't give you a hard time tomorrow."

"She'll be fine. I brought gifts for both of them and I'm not above bribery."

Finally, Carrie admitted she couldn't stay awake anymore, and Jonathan reluctantly got up to head back to his house. "I'm counting the days until we're all in the same house together," he said as he kissed her goodnight.

It wasn't until she was in bed that she realized she hadn't told him anything about the ladies' plans for addressing the city's housing problem.

CHAPTER SIX

Maria

Maria reached over and pushed the oversized button on her alarm clock. She sat up just enough to have a glass of water and take her pain pills and steroids before laying back down to fall asleep again. Another alarm would go in 45 minutes when the medication had kicked in enough for her to get up and start her day.

It was Friday—her favorite day of the week. She loved it when the ladies who worked for Jaz came by with all the projects they'd finished during the week. There was always a pot of tea and some cookies from the bakery for them to enjoy sitting around the table together while Jaz checked their work and Lisa added up their pay. Most of them preferred bank deposits, but a few found that cash was better.

Maria intentionally scheduled Susan for the last block of time. She wanted to have time to talk to her about her living situation. Last Christmas Susan confided in her and Jaz that she was saving to move out on her own. After spending the last four years as a virtual domestic servant at her daughter's house, she needed a better solution.

All three ladies were supportive of Susan's plans, even when she continued to change her move out date as her kids constantly gave her reasons why they needed her to stay. But Maria felt like she needed to have a real heart-to-heart. Susan was looking more and more worn down, and although the work she did for Jaz was still excellent quality, it was much less than it used to be. Something wasn't right, and Maria didn't want to see her friend suffering anymore.

Jaz and Lisa agreed to give Maria and Susan some privacy as soon as she was paid, and Maria had asked Susan earlier in the week to leave time to stay for lunch. Lisa put a quiche in the oven to heat up and left a salad in the fridge for the two of them. The rest was up to Maria.

"So, tell me how you're doing," she started. "I know you try to keep positive whenever you're over but there's more going on, isn't there."

Susan sighed, "Oh Maria, it's all such a mess. You don't want to hear about it!"

"I do, and I have all the time in the world for it. You know, Friday morning can be quite a whirlwind around here. I've been looking forward to a quiet visit with you all morning, no matter what you have to say."

"My daughter and her husband are having trouble. She's been spending a lot more time away from the house. I don't want to leave the kids alone."

"How old are they again?"

"Lucas is thirteen, Sarah is nine, and Janie is seven."

"And what about your son-in-law?"

"Actually, he's been trying recently. He even took Lucas out to the driving range last week and they both came home so happy."

"Have you changed your mind about getting your own place?"

"Oh, no! Not at all! I need it more than ever. I just... I don't like to leave the kids alone."

"Well, I'm no expert in parenting. But it sounds to me like as long as your daughter has you around to do her job, she doesn't really have a reason to step up, does she?"

"But the kids..."

The timer dinged for the quiche, "Would you mind grabbing the quiche? I'll get the salad." Together the ladies brought lunch to the table.

"I must admit," Susan started between bites, "It's quite nice to eat a meal in a clean, calm house. I try to keep things clean for the family but they've got so much stuff everywhere, it always feels so out of control."

"If you went out looking for a place, what would you want?"

"After squeezing myself into a spare room for four and a half years? I'd be happy for a shack with my own bathroom!"

"Well, if you ever want someone to go with you to look at places, Lisa said she'd be happy to. I would too, of course, but until this ankle heals, it's quite a bit of work to go anywhere."

"Oh, I couldn't take up Lisa's time like that!"

"She's planning to look at some places anyway." Maria told Susan about their project to set up affordable housing, without giving the details of how they came up with the idea. "It's important for us to know what's out there, and how much it costs. Going around with someone who's actually looking for a place would be really helpful. Do you have a budget in mind?"

"I look through the newspaper sometimes when I'm feeling desperate to get out. I think I can afford $700 a month for rent, as long as the extra costs aren't too much. Aside from gifts for the grandkids, I don't really spend any money so I've got a nice little nest egg ready." She smiled. "It would be nice to have more time to sew. I used to do it in the evenings, but I don't like to hide in my room when the kids are home alone."

They moved on to talking about Jaz's designs. "That girl is only limited by hours in a day. She has a whole list of new ideas, and whole lines to start!"

"I wish I could help her more," Susan admitted. "She says thank you to me more times in a month than my kids have done since I had to move in with them."

"Four years ago, if you had the option of moving in with them or having your own place, what would you have chosen?"

"Hmmm, I guess having my own place would have been much better. It was such a terrible time. You know, my husband would come over to my daughter's with his new girlfriend for supper and I'd be the one cooking and cleaning up while they all visited. It was so humiliating."

Maria's mouth dropped open, "No! That sounds like torture! How did you ever heal?"

"I haven't really, I suppose. No, that's not true. Having this job sewing has helped. Maybe more than I admit. It's nice to have something to do that I'm good at. That really helps." She looked down at her watch. "I should get going. Lucas needs his soccer gear for the weekend and I just got it in the wash before I left to come here... I really do give my daughter an excuse to not have to be a mom, don't I?"

"Anytime you want to look at places, Lisa's available. But no matter what, please stop by whenever you need a change of scenery. Oh, and let me send you a number." She looked down at her phone and tapped the screen for a minute before looking up. "This is the contact info for a friend of ours named Carrie. She's just graduated with a counseling degree, and she's really helped Lisa and I when we've faced challenges. Call her up sometime. You'll be glad you did."

"Thank you, Maria, and thank you for a lovely lunch, too!"

After Susan left, Maria cleaned up lunch. It took a while, but she managed. *For someone permanently in a wheelchair and without other people in the house to help, an accessible kitchen would make a huge difference* she thought.

Once in her bed, she put her wrist splints on, double-checked that her alarm was set to give her time to get up before Becky came home, and lay back with a sigh. She hoped her visit with Susan had helped. But as Carrie often reminded them, each person's choices were their own to make. Maria hoped Susan would choose what was best for her for a change.

CHAPTER SEVEN

Jaz

Jaz and Lisa made the most of their mid-day getaway. They went to Connie's—the café by the lake where Jaz used to hang out with her friends when she was still in high school. "You have to have the chili cheese fries!" she insisted.

Jaz fed Alex his bottle before their meal came and then propped him up in his stroller with some toys so she could eat.

"You really do need two free hands for this! But you're right. These are the best chili cheese fries I've ever had. So, it doesn't bother you to come back to your old hang-out place?"

"It doesn't, actually. The first time was hard, but I realized that I love my life so much now I don't really regret what happened before. So now I can just come and get my fill of grease!"

"Ew, when you put it that way..." Lisa paused with a forkful halfway to her mouth, "naw, I'm still going to eat it!"

"Oh my gosh." Jaz sat back later with her hands on her stomach. "I am so full. I can't believe I used to eat this every week!"

"How do you think Mom's doing with Susan?"

"If Susan really wants to move out, your mom will help her get there."

"I may have another piece to our housing puzzle..."

"What? We've been sitting here for forty-five minutes and you're just telling me now?"

"The fries made me forget everything! So, this week I met with the mortgage broker and the realtor who helped me get my house—"

"What's a mortgage broker?" Jaz was becoming more confident in asking questions. Turned out people really didn't mind being asked things!

"It's someone who can help you find the best mortgage—that's a loan you get to buy a house—for your situation. She only deals in mortgages, not other loans, and isn't limited to a single bank."

"Oh. OK, keep going."

"I've asked them for help in figuring out a mortgage for housing, and maybe even finding a property."

"That's great!"

"You know how I've been pretty focused on paying down my mortgage?" Jaz nodded and Lisa continued, "I can easily take $100,000 of equity from my house and use it for a down payment on another property. So that should take us a lot closer to seeing something happen."

"Wait, so you're using your own money?"

"Yeah, Jaz. Just like you." She answered dryly.

"Oh. Right." Jaz laughed. "Sorry."

"No problem. I asked Sandra and Frank to take a look at some properties that might work." She paused, and her face took on a sneaky look, "You remember hearing about Amy, who used to live in your room?" Jaz nodded. "Well, Sandra is Amy's mom, and she's single. And Frank's single. So..."

"What? You're playing matchmaker? Lisa! I had no idea!"

"I'm pretty good at it, too! Amy's married to my mom's old neighbor. Thanks to me."

"Oh my gosh! Wait... what if you set up your mom with someone?" Jaz immediately pictured a nice, middle-aged man—like a doctor—who would fall in love with Maria and take care of all her needs.

"Hey! That's different! Well, if I met someone I thought would be good for her I might try... but I think her and I will live out our days as single ladies."

"Count me in too!" Her imagination switched to living the rest of her life with Maria and Lisa.

"Don't you want Alex to have a dad?"

"Not really. I'm pretty sure I can give him everything he needs."

"Well, you're turning out to be a really amazing mom. Alex is lucky."

As if he knew he was the topic of conversation, Alex started to protest his confinement in his stroller. "You know, it's so beautiful out. Do you mind if I walk home with Alex? He hasn't even been to the lake yet!"

"Of course. I'd join you for the lake part, but I have some freelance work I want to get done before the weekend. And then I'll be home in time to get Becky from the bus."

After paying for their lunches they went their separate ways. Jaz turned the stroller towards the lake and took a deep breath. It *was* a gorgeous day, and she got to enjoy it with her son. Once she got near the water she took Alex out.

"Hey buddy! This is the lake. We'll spend a lot of time here when you're a little bit older. We'll go swimming, and play with balls, and maybe even make some little friends!" Alex kicked his feet in response. Jaz sat down right at the water's edge and put him beside her. He was fascinated with the new things to look at all around him.

She grabbed her phone and took a selfie of the two of them with the lake behind them and sent it to Maria with the title 'first time at the lake'. Maria quickly responded:

Oh, I wish I could see him right now, bet he loves it. We'll have to spend a day there with everyone once the kids are out of school. See you soon!

She almost laughed out loud when she pictured a trip to the lake with all her adult friends and their kids. Sometimes her new life was unrecognizable. "But it's a good little life, isn't it?" she asked her son. Kissing the top of his head, she got up and settled him into his stroller. He started to protest, so she quickly started walking, hoping he would fall asleep. "Sorry buddy, I should have brought another bottle. You're going to have to hang in there 'til we get home."

"Jaz? Jaz! Over here! Over here!"

Turning towards the sound, she groaned. It was Sherry, waving madly from a group sitting on the grass. It wasn't until she was already walking over that she realized Sherry was with all of her old friends— likely all on summer break after their first year of university. Jaz debated turning around and walking away but it was too late. Everyone had seen her.

"Oh my God, I was just talking about you! Guys, look, can you believe Jaz? Seriously, you look like you're twenty-five or something."

"Uh, hi!" she realized Ellison was also there, avoiding making eye contact. But all the girls popped up and crowded around the stroller. Startled by the all the faces so close to him, Alex started to cry. Jaz quickly unbuckled him and picked him up. "Hey, you're OK," she whispered.

"I was just telling everyone about how I'm modeling for you! Your clothes are *so* cool!"

"Yeah, thanks. Have the rest of you seen them?" Jaz felt suspended between two lives as she tried to make small-talk with the people she used to consider her best friends while holding her four-month-old son. The other girls talked about her clothes and squealed over Alex's outfit. She had to admit, he looked adorable, but then she made sure he was always well-dressed.

After a few minutes, she pulled herself away, vaguely answering invites to 'hang out sometime'. Buckling Alex back into the stroller she headed for home, only to be interrupted again by Ellison jogging over.

"Jaz, wait!"

She slowed but didn't stop. As he came up beside her, he put his hand on her arm. Jaz looked down, and then up at the guy who had changed her entire life without being affected at all. "What do you want?"

"I, um..."

"Did you want to see my son?"

He flinched as if she'd hit him. "He, um, I..."

Jaz stopped walking, "Look at him, Ellison. Just for a second." She turned the stroller towards him and looked carefully at the two of them. Alex looked up with trusting, brown eyes that had never known rejection.

"He's, um, wow. He's so small."

"Trust me, he didn't feel small when I gave birth to him." Jaz didn't know what to do. Criticize Ellison? Tell him to get lost?

"Does anyone know? About me?"

Jaz rolled her eyes. At least now she knew he was only interested in his reputation. She'd put him at ease and be on her way. "One person, who's never met you and never will. OK?"

"Oh, yeah, great."

She turned the stroller towards home again. "Bye Ellison."

"Wait! He, uh, he kinda looks like me, doesn't he?"

"He does. And one day, someone else might realize that too. So you probably need to figure out what you're going to do."

This time she started walking and didn't stop. She was glad for the movement while she tried to process what had just happened. Her life now was so much better. She loved being a mom, having Alex to love, and sewing every day. And she loved being surrounded by people who accepted her completely and didn't care about appearances. There was nothing she would change, even if she could go back.

It didn't seem fair that Ellison hadn't changed too. After a minute, she smiled to herself. Maybe he was the one who was missing out.

CHAPTER EIGHT

Lisa

"Hello?" Lisa caught her phone before it went to voicemail.

"Lisa! Oh my gosh! I don't know whether to kiss you or yell at you!"

"Amy?"

"Yep. And you'll never guess who just left our house after a visit? My mom *and* Frank. Apparently, you've asked them to help you out?"

Lisa laughed. "So? Any more sparks between them?"

"Well, Frank seemed really nervous, if that was any indication."

"OK, I admit, I did consider the fact that they were two well-matched, single adults when I asked for their help. But they're also in a field I genuinely need some expertise from. So, if they don't fall madly in love, at least I get what I want."

"Yeah, mom told me about your idea. And I absolutely love it! Whenever you buy property Jesse and I will help with fixing it up. Well... Jesse can help. And I guess I can hand out band-aids or something!"

They both traded updates on their lives for the next twenty minutes, and Lisa hung up the phone with a smile. She'd met Amy when they were both renting rooms in the same house six years ago, and they had hit it off. When Lisa bought her own house, Amy came and rented a room from her until Lisa successfully connected her with Jesse. *Hey if I can match make once, I can probably do it again!* Frank was kind and helpful, and so was Sandra when you got past her professional veneer. Who knows, maybe there would be another wedding soon.

But when Sandra phoned later on that night it wasn't such a happy conversation.

"The good news is that there are multifamily properties for sale. But nothing for under a million. So you either need to raise a down payment of at least $200,000 and be able to present a strong mortgage application, or you need to start smaller. We didn't have time to look at any smaller properties, but there are some duplexes—or even single apartments for that matter—that can still meet your goals. Just on a smaller scale."

Lisa hung up the phone feeling completely discouraged. Had she made the right decision by quitting her job? Even with her increased free-lance business and working for Jaz she was making less than she did as a full-time employee. And there weren't any end-of-year bonuses for freelancers. If only she could take more equity out of her house to get the $200,000 they needed.

She sat for a few minutes, trying to figure out what to do. This project might have been Jaz's idea to start, but Lisa really wanted to make it work. Being able to give Chris, Carla, and Becky a safe and affordable place to live when they desperately needed it had sparked something inside of her. It made her feel like her life was adding up to something more than just putting in time at work and taking care of her mom. She wanted to create more of that spark!

It was time to get another view of her finances. She picked up her phone again and texted Carrie:

Hey there! I hope you're having a good day. When you get a minute can

you send me your friend Jenny's number? The one who's a financial advi-
sor? I need some advising!

"All right," she muttered to herself. "Now quit sitting around and get some work done!" Taking her own advice she pulled out her laptop and got lost in the numbers and accounts of her clients.

When her phone buzzed a reply two hours later, Lisa was already feeling better. This was why she loved bookkeeping. Numbers were always so predictable. And whenever she found something that didn't fit, she'd search until she figured out how to make it fit. If only life were the same! She finished her work, added Jenny to her contacts, and send her a text:

> *Hi Jenny! This is Lisa, Carrie's friend. Can I make an appointment to come see you? I need some financial advice.*

It surprised her when Jenny immediately called back.

"Hi, Jenny! Wow, you're fast with the responses!"

"Hey Lisa, I happen to have ten minutes between clients so I thought I'd call. Can you give me a quick idea of what you want to go over? Then I know how much time to set aside."

"Yeah, of course. So, I'm trying to figure out how much equity I can take out of my house to fund an affordable housing project with a few other people. It's not so much myself I'm worried about, but I want to protect my mom and not create a situation that might leave the house underwater if something happened to me."

Jenny was quiet for a minute, "Can you say that first part again?"

"Sure. I've got really good equity in my house, and I want to figure out how much of it I can use as a down payment for an apartment building or something to create affordable housing."

"I *thought* that's what you said. Is this for a charitable organization?"

"No, we want to stay away from that so we can make quick decisions and have more flexibility."

"I see. And who else is involved?"

"Well, I want to provide the down payment. Jaz—that's the clothing designer who used to live with Carrie and lives with us now—is bringing in enough income to cover monthly costs. My mom is available to help with anything besides finances. We've asked Carrie to help with counseling people in transition. And I have my former mortgage broker and real estate agent looking at properties."

"Wow! That's quite a list. How much were you hoping to take from your house equity?"

"Well, I know I can do $100,000, but it looks like we'll need at least double that. Which is a bit more ambitious than I thought at first. But it's not impossible!" she quickly added.

"OK... I think this is bigger than a one-on-one consultation. Can we set up a get-together with everyone who's interested and go from there? I know my husband would be interested, and Jonathan too if Carrie hasn't already suggested him. What do you think?"

Lisa felt a weight fall off her shoulders. "More people helping would be amazing. I'm happy to have it here at our place. If it's nice, the kids can play in the backyard. We should do it soon before summer holidays start."

"Sounds good! I know for us Sunday afternoons work well. But whatever works for most people, we can fit it in."

"Thank you, Jenny! I'll text you with a date and time later on today." Lisa put down her phone and sat back in her chair with a smile. She had just assumed it would be her, Jaz, Carrie, and her mom, with Sandra and Frank playing a smaller role. With more people involved, she was starting to think they could actually make this thing happen.

Hearing her mom's after-nap alarm clock ring, she went to her room to talk about the latest development.

CHAPTER NINE

Carrie

Carrie finished putting a coat of glossy lime green paint on a frame and stood back to look at the results. It was one of three small frames, all different shapes but all painted the same bright color. She had missed creating new frames from old cast-offs during the many months she'd been so focused on grad school, and reveled in the chance now to tune everything out except for the project in front of her. There was just enough time to clean up before getting the kids from school.

Seeing a text from Lisa that had come in when she was painting, she replied with Jenny's number and then left the house. The summer weather was definitely on its way and she was happy to finally wear the sporty skirt Jaz made for her last fall. It was almost too short for someone her age, but Jaz had assured her she could pull it off. She paired it with a bright pink t-shirt that matched the pink stripes on the sides of the grey skirt, and a pair of white runners.

It was silly to feel so good about wearing nice clothes, but after years of digging through thrift stores for the cheapest clothes she could find, she loved having some new things to wear. And it didn't hurt that she was wearing something from the city's hippest new designer! Jaz's success still made Carrie smile every time she thought about it.

She really needed some reasons to smile. Her second week at the women's outreach center hadn't been any easier than the first. The women at the group therapy sessions each day seemed cold and unresponsive, the psychologist told her to get her head out of the clouds when she asked him for suggestions to reach the participants, and during her client visits at the clinic she had to report a young man's parents for suspected abuse.

She knew she'd run into challenging situations, but she hadn't expected the feeling of helplessness that came with it. No matter what happened next, a family would be disrupted because of her actions. The supervising psychologist assured her that she was doing the right thing, but it still left her feeling like she was making things worse for the situation, not better.

At least Jonathan had been around to spend the afternoons with the kids, and to listen to her concerns about her practicum.

Standing by the school gates, she chatted with the other parents. Now that they knew the guy picking up Katie last week was her fiancé, everyone wanted to know how they had met, and all about their wedding plans.

"And you have to tell me where you got that skirt! It's too cute!" one mom gushed.

"Oh, thank you! It's actually a local designer who sells her clothes on Instagram. Here, let me show you..." Carrie pulled out her phone and got them to follow the Jazzy Clothing Company before the bell rang.

As usual, Katie came tearing out the door, full of enthusiasm about the day. "Hi Mommy!" she hollered while she was still ten feet away. Carrie smiled and waved as she heard other parent's laughing. Katie's bubbly personality was already legendary around the school, and she was only in first grade!

It was another few minutes before Matthew found them, and then the teacher walked out with Magnus. Carrie was back to watching her friend Kara's son Magnus after school on Thursdays and Fridays. As a very shy child, he was still finding first grade overwhelming.

"Hi Magnus," Carrie said softly, crouching to talk to him. The teacher crouched as well, creating a very small bubble to talk to him.

"Magnus, you did really well today!" She turned to Carrie, "There was an assembly with Polynesian dancers and drums that were loud, but Magnus just covered his ears and enjoyed watching."

"I liked their outfits," he said, "but they were very loud."

Carrie smiled her thanks to the teacher who always treated every student with respect and understanding. Sometimes dealing with Katie and Magnus felt like too much, and this lady had 25 of them every day!

Walking home, Katie bounced around in front of Carrie and Magnus talking a mile a minute about her day. Matthew went on ahead, asserting his independence just a bit. He had his own house key now, and already had his coat, shoes, and schoolbag neatly put away when Carrie and the other kids walked in the door.

"Ooooh look, Mommy! You did more shiny frames!" Katie exclaimed, getting as close as possible to the wet frames without touching them.

"Uh, Katie?" Carrie waited to see if she'd realize what she had forgotten.

"Oooops! Silly me!" She came back to the front door before kicking off her pink sparkly shoes and throwing her backpack on top of Matthew's. "What's for snack Mommy?"

"Fruit and cheese. Wash your hands and then you can put it on the pretty plate." Their last trip to the thrift store to look for frames for Carrie's business had resulted in a vintage serving platter making its way into their house. At the moment Katie was determined that every possible food item be laid out on the platter before they ate.

When they were all sitting down, Carrie insisted Katie take a breather and let the boys talk about their days. Magnus was getting better at talking about his day and seemed to enjoy having everyone's attention. His older twin brothers were fourteen now and didn't have time for a shy little brother to find his words.

After Kara picked him up, Jonathan joined them for their Friday night pizza tradition. It was almost three years ago now that Katie had first invited him to join them for pizza—in front of a mortified Carrie standing in the grocery aisle. But things had worked out pretty well, all things considered.

"Daddy Johnny," Katie started, "can we play Candyland after supper?" She used her nickname for him every chance she got, immediately switching from 'Uncle Johnny' which she had called him until he proposed to Carrie.

"Come here Katie," he said, sitting down at the table. She climbed into his lap and wrapped her arms around his neck. "I have played enough Candyland in my lifetime. It's time for a new favorite game. What do you think?"

Katie's face fell. "But I *love* Candyland!"

Carrie and Matthew exchanged glances. It really was time for some different games.

"How about we go to the toy store after supper and pick out some games? I'll bet we can find you a new favorite."

Katie looked at him in shock, "We don't go to the toy store unless we have birthday money! And my birthday money's all gone!"

Now it was Jonathan's turn to look shocked, but he recovered quickly. "You don't need birthday money now Katie. It's my daddy job to pay for your new games!"

"Really? My old daddy didn't do that."

"Well I do," he said with finality. "Now, let's get the table set before the pizza delivery guy comes."

Carrie gave his hand a squeeze as they set the table. She sometimes tried to ignore how desperate her financial situation had been until the kids said something to remind her how much their lives had changed.

Being able to provide a decent house and life for her kids was an amazing feeling. Having such a great guy as part of it felt too good to be true.

After a game of Scrabble Junior that was a welcome change from Candyland, Carrie followed Katie upstairs to tuck her in. When she came back down, Jonathan and Matthew were playing chess at the table.

"Your phone buzzed Mom."

"Oh, thanks." She picked up her phone and then put it down and sighed.

Jonathan looked up, "What's wrong?"

"It's nothing wrong, really. Jaz, Lisa, and Maria are working on this idea to provide affordable housing."

"OK..."

"And they want me to help. Actually, it looks like they want everyone to help!"

"You don't look very happy about it."

"It's a great idea. Amazing, actually. But there's nothing I can offer, and they seem to think differently." She rested her head in her hand. Just the idea of reaching out to another needy person who didn't want her help was enough to make her want to run the other way.

"Mom, maybe the people at the women's center are different than the ones Jaz and them are trying to help. You should be more open-minded."

"Oh Matthew," she resisted the urge to ruffle his hair, "you may be right. But after always feeling like I get in the way when I'm there, I'm not feeling so confident in my counseling abilities."

"Is the feeling based on fact?"

Jonathan burst out laughing. "You're awesome Matthew! That's exactly what I was thinking, but I wasn't brave enough to say it!"

Carrie couldn't stop the smile. "All right you two. No Matthew, my feeling is not based on fact. I just need to figure out how to connect with those people. And I did have some really good sessions at Kara's clinic. I'll try to focus more on the facts. Anyways, the meeting to talk about this housing idea is Sunday at two in the afternoon, but only if we can make it. Apparently, they'll reschedule if we can't—guess they really want us there."

"By we you mean all of us?"

"Yep, she said to make sure you can come too, Jonathan. It was Jenny's idea to have more people involved. I don't know how she's mixed in with this! And I guess they'll set up the kids to play in the backyard."

"Well, we don't have any plans. Why don't we go to church and then grab some lunch out before going over? Make a day of it?"

"OK. I guess it doesn't hurt to see what they have to say. And I'll feel better having you there."

"Mom, can I listen at the meeting too, instead of playing with the kids?"

"Of course!" Carrie knew that Matthew was far more aware of the impact of poverty than most kids. He was old enough to understand their money problems when she left her ex-husband. While she wished he didn't still worry about money, she was glad he could empathize with others who were struggling to afford housing.

CHAPTER TEN

Maria

Maria lay in bed, her heart already beating faster with excitement. It felt like today would be the start of something big. Jaz and Lisa had invited everyone they thought might want to help create housing solutions in their city, and Lisa insisted that Maria manage the discussion when it was time.

For her part, Maria had ordered a variety of pastries from the bakery, chosen pretty paper plates and plastic cups, and stocked the kitchen with enough tea and coffee to last for a month of Sundays. She didn't really know anything about hosting a meeting, but these were all good people, so she was sure it would be just fine.

By 2 pm, the living room was full. All the kids except Matthew were sent outside with cookies and juice boxes, every seat was taken, Chris had brought up extra chairs from their suite, and a few people were even sitting on the floor.

"Well," she started, feeling a bit intimidated, "this is quite the group of people!" She paused and looked around the room. Everyone smiled their encouragement.

"In a nutshell, we believe we can purchase some sort of housing, and make it into something that provides a safe place for people who need it. The purpose of this little get-together is to talk about what we can all offer and to see what ideas we can come up with. Let's start with each person and say a few things related to what you think of our little plan and how you might want to be involved. Carla will take notes as we go along since I'm not so good with handwriting." She turned to Lisa who was sitting on the floor beside her wheelchair. "Why don't you start Lisa?"

"Sure! I'm a bookkeeper, and I can manage all the finances. I also worked in accounts at Golden Lion Investments so I have experience handling the bookkeeping for investment properties. But my personal story is probably more why I think this is such a good idea. I ended up on my own at 18 and had to deal with some kinda crazy roommates at the place where I rented a room. It's hard to find good, safe housing. And I know it's even harder for people who have a family to take care of. And then I found out later on that my mom couldn't leave my dad —even though he was terrible to her—because she didn't have anywhere to do. If I had my way, I'd make sure that no one was trapped like that ever again." She took a shaky breath and then turned to her friends Manuel and Betsy and smiled.

"Hello! I'm Manuel and this is my wife Betsy. I'm retired now, but I used to own a property maintenance business. And Betsy is a retired nurse."

The introductions continued around the room. Carrie, of course, was finishing her practicum to be a counseling psychologist. "I was in a similar situation as Maria. I needed to leave an abusive relationship, but without money for a down payment and rent I was trapped. Then, when I managed to move out with the kids, we lived in pretty rough subsidized housing, and making ends meet was still a huge struggle. It's crazy when you're trying to get over the past *and* you have to worry about whether you'll lose the only home you have because of finances." She put her hand on Matthew's head, who was sitting on the floor leaning against his mom's leg. "Matthew can tell his own story, but as a Mom I felt terrible that he was exposed to the stress of budgets, bills, and no money. That's hard on a kid."

"Well, it wasn't *that* bad," Matthew started. "Living in the townhouse was better, because my dad couldn't hurt my mom anymore and we didn't have to be scared of him. But before that, when we all still lived together it was bad. Every day I wished we didn't live there. So now that Mom and Jaz and everyone have money to help other people, I think we should do it!"

Jonathan was next to talk, but there was silence as he visibly struggled with his emotions. He turned when Carrie reached to wipe a tear away and gently took her hand in his. "It's weird. I remember the first time I saw Carrie and the kids at her townhouse. I mean, yeah, it wasn't anything nice, but the feeling there..."

He paused and smiled, "Well, I could just tell how much love was in the place. If I had known how much she was struggling, I would've done anything to make it better. Getting to know Carrie has shown me a whole different world that people live in. And hearing stories like yours, Maria, it makes me determined to do whatever I can to help."

Jenny spoke up next, "So I'm Jenny. And I work as a financial advisor. I know that good plans can make a lot of things happen, and I'm happy to help with that. My own parents were terrible with money—even though my dad had a good job—and I spent my childhood being moved around, either because we had been evicted again, or we were about to be evicted. My parents are doing really good now, and they just bought their own home a few years ago. Having a nice, safe place to live is a huge deal." Jenny's husband Max lifted his hand in a quiet greeting to everyone and turned to Ken and Kara.

Ken was a stay-at-home dad. "I guess I take our home for granted," Ken said, "I can't really think about what it might be like to not have that."

"I'm a physician's assistant," Kara started, "and every day I see people whose health problems are made worse by their housing. It would be fantastic if we could do something about that."

"Plus, she knows everybody in the city!" Carrie quipped, and everyone laughed. It wasn't a secret that many of them knew each other because Kara had connected them.

Sandra and Frank introduced themselves, and then Amy and Jesse. "I don't know how much I can help since I'm studying nursing full-time, but whatever I can do I will."

"And I'm in construction," Jesse added. "No problem to pop up here for a day or two at a time."

"We're in construction too," Chris started. "Carla and I specialize in home renovations, and along with Jonathan's help, we're getting pretty good at adapting homes to be accessible. We lost our own home a few years ago during the downturn and it was devastating. Our only option was to move in with my parents, but they couldn't handle Becky's special needs. Every day with them was a nightmare, and it really took a toll on all of us, but especially Becky."

"You know, Lisa and Maria have already made a difference for us." Carla's eyes sparkled with unshed tears. "They insisted we move into the suite downstairs the second they heard about our situation. And when we got here, they had stocked the kitchen with groceries, bought flowers, and had a helium balloon for Becky. I can't even say what a relief it was to have our own, safe space. We'll do whatever it takes to make that happen for someone else, and we'll never, ever forgot the kindness they've showed us."

As people cleared throats, and wiped eyes, Lauren's blunt voice was a welcome interruption. "I don't know why Jaz invited *us*. I'm an artist, and Dustin stays home with Brittany. I mean, the idea is cool and all, but we don't exactly have skills."

"As far as I know, you're the only ones here who have lived in a shelter," Jaz explained. "And you figured out a way to get out of that situation. Plus, you understand how accessibility has made Dustin's life easier, and we'd like to make at least some of the units accessible if we can. So I thought we needed you the most, you know, to keep it real and make sure our ideas will actually make sense."

"Huh," Lauren answered, and then seemed to have trouble talking. Dustin reached over with his good hand and rubbed her shoulder.

"So it's to me now," Jaz said. "Well, I guess I just learned that having a safe, affordable place to live can make the difference to someone staying trapped in a bad situation, or being able to get out. And I want to do something about it. I mean, I was only homeless for a day before Kara and Carrie rescued me. But it was really scary. I never thought about that stuff before, and then suddenly I was in a situation where I don't know what would have happened to me if strangers hadn't helped me out. I don't want anyone else to go through that."

"It's really amazing how perfect you all are, and how right it is that you're all here today." Maria tried not to get too emotional, but it was hard after hearing everyone speak so openly. "I guess you sort of know that I spent years feeling trapped and hopeless. I didn't have any way to earn money because of my health, and my husband controlled all the money. I *had* managed to put a little bit aside by returning things to the store for cash when Robert was at work. But then he found my savings..." She gazed out the window, momentarily lost in a memory before visibly shaking herself and forcing a smile on her face. "Now that I live in such a lovely house, and I get to spend my days with good, kind people, I really want to give back somewhere. And this project is the perfect place to do that."

"Well, I'm not entirely sure what happens next! Maybe Lisa and Jaz, you can talk about what you have so far regarding money?"

"Sure," Lisa answered. "I can take $100,000 in equity from this house to go towards a down payment for a property. Possibly more, but I'm not sure."

There was a shift in the energy in the room as everyone began to realize how much she was willing to put on the line.

"And I can pitch in up to $5,000 a month for the monthly expenses," Jaz added.

Maria looked around the room at everyone's faces. They ranged from shocked to emotional—hopefully happy emotions, but it was hard to tell. "Sandra, how far will that get us?"

"Well, the actual qualifying for a mortgage is still a big question. But with the down payment and the monthly costs, we can comfortably look at a property of about half a million."

"How many units would that have?" Jaz asked.

"That would be a duplex, so two. Maybe a fourplex, but at that price it would be quite run down. Frank and I looked at a ten unit apartment complex that's about an hour's drive from here. It's for sale for just under a million and wouldn't need much work to get ready. But it's only got two units empty right now. The others are in leases that vary in length."

"So, as far as actually providing housing, it would be the same availability as buying a vacant duplex in the city." Lisa summarized. "But I think the needs in the city are greater because the costs are so much higher."

"Are there any vacant apartment buildings in the city?" Jonathan asked Frank.

"Oh, I very much doubt it. I can look this week. But even run-down apartments are full, simply because it's all people can afford."

"That's not what we want though. We want nice, safe places." Jaz was determined the housing would be nicer than the scary, dirty places she saw on TV.

"Let's step back and identify what it is we *do* want," Maria suggested.

They spent the next hour talking about different options. Maria smiled as she listened to the exchange of ideas. Only two years ago she spent her days in pain, sitting by a living room window in a house she hated, imagining a different life that would never be hers. Now she was surrounded by kind, caring, ambitious people who were all focused on making life better for others. Reality was much better than anything she had tried to imagine.

"All right, we've got a good idea of where to start. It seems like you'll have the most work right away Frank." She looked at him and smiled.

"That's fine with me," he smiled right back.

"So we're looking for any multi-family property in the city that's currently vacant and needs some work." She continued, "If we can't find anything vacant, we'll look for options that have some vacancy. With all the experience in the room as far as fixing things up we should be able to improve the property enough to use the equity to buy the next property."

"Easy peasy!" Lauren joked, and everyone chuckled.

"Well," Maria paused, "why not? Sure, it will involve some effort. But with so many good people involved, and everyone doing what they can, maybe it can be easy."

"Can we talk a bit about finances?" Jenny asked. Seeing Maria nod, she continued, "I'm just thinking out loud here, but if we're not operating as a charitable organization we have a lot more freedom to work outside the box so to speak... If Lisa and Jaz are contributing the bulk of the funds, I think they should be on the property title. That way they own the equity. But with Jaz just starting her business and having no income history they'll need a co-signer to qualify."

"We can help with that," Manuel had been listening intently through the entire meeting, but spoke up now—his gaze directed at Jaz and Lisa. "Betsy and I are so impressed with you two. We'd like to offer $50,000 to help with a down payment, and $20,000 for whatever you need to get things move-in ready. And I'm happy to co-sign on the loan. That should help you qualify. This city is the place where we've found our own home and certainly done well. It's an honor to give back."

"Oh, that's wonderful! Thank you! Jenny, that must move us further along."

"It does, wow!" Jenny answered enthusiastically. "Can we set something up so those who are putting money in can get reimbursed?"

"The girls should do that, but Betsy and I are much further along so we'll leave it as an investment in our city." Manuel looked at Sandra. "Before we go, let's set up a time for you to collect all our info for the mortgage application."

"So, we're really doing this?" Jaz asked carefully. She was having trouble following the talk about equity, investments, and mortgages, but she felt the passion in the room and that was all that mattered to her.

"I think we are!" Maria reached out to squeeze Jaz's hand.

Jenny smiled at Jaz. "There's another money matter we should talk about. How do we set up the actual rent?"

"Well, none of us are in it for the money. But we need to have some guidelines. And from my experience, they need to be clear right from the start. That way the residents know what to expect. Beyond that, I'm not sure what to suggest." Lisa turned to Carrie. "What do you think?"

Carrie sat for a minute before answering. "For me, the amount that the subsidized housing agreement set out for my rent really was more than I could actually afford. Although I it *does* need to be proportional to income. And pulling together a damage deposit really restricts someone's ability to get into housing..."

"Let's just say no damage deposit," Jaz suggested.

Everyone looked around and began to agree.

"And maybe make it a thing that when they're doing better they do something for someone else?" Matthew offered. "You know, like paying it forward."

"Great idea!" Lisa smiled at him. "So I'm thinking we ask each person individually what they can afford and then set the rent lower than that —something like 20% less. Remember, we really can do whatever we want."

"Does everyone agree?" Carla asked and looked around before adding it to her notes. "All right, it's written down, so that's as official as we need to make it."

Maria cleared her throat. "I suppose the last order of the day is for those who want to work in certain areas to have a little chat and make sure everyone has everyone else's contact info. For lack of a better method, can all of you make sure Carla has your email address, and we'll send out a summary to everyone? All right, let's have the construction team in the kitchen, the mortgage team at the dining room table, and the everything else team here in the living room. Oh, and grab more pastries and tea or coffee!"

Soon the house was full of the comfortable sound of conversations, ideas, and growing excitement. Matthew slipped outside to be with the other kids. Carrie, Lauren, Dustin, Jaz, Maria, and Carla all stayed in the living room and the talk turned to specifics for a property location. Things like access to public transportation and affordable shopping, good schools, and parks were at the top of the list.

CHAPTER ELEVEN

Carrie

"You sure have an amazing group of people there." Jonathan, Carrie, and the kids were driving back from the most interesting meeting Carrie had ever attended.

"It is quite something the way they all feel the same about the project," Carrie acknowledged. "That was what I needed today. The chance to feel a part of something that will make a difference."

"I'm glad it helped. Katie, did you get enough play time in?" He looked in the rearview mirror at her.

"Yep! I liked playing in Becky's playhouse! Can I get a playhouse too Daddy Johnny?"

Carrie tried to hold back a snicker. Katie was quickly realizing that 'Daddy Johnny' had trouble denying her anything she asked for. It was nice to see her daughter finally get the experience of having a daddy who doted on her.

"I don't know Katie. Maybe."

"Maybe's better than no," she told Matthew.

"Mom," Matthew started, "can we give money too? *We* don't need more things. Well, a dog. But after that, don't we have everything we need?"

"Oh Matthew, I love the way you see the world! I guess that's something Jonathan and I need to talk about." She caught his eye for a minute before he turned back to watching the road. Money was one of the many things they needed to talk about. With starting her practicum, and Jonathan away working for a week at a time, they really hadn't had enough chances to talk recently.

She rested her head on the headrest and tried to go over her own finances. She knew the *Framed* business was doing well since she hadn't worried about paying all her bills in a long time. And she didn't have to save every spare penny for grad school anymore. But she did still have student loans and a credit card from her last marriage to pay off. She decided to prioritize figuring out where she was financially.

It seemed like Jonathan was thinking the same thing. "I'd love to take some time to talk to you about future plans and finances. Can I book you in for a working lunch on Thursday? I'll bring takeout over."

She smiled at him, "It's a date! That gives me time to figure out where I'm at with everything."

The next day she tried to give herself a pep talk as she drove to the center. "You got this! Even if they all still don't want to talk, at least you're showing up and trying to be available. That's got to count for something."

When she walked into the group meeting room she was shocked to see over a dozen women waiting for her. "Hi everyone!"

There were a few murmured responses. "So, for those who haven't seen me before, my name's Carrie, and I'm working here under Dr. Bradley's supervision. Who, uh.." she turned to the corner where he usually was, but it was empty, "Who isn't here yet..."

"No loss there," Julia snickered.

"Could we start by everyone saying their names? I'm going to write them down here, but I won't write about anything you say. It's just to help me get familiar with who you all are." Dr. Henshaw from the clinic had advised Carrie that having someone writing while a client was talking could be intimidating. She immediately quit taking notes at the group sessions unless it was necessary.

"Not interesting enough for you to write about?" The voice came from a head bowed down over a phone.

"Actually, I find people in general interesting." Carrie paused for a minute, then decided she had nothing to lose by being blunt. "But my supervisor at another practicum said writing while people talked wasn't a good idea. So I stopped. Can we start with you, and go around to say names?"

The face in the phone spoke again after introductions. She hadn't looked up once. "What are you supposed to be doing here anyways?"

"Well, I just graduated with a degree in counseling psychology. That's kind of the talking side of psychology. I don't give prescriptions or anything. My job here was, um, is to work under Dr. Bradley's supervision as a counselor. But it's not like you all are beating down the door to talk to me, so I guess I don't really know what else I'm supposed to do."

The silence that followed almost made Carrie want to giggle. She could probably tell them she lived in a cloud and slid down rainbows for fun and they wouldn't pay attention.

"Is there any reason for the big turnout this morning?" she wondered out loud.

"Mrs. M is back," Julia offered. "Everyone likes her. It's worth hanging around here all day so we can have whatever she cooks for supper."

"We help cook, too, idiot." The face in phone replied.

"Oh... that's the lady who runs the cooking class?" Carrie wondered if that was the only person at the center that any of the clients even liked.

"Whoop de do! The counselor's a genius."

"Not smart enough to avoid getting tricked by an idiot and marrying him, but whatever." She wished the hour was over. Nothing she did here would make a difference. But the face in the phone suddenly looked straight at her and Carrie was shocked to see it was Char. Both eyes were bruised and there was a nasty cut on her forehead that probably needed stitches.

"He used words," Carrie said quietly. "Not fists." She waited, unsure whether to ask about the injuries or not.

"They say the words are worse. But some guys sure know how to throw a punch."

"I don't know what to say," Carrie admitted. "What happened?"

"Well, he wanted me to sleep with his dealer and I didn't want to."

Julia rolled her eyes, "What, *now* you have standards? Coulda fooled me."

"Shut up Julia."

"How many of the rest of you have to deal with physical violence?"

A few of them raised hesitant hands. "What makes it stop?"

"Jail? Not that it stops for good, but it's a nice break. And it's nice to know where you're going to sleep while you're in."

"Wait, you mean if *you* go to jail?" Carrie was having trouble understanding what she was talking about.

"Duh. You didn't think the guy would get caught did you?"

"Huh. Guess I was lucky when my ex went to jail. And... it was a pretty nice break." She thought back to the eighteen months when she hadn't needed to deal with Don. Much nicer than being forced to take the kids for a supervised visit every month and knowing they had to see him.

"Do you think that makes you just like us? Cause I can tell you right now you're not." Julia snapped.

"No. It does help me see how fortunate I was. But I know that all of your experiences are different than mine. I just don't know *how* different without hearing your stories." She held up her hand to stop the next comment. "And I'm not saying you have to tell me. Only that I really don't know anything about you, and I'm not going to assume anything."

Wanting to move to a less threatening topic, Carrie asked, "What about Mrs. M? What do you like about her?"

"She acts like she likes us." Julia offered. "I mean, maybe she doesn't but it really seems like she does."

"She didn't put mushrooms in the stir fry when I told her I didn't like them. My mom would purposefully make food I didn't like, just to make me eat it. Bitch."

"I like that she doesn't preach at us."

"And her lasagna. Oh my god."

"Now we're getting somewhere! OK, what's everyone's favorite food of hers?" Carrie was desperate to find some common ground to end the session with. And it worked. At least favorite food was a neutral enough topic that everyone felt comfortable talking about.

Waiting for everyone to make their way to the front office after the session so she could turn out the lights in the room, Carrie realized that Char was holding back. "Hey," she smiled. She didn't actually get a smile in return, but at least it didn't scare her off.

"Can I ask you a question?"

"Of course."

"Your ex. How did you get away?"

"Long version or short version?"

"Both."

"Let me go sign everyone out that was here for the group session and then I'll tell you."

Ten minutes later they were back in the group session room. Carrie sat down first so Char could choose how close to be. She sat down one chair away from Carrie.

"Like I mentioned, my ex used words to hurt me. Everything I did was wrong, and everything that he did wrong was my fault. It was a long slow process for me to realize everything *wasn't* my fault. And then it was a long slow process to save enough money to be able to move out. He wouldn't let me have a job, or babysit other people's kids or anything, so I did things like cash in pop cans and take a few extra dollars in cash out whenever I did a debit card purchase."

"But didn't a part of you want to stay? I mean, you loved him and all..."

"It seems like that's where it was different for me than a lot of others. I didn't want to stay at all. And I truly didn't love him anymore. I wouldn't have believed it was possible to stop loving someone until it happened to me. Tell me, Char. Did you feel loved and safe growing up?"

She snorted, "Are you kidding? The only safe place for me was when my parents passed out. And it took a long time for them to get there."

"It wasn't like that for me. I had—still have—really nice, loving parents. I think that's why it was easier to leave. I mean, it took years to clue in that our relationship was abusive, but when I did I totally switched my focus to making a plan to leave."

"How long did it take? To leave?"

"Almost two years."

"Shit. I won't make it two years."

"Do you have a plan started?"

"No. But I think I want one."

Carrie took a deep breath. "I'm going to need help with this. You know

I'm new at all of this right?" Char nodded. "And the time you decide to leave—even if you haven't left yet—is when you're most at risk for more harm."

"Yeah, guys get pretty pissed off when they think they might not be able to mess with you anymore."

"You got that right. Are you OK if we talk to Donna about this?"

"Not yet. Julia's really nosy, and if she sees me talking to two of you in one day, she might go blab something."

"Alright. Do you have the number to the crisis line?" Again, Char nodded. "Use it at any time, OK? And I'm here Mondays and Tuesdays for the next five and a half months."

"You counting?"

"Well, this is the first real conversation I've had here. But maybe I'll figure out how to be more useful."

When they came out of the room, Carrie recognized a friendly face. "Mary!"

"You *know* Mrs. M?"

Carrie nodded. "She rescued me many times last year while I was studying for my master's degree by taking my kids to her house for baking fun!"

"Carrie! Char! So nice to see you both!" She reached up and gently touched Char's face. "Oh my dear. That looks painful."

Char's chin trembled for a minute before she clenched her jaw, "It's OK. Worse than it looks, hey?"

"So I see you've met Carrie. Isn't she wonderful? Carrie! Is that a ring I see on your finger?"

"Yes, Jonathan threw me a graduation party a few weeks ago and totally surprised me with a proposal!"

"I'm so happy for you!" She turned to Char. "It's nice to know there are still some happy endings out there, isn't it?"

"I guess," she said before walking away.

"We'll catch up later," Mary promised. "I'm going to see who's interested in baking some cookies."

Carrie stopped to check in with Donna. It seemed like the whole center was happier now that Mary was back. Once she finished her reporting, she followed the pleasant sound of voices chatting and utensils clinking to the kitchen.

Sitting in a corner of the kitchen gave Carrie a chance to quietly observe everyone. With Mary's kindness and gentle instruction, she saw them let their guard down and enjoy the simple activity of baking cookies. She wondered how many of them had any memories of doing things like this as children.

A few still held back, but when it was time to pass around warm, fresh-baked cookies, everyone stepped in. It was Julia who saw Carrie in the corner and brought her two cookies on a napkin. "You didn't actually help with anything. But here."

"Thanks!" Carrie took a bite and closed her eyes to savor the moment. When she opened them again, everyone was watching her. "What?"

"Are they OK?" one of the younger girls asked.

"They're fantastic!" With her approval, everyone went back to eating.

Mary handed out takeout containers to everyone, and they all began to pack up the remaining cookies. "We'll start making bread at three, and then lasagna at four-thirty. Let's aim for dinner around six?"

There was a murmur of agreement. "All right, let's get going. These are best served fresh."

"Where are you going?" Carrie asked.

"We take the rest of these to any panhandlers or others hanging around the area," Julia explained. "That's Mary's thing, you know, giving back and shit."

CHAPTER TWELVE

Jaz

Jaz looked around at her sewing room. Normally she didn't mind having projects everywhere, but things were getting out of control—even for her! Now that they were getting going on their housing project she was more determined than ever to grow a business that would make even more money. After all, the more she made, the more she could help.

She tried to separate clothes into different piles but soon forgot which things went where and had to start over again.

"Aargh!" she shouted and then clamped her hand over her mouth. Sure enough, she heard Alex start to fuss. With a sigh, she turned to her bedroom where he was supposed to be napping.

"Hey you," she said, reaching down to pick him up. As frustrating as it was to be interrupted in the middle of trying to get something done, his adorable face made her smile. "I thought I'd get more sleep out of you. That's what I get for yelling, I guess."

After feeding him she went downstairs. Maria was at the table with her laptop, messaging clients. "Everything OK?" she asked.

"Yeah, I was trying to get organized, but I forgot which things went where and had to start all over again." She passed Alex on to Maria and went to bring his bouncy chair over to the table. He loved being able to see his favorite people while he played.

"What categories are you using?"

"I want to separate everything into the different lines of clothing. I feel like it's all getting jumbled together and I can't keep track."

"It sounds like a good idea—getting organized, I mean. How can I help?"

"I'm kinda stuck. What do you think?"

"Well, why don't we list out all the lines you have and the pieces under each of them? We can use some printer paper to make signs and tape them all to the sliding glass doors!"

Jaz giggled, "OK!" Soon she had signs for Maternity, Baby & Toddler, Kids, Men, and Trendy Young Adult taped to the large glass doors. "I know 'trendy young adult' is wordy, but it works for now."

"Wonderful! Now, can you list the pieces that fit under each one, and the prices?"

"OK, but I'll need you to look up prices for some stuff as I go. I used to remember everything, but there's too much stuff now!"

Together they started to fill the sliding doors with labels. Then Maria suggested they use a different colored sticky note beside each project to show which seamstress did most of the work.

"What's going on here?" Lisa came in with her backpack over one shoulder. Some afternoons she went to a café nearby to work, claiming it was the best way to focus.

"I'm trying to get organized," Jaz admitted, "Things are getting a little crazy and I'm losing track of stuff."

Lisa stopped to say hi to Alex and give his cheek a kiss before going to the window and reading over everything. "What a great idea! I was thinking about doing some sort of spreadsheet with all of this, but having it out here to see is really helpful for a start."

"I wonder," she continued, "how many listings do we have for each item?"

Maria went through the online site counting, and Jaz added in the numbers for each piece.

"And how many of each do we expect to be returned on Friday?"

Jaz turned to her slowly, "I have... no idea!"

"Well, I guess we have more work to do. What if I make up an inventory spreadsheet for everything, and we can track what's going out and coming back in? I'm sure the ladies are all honest, but it can't hurt to keep better track of things."

"Yeah, that's actually a good idea! And what if we started keeping track of how much of each thing we sell in a week so we can plan ahead? Last night I was scrambling to make more baby bandanas because we sold out."

"We definitely don't want you working on things the other ladies can easily do. I hate to say it Jaz, but the way things are growing you may need to spend more of your time planning and less on sewing—except for Carrie's wedding dress, of course."

"If it means we can make more money, I'm game. Have you heard anything from Frank and Sandra about properties?"

"Not yet. But it's only been two days since our meeting!"

"I know. I just want something to *happen*, you know?"

"It will, it will." Maria assured her. "But the better organized you are, the better position you'll be in when things do happen. I'm all done with replies for now, and you're pretty full for appointments for the rest of the week. Lisa, can you make a spreadsheet for me to fill in that tracks how fast everything sells?"

"For sure!" She sat down and pulled out her laptop. "And then I'll put your lovely window chart into spreadsheet form too and set it up so you can both add to it. Jaz, do you have more ideas for projects than what's up there?"

"You're kidding, right?" Jaz bumped her shoulder into Lisa, "How many lines can I fill with ideas?"

They all got to work, with Jaz occasionally running upstairs to check on materials she had stacked up for future projects. An hour later Alex was more than done with his bouncy chair, and Lisa had a list for Jaz of everything they needed for inventory.

"Wow! This is great!" She unbuckled Alex as she talked. "Now I can make sure I have everything ready for the ladies on Friday to fill-up what we need the most! Probably way better than me randomly putting things together."

She moved over to the living room where she rolled out a playmat for Alex and lay him on his tummy. While he kicked his legs and rocked back and forth she gave herself a little lecture. It had been fun to start multiple projects and throw things together to hand out on Friday. But now she needed to get serious about her business. People would be relying on her soon, and she needed to act like a proper businesswoman.

On impulse, she texted her dad:

> *Can you and I take Alex for his walk tonight or tomorrow night? I have some things I want to talk to you about.*

Her dad had been in the corporate world his whole life. Maybe he'd have some advice for her.

"Oh my goodness!" Maria interrupted her thoughts after looking down at her phone. "The TV station wants to come on Friday to film us for their Go Green segment. That works OK, right?"

They all looked at each other for a minute before bursting out laughing. "I guess it will have to be!"

"You'd better get everything possible listed between now and when they air," Lisa warned, "because things are about to get even *more* crazy!"

A new energy took over the room as they continued to work. Lisa started to set-up the new tracking spreadsheets, and Maria and Jaz looked through their inventory, trying to decide where Jaz should focus her sewing time for the next two days. When it was time for Becky's bus to come, Jaz went out to get her with Alex on her hip, and then set him up on the floor in the living room with Maria supervising both kids so she could start sewing.

That night, Jaz and her dad talked about running a business while they walked around the lake with Alex in his stroller. He was big enough to be propped up to look around, and loved all the new sights and sounds along the way.

"While I still wish you'd focus on providing for yourself and Alex, I can't help but be proud of you for what you're trying to do," her dad started. "Just make sure you're planning for your future and his, OK?"

"I am. Lisa has me putting money into a savings plan for Alex, plus taking 30% of the net profits every month instead of a flat rate. That way my own net worth is growing along with the business. I wish I would have taken a business class in high school though. The sewing and designing part is easy, but the other stuff is a lot harder."

"Well, it sounds like having Lisa working for you is helping. What if I took on a role as advisor, maybe with a few others that have experience? We could meet once a month, and you show us where you're at and we'll give you some advice?"

"Daddy, that's a great idea! Thank you!"

"I'm happy to help where I can. I'll see if Ellison's dad is interested too. He's just been promoted to vice president at his job, so he'll have lots of good advice to offer."

Jaz just about choked. But she couldn't think of anything to say so she nodded and they continued walking. She was up late into the night sewing and trying not to think about having extended contact with the grandfather of her son—even though he didn't know he had a grandson.

CHAPTER THIRTEEN

Lisa

"Hi Frank!"

"Lisa, hello. I hope I didn't catch you at a bad time?"

"Nope, we're just finishing up breakfast here. What can I do for you?"

"Well, I have a few properties I thought you might want to take a look at."

Lisa gave a thumbs up to her mom and Jaz who looked up as soon as they heard Frank's name. "Sounds great! I can work my schedule around whatever suits you."

"OK, let's look at Friday morning then—"

"Oh, sorry, anything *but* Friday. The local TV station is coming over that day to do a feature on the Jazzy Clothing Company for their Go Green week!" Lisa couldn't keep the pride out of her voice.

"That's wonderful! You'll have to tell me when it airs so I can be sure to watch it! Should we wait until next week then? These are not hot properties. I don't expect anything to change if we wait a few more days."

"What about today or tomorrow? I don't really have any prep to do for Friday, I just need to be here on the day to watch the kids."

"Let me see what I can do and I'll get back to you."

Lisa agreed and hung up. "I guess this week we start looking at properties!"

"Oh, that's so exciting! What a week it's turning into!" Maria looked down at her phone, where she had numerous lists going in preparation for Friday's excitement. "Now, it looks like the only one of the ladies who doesn't want to be filmed on Friday is Susan. No surprise there. If her kids found out she was sewing for a proper company they'd probably try to stop her."

"I want to get a place right now for her!"

"I know Jaz, but we've got to keep an eye on the bigger picture." Maria reminded her. "I want to get her out too, but we can't force her." She looked at Lisa. "Did Frank say anything about the properties?"

Lisa shook her head, "I guess it'll be a surprise. In the meantime, I'm going to try and get my freelancing work done early, just in case." She stood up to start clearing the table, and Jaz joined her.

"Isn't it weird that on the day we get everything with the business organized we get the booking from the TV station?"

"I don't know," Lisa answered. "Is it a case of 'luck favors the prepared'? Or good things come to those who work for it?"

"Either way, it's kind of exciting! I'm going to spend the morning getting all the current inventory listed, and then I'll do some more sewing."

"You were still sewing after I went to bed..." Lisa exchanged a glance with her mom. They both noticed that Jaz worked later into the night when she was worried about something. "Everything OK?"

Jaz deftly took apart Alex's bottle and put it in the dishwasher before answering. She smiled, "I can hardly remember when I used to have two hands to do anything!" Her smile faded before she continued, "I asked my dad last night if he could give me some business advice. I thought it might be a good way for him to see that I'm doing good, and give some tips or something." She propped Alex on the counter with one arm still around him while she wiped away crumbs with her free hand.

"What did he say?" Maria asked gently.

"Oh, he was more than happy to help. But then he said he'd ask someone else too..." she bit her lip, clearly conflicted about what to say. "Um, someone who's actually related to Alex but doesn't know it."

"Holy cow," Lisa breathed, "You're talking about his other grandpa, aren't you."

Jaz nodded, "I promised the sperm donor I wouldn't say anything. But I didn't think I'd ever have contact with his family. And it's too late to take back my request for help. I wish I hadn't said anything!"

"The only reason you did it was to build your relationship with your dad. There's nothing wrong with that. And maybe this will be a good thing! You can see if this other person is someone you want in Alex's life. It's just my opinion, but I say whatever's best for Alex overrules any promise you made to anyone else."

Jaz looked at Lisa, "I never thought of that. But you're right. Alex comes first." She let out a sigh, "Um, that helps. Thanks."

Lisa came over and gave her a side hug, "Our life was so boring before you came, I don't even remember what we did! But now we all need to get cracking on our morning! I'll call you down for lunch if you forget to eat."

She watched Jaz head back upstairs with Alex, hoping she gave the right advice. Dads could wreck everything if they wanted to. Jaz's dad seemed decent and kind, but time would tell whether he would support his daughter and grandson.

Giving her head a shake she went to the recently purchased buffet in the dining room. With two businesses being run from the house, the paperwork and laptops needed a place to be put away at the end of the day. Without space for a home office, the buffet was the next best thing. From the outside, it looked like a nice piece of furniture with a healthy-looking peace lily on one end and a collection of cream-colored candles at the other. But when the doors opened, they revealed an immaculate set of hanging files, office supplies, and a slide-out shelf for the printer. It had the added benefit of being accessible to Maria in her wheelchair.

She pulled out Maria's laptop first and set it in front of her at the table before getting her own out. They had gotten into the routine of working side-by-side in the mornings after breakfast. Maria would give Lisa updated sales numbers and reply to all the online inquiries until Jaz came down with the previous day's online orders. Then she'd switch to lining up shipping labels.

Lisa would update the numbers and send Jaz a short summary before switching to her freelance work. The extra time to focus on the clothing company gave her the chance to better understand how Jaz thought. She was quick to catch onto things and had a good business mind, but she preferred to see summaries in a quick text, rather than on a spreadsheet.

The two women worked contentedly beside each other for nearly an hour, only pausing to comment on the number of online orders. Jaz had to make two trips downstairs with everything.

"If you want, you can use a laundry basket and save yourself an extra trip," Lisa suggested. "It looks like this is the new normal for orders."

"Good idea! Yeah, I'll start that tomorrow."

When Frank called back, Lisa was completely wrapped up in reconciling her newest client's bank statement and needed a nudge from her mom to realize her phone was buzzing.

"Hi Frank!"

"Good news! We can fit in the viewings tomorrow starting at one! I'll see if I can find anything else, but there's definitely three on the list right now."

"That's great! See you tomorrow then!" She scribbled a note to herself to make sure Jaz could get Becky from the bus the next day before telling Maria.

"I have a good feeling about this!" she replied.

Too excited to wait inside the next day, she went out in the front yard just before one. As a teenager, she hated yard work, but now she liked to think she was getting a bit of a green thumb. Having her own place made all the difference. She walked around, dead-heading any fading flowers from the pots that stood on either side of the porch and the flower beds that bordered the lawn. This year she was trying to fit as many colors as possible into her gardening plan, and the yard was a rainbow of brilliant colors. Neighbors often stopped to tell her how much they enjoyed her efforts.

When Frank pulled into the driveway, she dusted off her hands a little reluctantly before getting into his car.

"Your yard looks more stunning every time I visit!"

"Thanks! Planting flowers becomes a bit of an addiction! And now that I'm not clocking into a job downtown every day, I have more time to putter around my yard. But enough about that. Tell me about the places we're seeing!"

"Well, it's a bit of a mixed bag. First off, we're going to see an apart-ment building. It's not big—only twelve units—but I want you to get familiar with these types of properties. Then we'll look at a duplex and then a fourplex that's been on the market for a while."

Lisa was armed with a list of practical things to look out for such as playgrounds, public transportation, and busy roads. She hoped she could view the properties through the eyes of seniors, and people with kids instead of just development potential.

The apartment was easy to rule out. Not only was it on the corner of two busy roads, but it didn't have any green space around it and the nearest proper grocery store was at least a twenty-minute walk away. Lisa knew from her own days as a student on a tight budget that having access to reasonably priced food was essential. When people could only get to a convenience store for their shopping they were limited by price *and* selection.

Although the duplex was nice, and one of the units would be vacant at the end of the month, Lisa couldn't get excited about it.

The fourplex was a different story. As they drove through the neighborhood, she liked what she saw. Many of the houses were big, but they weren't flashy or pretentious and most of the yards were well kept too. There was an elementary school with a colorful playground just up the street too.

"Now, this one doesn't have any grocery stores close by," Frank interrupted her thoughts, "but there's a really good bus service that runs regularly." He drove past an unkempt yard and stopped in front of an even messier looking property. "I'm not sure about the whole story here, but it sounds like someone bought it as an investment property and then forgot to invest any money in it. Apparently, the last remaining tenant moved out quite a few months ago."

Lisa tried to be objective. There was a decent-sized, rather overgrown front yard with a pathway in the middle of the property that led to two front doors side by side. The pathway turned both ways and wrapped around the building.

"Are the other two doors around the back?"

"I think so. Let's take a look."

They walked around the building to the backyard where the other entrances were located before Frank produced the keys. Each unit had a kitchen, half bath, and living room on the first floor and either two or three bedrooms and a full bath on the second floor. Looking out onto the neighbor's yard, Lisa saw a girl of six or seven with her arms spread out, slowly spinning in circles and looking at the sky.

It was such an unusual scene that she continued to watch. The girl was dark-skinned but in some ways reminded her of Becky. Maybe it was the way she moved. Her black curly hair stuck out everywhere and she was wearing a nightie, with an image so faded it wasn't recognizable. Lisa briefly wondered why she wasn't at school before turning away from the window.

CHAPTER FOURTEEN

Carrie

Thursday! Carrie woke up feeling happy. Her practicum was over for the week, she had the morning to work on painting frames, and then lunch and the afternoon with Jonathan. *This* was something she could get used to!

After dropping the kids off at school she hurried home, eager to get more projects done. All the frames in her inventory were listed for sale on her website already, so she was overdue to bring her numbers up. And this evening Lauren would be over with another batch of upcycled paintings. Carrie smiled as she covered her kitchen table with the old shower curtain and then started priming frames.

It was hard to believe how far Lauren had come since Carrie met her almost two years ago. From terrified about giving birth, to struggling to care for a suddenly disabled husband and new baby, to creating amazing works of art from the paintings everyone else donated to the thrift stores, Lauren really was her own version of upcycling!

By eleven Carrie had all the frames primed for her next project. She texted Jonathan that she'd rather meet at his place, since her table was in use, and then grabbed her laptop to go over her finances before meeting with him.

Her new and improved financial position still surprised her. The times when she hid a few dollars whenever she could, trying desperately to save enough money to get her own place without her husband finding (and spending) her money were long gone. And so were the months of only having a few dollars to spare after paying the bills. She remembered Kara's thoughtfulness in always paying her cash on Fridays for the childcare Carrie provided, and the thrill of selling the first coffee table she pulled out of a dumpster and cleaned up.

But things really took off when she found a stash of cash in a discarded end table drawer. That had paid for her to finish her undergrad degree while continuing to babysit and fix up furniture. Then she discovered her talent for turning old picture frames into works of art. With a smile, she thought back to the first time she bought groceries without adding up every penny. Taking her kids to McDonald's because she could, buying Christmas gifts for her family—those were luxuries she would never take for granted.

While her first year of grad school required painting and selling frames in every spare minute she wasn't studying, by the second year, she only had to sell enough to cover her expenses after she proudly paid in full for grad school from her earnings.

Her agreement with Lauren helped ease financial pressure immensely. Carrie kept a 20% commission from everything of Lauren's she sold, in exchange for listing her paintings on Carrie's *Framed* website. It was an agreement that worked perfectly for both of them. Lauren had no interest in the business side of selling her paintings, and Carrie appreciated the variety they brought to her inventory and the extra income.

In the last few months of grad school, Carrie had completely ignored her business bank account, only transferring out enough to cover her monthly expenses. But she was using her evenings now to slowly catch up with everything. Her friend Jenny had coached her on budgeting, financial planning, and even business management so it didn't take too long for her to finish up her summaries and know exactly where she stood.

But she still went back to double check her numbers, just in case. Even with the extra spending she had done on take out and frozen dinners in the last month, her bank account was solidly in the black. The one month of emergency savings that she kept as a buffer hadn't been touched, and her business account had over $4,800 in it after transferring out enough money for June's expenses.

She was excited to go into marriage able to completely provide for herself and the kids, and she was determined to always keep it that way. Never again would she be trapped because she didn't have an income.

It was less than four years ago that Carrie had left her marriage, but the memories of what it was like to *not* be able to leave when she needed hadn't faded. She knew the desperation of looking at her tiny emergency fund and knowing it would be a long time before she could leave. And she knew the heartbreak of seeing her ex continue to make her kids feel terrible, even when they didn't live with him anymore. Although they still had supervised visits once a month, knowing the rest of the time they were safe from him was worth everything to her.

Grabbing her laptop, purse, and keys, she walked around the corner to Jonathan's house. The little tingle in her stomach was a bit stronger than usual as she thought about spending the afternoon with him. They'd both been so busy the last few weeks that there hadn't been much time alone. Today they had a blissful two and a half hours before needing to go pick up Katie from school.

"Hello?" she called as she opened the door.

"Out here!" came an answer from the back deck. "Hey there," he said as he walked in to meet her. He took her things out of her hands before kissing her a proper, long hello. "I've missed you all morning."

"Silly man," she said, and then felt a little shy. "Wow, I feel weird. We haven't really had any time together lately."

"Tell me about it! Come on outside, I've got lunch ready." The patio table was set up with takeout from the deli. "I thought it felt like a picnic day. You OK with sandwiches?"

"Only if there's a proper corned beef sandwich with extra pickles on the side!"

"But of course my lady. Nothing but the best for you!" He bowed before pulling out her chair. The takeaway packages were opened up at each place setting, enticing her with fillings spilling out the edges of the rye bread, and pickles and chips on the side. Glasses of iced tea were already showing a little condensation.

Carrie sat down and kicked off her sandals before stretching her feet out. The patio was warm on her toes, but the bright orange umbrella over the table shaded their lunch. She noticed the smell of fresh-cut grass that came from the tidy back yard, before taking a bite of her sandwich. "Wow, I didn't realize how hungry I was. Thanks!"

As they ate, they skirted around the issue of finances before Carrie couldn't stand it anymore. "All right, we've got to have *the talk* about money. Shall I go first?"

"Please."

"Well, the bad news is that I still have student loans from forever ago. I checked before I came over. Total owing is $3,480. And, I got stuck with a credit card debt after I left Don. That's still at $6,500." She felt the familiar angry tears threaten to come—the ones she always felt when she thought back to how helpless she had been, and how she was still paying the price for her ex-husband's recklessness.

Clearing her throat, she continued. "The good news is that I can cover my monthly expenses easily with my *Framed* sales. And I have a month's expenses in my checking account as emergency funds and $4,800 in my business bank account."

"What do you think of Matthew's question about helping with the housing project?"

"Well, until he suggested it, I hadn't thought about it at all. I'm so used to not having any money to help others. But... I looked at things carefully today before I came over, and I can easily do $500 a month." She laughed. "I can't believe I can even say that!"

"What if all your income was yours to do what you wanted with?"

"What do you mean?"

"What if you could spend your *Framed* profits on anything? Then what would you do?"

She looked at him, "Jonathan, I know where this is going. But it's really important that I contribute and pay my own way."

"Do you remember when I took you to see that house that Chris and I were in the middle of flipping?" Carrie nodded and Jonathan continued, "And do you remember how you inspired me to get my own finances in order?"

"Well I didn't—" she started.

"—Yes, you did. You changed my life long before you made me the happiest man in the world by *finally* agreeing to date me. I took care of some stuff that needed taking care of, and Jenny helped me with figuring out the rest. Because of you, I'm actually in a position where I can make things easier for you and the kids."

She leaned over and kissed him softly. "Well, you still did all the work to get where you are now."

He gazed at her for a moment with a smile on his face before continuing. "OK, let's talk about that. I owe just over $100,000 on the mortgage here, and it'll be paid off before Matthew graduates. Everything else is clear, thanks to you—it's crazy how I didn't even consider how much debt I had. But I've paid it all off now." He nervously pushed his blonde wavy hair off his forehead. "Um, I *was* hoping you and the kids would want to move in here..."

Carrie tried to keep a straight face. "Well...I don't know...I mean, it's OK I guess..." She laughed and lightly punched him in the shoulder.

"I'm *joking*! I've been salivating over this house since you gave me that first tour when it was still bare floors and blank walls!"

"Phew!" He leaned back in his chair and put his hand over his chest. "But you know, if you want to pick your own home, we can do that!"

"I don't. I love your house. I mean, it's missing some color and a few girly things thrown around, but other than that it's perfect. And I love that we can keep the kids in this school."

"I'll have your name added to the property deed then. And can you get the name of the company that did Maria's bathroom? I think we can put in an elevator, or maybe one of those stairlifts, and renovate the middle floor bathroom. Then your parents can visit whenever they want."

"Oh Jonathan, really? You just finished renovating!"

"Doesn't matter. I know you've been dreaming about having a house your parents can visit you in, and if it means we put a few more holes in the wall so your mom can get around in her wheelchair, then that's what we'll do!"

"I can help pay for it!"

"You can, but you won't." He held up his hand to stop her protest. "That's not up for discussion. I have money set aside for that and anything you want done to the house. I want you to be happy Carrie. You've spent enough years pinching every penny, and denying yourself anything nice, so you can take care of your kids. Now that we're in this together, it's time for you to relax a bit."

"I can't even really process what you're saying. It's too good to be true."

"Want to switch to wedding talk? Or honeymoon talk?" He winked at Carrie and she found herself blushing like a teenager.

"Uh...." she held her hands to her cheeks for a moment before looking back at him. "The things you do to me..." she answered quietly.

He reached for her hand. "You know how lucky we are to have found each other?" she nodded. "I just want you to be happy." he finished.

"Oh, I am. OK," she took a big breath and changed the topic. "We both have super small families, and the guest list beyond that won't be too big... There's a little church not too far away. What about seeing if we can have the ceremony there, and then come back here for a reception in the backyard?"

"Are you sure? We can find something fancier."

"Nope. Simple and elegant is what I really want. Oh wait... November. It'll be too cold for the backyard by then! We'll have to think of something else that might work."

"We'll find something. Hey, speaking of work, how did practicum go this week? Are the people at the center finally talking to you?"

"Actually, they are! Well, one of them. And remember Mary from church? She's back from visiting her grandchildren and teaches cooking there on Mondays! They all love her, so when they found out I knew her too, it's like I got my first little bit of street cred!"

"It was so neat," she continued, "Mary bakes cookies with them, and then they pack them up and deliver them around the area to any panhandlers or homeless people. I saw a few of the girls show something close to happiness about being able to do something nice."

She reached back and tried to rub some of the tension out of her neck. "But I really don't know if I can do any good there. I'm not *trying* to force anything, but it feels like every time I say something or do something the women push back at me. I wish I could connect with them, and somehow let them know I'm on their side."

CHAPTER FIFTEEN

Maria

The alarm clock surprised Maria. She was so eager to hear about the properties Lisa was looking at that she hadn't expected to fall asleep after lunch. Gingerly she stretched and tried to make some slow circles with her bad foot. It was healing slowly after her fall and even though the cast was off now, she was very cautious about using it. She needed her mobility more than ever with everything that was going on. By the time she moved herself to the living room, Jaz was walking in the door with Becky.

She heard the clunk of Becky kicking off her shoes almost immediately.

"Come on, let's go to the bathroom," Jaz insisted.

Maria smiled. Jaz was now comfortable helping Becky out, and somehow managed it even with Alex. She hoped that one day Jaz would find a partner who would be a good match and support her with all her ambitions. It was something she still wanted for Lisa too, but she really couldn't imagine a man that would complement Lisa and still give her the independence she needed.

When Becky walked into the room with a cookie in each hand and a big smile on her face Maria put her wishes aside. Right now she had her sweet little friend to focus on. That was good enough. The two hours she spent with Becky every weekday afternoon were always rewarding. Maria had once dreamed of becoming a preschool teacher, and she loved the chance to work with Becky and help her develop new skills.

Chris and Carla kept her informed of Becky's learning goals from school, and together with Becky's teachers they were all working together to improve her communication. Some days Maria would repeat the same little lesson over and over without seeming to make any progress. But other days it was like a light turned on in Becky's head, and she would fully grasp a new skill.

With all the resources available online, Maria was learning new things to pass on to Becky. Now Becky often used basic sign language to ask for food or a drink, tell Maria if she was happy, sad, or angry, ask to watch TV, and say 'I love you'. While she still usually reserved that phrase for her parents, every once in a while she would spontaneously sign it to Maria. Those little moments made her heart sing. If Maria had her whole life to live over, she would have taken baby Lisa, left her husband, and found a way to become a special needs teacher.

When Lisa returned from her afternoon with Frank, Jaz came down with Alex and put him on the floor beside Becky, and they gave Lisa their full attention.

"I think we have a contender. It's a fourplex that's been vacant for a while now. I like the neighborhood—there's an elementary school with a huge playground and good bus service. Most of the other houses in the neighborhood are modest, but nice. Oh, except for the house next door which has a pretty rough looking yard."

"At the front are the entrances to two units, and then the other entrances are at the back. Each has a small living area, kitchen, and half bath downstairs and two bedrooms and a full bath upstairs."

"No units that are completely on the ground floor?" Maria didn't think they could provide anything accessible if it had stairs.

"No, not at the moment. I don't know... There might be a way to renovate to have one ground floor only unit, but I can't picture it. We'll need someone with some imagination to help with that. The only other problem is the price. It's listed at $695,000 right now and Frank feels it's too high considering the state it's in. I guess the good news is that no one else wants it at that price either, so it's been on the market for a while."

Jaz took away a hair elastic that Becky was trying to give to Alex and replaced it with a baby toy, "Here, try this instead," she said before looking up. "So what do we do next?"

"Let's send an email out to everyone with the information we have so far and see what they say." Maria suggested. "And then if there's interest Frank could schedule another viewing with everyone who wants to see it in person?"

"Good idea Mom. That takes all the pressure off me to make any sort of decision. I'll go do that now and send it off before I make supper."

"Remember Susan's supposed to come by sometime tonight to bring her work and pick up the next set so she's not here when they're filming tomorrow."

"Right, thanks. Will she want to come for supper?"

"I asked, but she said she has to be home to feed the kids, and then she'll be over whenever her daughter gets home from work." Maria felt herself worrying again about her friend.

Susan didn't arrive until almost nine that evening. She apologized profusely for the late hour. "I didn't realize my daughter had planned to go out for drinks after work. I had to stay until the younger two were in bed."

The other women exchanged glances but said nothing.

"Well," Maria said brightly, "We're always happy to have you here, no matter what the time. Why don't we get right to it so you can get yourself to bed. You look about ready to collapse!"

When Susan left, the three of them sat silently at the table. Finally, Jaz spoke, "Do you think she'll ever leave, even if she has a good place to go?"

"I don't know. They have such a hold on her. She knows deep down that it's not right, but I don't know if she'll be able to cut that dependency. All we can do is offer her a solution. It's up to her whether or not she takes it."

Maria lay in bed thinking about all the good people in her life while trying to ignore the pain that was coursing through her body. Sure, they had struggles, but she felt overwhelmed with the fact that her life was so full. Her last thought as she drifted off to sleep was how nice it was to be so tired she actually fell asleep when she went to bed.

The next morning she was wide awake before her alarm. After taking her pills she lay back and thought about the day. Not one for daytime television anymore, she had taken time over the past week to watch a few shows with the host who would interview Jaz about her business. He seemed to do a lot of reporting on the environment and had challenged some companies who called themselves green but didn't always follow up with actions. She hoped he would see Jaz and her business for all the goodness it created.

When she felt her medication start to kick in, she carefully got up to shower and get ready for the day. She wasn't expecting to be in sight of the cameras but she still wanted to look her best. As she stepped into the shower and used the grab bar to slowly lower herself onto the shower chair, she said a prayer of gratitude for Lisa who had worked so hard to provide her with a safe and beautiful place to live. Needing Robert's help to do things like showering had made her feel like a child and a nuisance. Now, even though her rheumatoid arthritis was progressing, she took care of all her personal needs herself thanks to her accessible bathroom.

She dressed in a soft grey skirt that Jaz had altered to look fitted when

Maria was sitting in her wheelchair. It had a small slit on either side and an elastic waistband that was loose enough to pull on herself, but still fit comfortably. It came just below her knees, allowing her to shift in her seat without always needing to pull her skirt down.

Her top was another Jazzy Clothing Company creation. It was a soft rose floral pattern accented with random white flowers. Maria often struggled to get tops on, and Jaz had worked tirelessly on a way to alter them without losing any style. Finally, she came up with a genius solution. On one arm she cut the sleeve all the way from the neck down and finished the seams. Then she added three tabs with Velcro closures so Maria could slip the shirt through one arm and close it over her other arm. In typical Jaz fashion, she had added a white fabric rosette at each connection which made the design look intentional and stylish.

The last challenge with the shirt had been the Velcro along her shoulder that sometimes came loose when Maria was moving around too much. Jaz added a button closure hidden by the top rosette, making the shirt secure and practical. While Maria needed help to do up and undo the button, she could still get dressed and undressed on her own.

She finger-styled her short hair, put on a little blush, and smiled at her reflection. At 45 years old, it often surprised her to see her reflection. She felt a lot older than that, probably because of all the hard years when she was married. Part of her transformation after Robert died was to slowly let go of the mousy look and attitude that she had lived with as his wife. It took time to find her true self and begin to let her sunny personality out, but now that she had there was no turning back.

Maria sighed. No matter how good she felt about her life now, the reality of her health was a different story. She wouldn't get better, that was for sure. And slowly her mobility would decrease while the pain increased. But today was a good day and she determined to enjoy it.

CHAPTER SIXTEEN

Jaz

Jaz looked up when she heard Maria's bedroom door open and smiled as she watched her wheel herself over. Creating accessible clothing was the biggest challenge she had faced so far with her business, but she could tell it was starting to work.

The color of the top suited Maria's sweet personality, and the grey skirt was stylish enough for anyone to wear. Paired with grey flats, Maria looked the part of a capable Executive Assistant. Jaz reached over and did up the button hidden by the rosette before giving her a hug.

"You look so pretty!"

"Thank you! And you and Alex are looking wonderful too!" She reached out her arms and Jaz set Alex in her lap before going to get tea for both of them. After reading that she shouldn't wear white or black on camera, Jaz had struggled to decide what to wear. Her signature look of simple basic pieces paired with bright vintage earrings was made almost entirely of black and white items.

Finally, she decided on a light blue wrap dress made from a men's shirt. Now that she had her tiny figure back she could highlight it with a wide purple band around the waist. A pair of bright yellow feather earrings gave her look a pop, and her straight dark hair was in its usual short bob.

Alex was dressed in a red button-up shirt and a little purple bow tie, khaki shorts and his slippers that looked like loafers. She wasn't sure if he'd be in any of the interview shots, but he'd certainly steal the show if he was!

Last night she forced herself to go to bed before midnight after spending many nights in a row working on adding to her inventory. It felt like she had done everything possible to be ready for the day.

All the listings were at their new, increased prices that Lisa had suggested a few weeks ago, and the finished products that the seam-stresses brought today would help boost the inventory if sales were as high as Carrie warned them they might be. Her own feature on the same show the year before made a huge difference to her income when she was trying to finish paying for grad school.

When the TV crew knocked at the door, Jaz, Maria, and Lisa were ready for them. Lisa went to let them in, and soon they had set up and were taking various shots of the front yard, the house, and Jaz's sewing room.

The ladies arrived with their finished products before ten, and with all of them sitting around the table showing their projects and listening to Jaz explain their next set of tasks, they soon forgot they were being filmed. Alex was passed around to each of them in turn, and there was a feeling of teamwork and hope that soon had the camera crew and TV host smiling.

After the seamstresses left, Lisa took Alex up for his nap and Jaz and Maria sat down for a more personal interview. The host introduced himself as Mark Campbell, environmental and special features host, and got right down to business.

"What makes your business a Green Business, Jaz?"

"Well, it's a combination of things. To start, we're working with products that have already been through the production cycle once. I source my supplies from thrift stores, and sometimes online auctions where people are selling things they don't want anymore."

"Second, all our seamstresses are local women who work out of their homes. For that matter, Maria and I work from home too. Using the buildings we already call home to do our work saves on commuting and reduces the number of buildings we need to keep the economy growing."

The host smiled, "Surely you don't think your little business contributes to the economy? Isn't this more of a hobby?"

Jaz turned to Maria, who answered with a warning in her voice, "This 'little business' supports the women in this house, five seamstresses, and generously contributes to the good charities that run the thrift stores where Jaz buys most of her supplies. I'd say that's not bad for a 19-year-old whose business is less than a year old!"

He nodded in agreement. "Alright, you've convinced me. And congratulations are in order! Jaz, where did you learn to sew? It's not a skill many people your age have."

Jaz told a shortened version of her grandma's story and how it had influenced her life—how impressed she had been by the way her grandma made every client feel important and stylish. "I never thought I'd actually follow in her footsteps, but I'm very proud to operate this business in her honor."

"And where can our viewers find your clothing?"

"It's all there on Instagram. Just search Jazzy Clothing Company and scroll till you find what you love. We also offer personal shopping appointments so clients can take their time choosing pieces that are perfect for them!"

"And we'll put the link on our news pages as well, so people can find you. From a small cottage industry running a Green Business in the heart of our city, I'm Mark Campbell."

Both camera operators turned off their cameras, and Jaz and Maria both let out a sigh of relief.

"Did we do OK?" Jaz asked the interviewer.

"More than OK. There's a real community feel to what you're doing here that our viewers will love. Now, just one more thing while the crew packs up," he paused.

"You'll have to spit it out!" Maria said with a smile.

"I, well, my wife is five months pregnant and she's been feeling really, well, not very good about how her body's changing. Do you have anything in your maternity line that I could buy as a gift for her?"

With a smile, Jaz asked him to follow her back upstairs to the sewing room. He pulled out his phone to show Jaz the hundreds of pictures he had of his wife, and Jaz quickly offered a variety of options. He bought one of the jean jackets that Jaz was well-known for, a wrap dress, and a maternity T-shirt that said 'Oh baby' in Greek.

"This is perfect! We went to Greece on our honeymoon and it's her favorite place in the world. Thank you!" Jaz processed his payment using an app that took credit card payments. Lisa had insisted Jaz offer it to her clients, and it made her feel even more like a professional.

That evening the three ladies sat at the table long past supper, talking about the day and wondering what kind of impact they would see when the show aired in a week's time.

"At least we still have time to increase the inventory," Jaz mused. "And thanks to your new spreadsheet Lisa we're way more organized about what to send out to the seamstresses. I almost think we're ready for another few people to join us. Do you know anyone else, Maria?"

She shook her head, "That's the limit of my contacts I'm afraid."

That night Mark Campbell's wife was on Instagram raving about her new clothes. She also sent Jaz a private message thanking her. "For the first time I'm excited to go out on a date with Mark while I'm pregnant. Thank you!"

CHAPTER SEVENTEEN

Carrie

The same day the camera crew was at Lisa's, Carrie was lost in her own world, working on frames. After weeks of feeling like she was floundering, she was now on a new mission—to pay off her student loans and old credit card debt. Now that she had a new goal, the old fire that had driven her in the past few years was back. It was fun to have a purpose and to think big again.

Just as she finished priming the seventh frame in a set, the phone rang. She quickly wiped off her hands and answered it. "Hello?"

"Hello, is this Carrie?"

"Yes."

"Carrie, my name is Susan. We have a mutual friend Maria who suggested I give you a call."

Carrie moved to her favorite armchair in the living room and sat down with her legs stretched out in front of her. It felt good to get off her feet. "Of course, how can I help you?"

"Oh, well, I was wondering if I could talk to you sometime. Do I need to make an appointment?"

There was something in her voice that rang a bell in Carrie's mind, even though she couldn't quite place it. "I'm completely free right now. Does that work?"

"Oh! I suppose so," she paused for a moment. "The thing is, I'm in a bit of a situation. I think, well, I'm not sure..." Her voice trailed off.

"How about you start by telling me about where you're at today?" Carrie asked carefully.

"Well, I live with my daughter and her husband and their kids."

"What caused you to move in with her?"

"Well, my husband decided he liked his girlfriend more than me and left me. He kept the house and I had nowhere to go except my daughter's."

Now Carrie recognized what she heard in Susan's voice. It was the sound of someone who felt trapped. "Oh wow. Do you mind telling me how old you are?"

"I'm 62."

"And how are things working out at your daughter's?"

"Well, that's the problem. They're not working out very well at all. I'd like to move out into my own place—even if it's just a little basement suite or something—but my daughter and son-in-law keep insisting I stay. And in the last few months, they've been having some troubles and I'm the only one around every day to care for the kids."

"How old are they?"

"Lucas is thirteen, Sarah's ten, and Janie is seven."

"Tell me something. What do you *really* want?"

"Oh, I want everyone to be happy!"

"OK, and what do you want for yourself?"

Carrie heard her take a shaky breath, "I just want a break from all this. I'm so tired."

"Tell me what that looks like for you. If you could have what you want, what would your day be like?" She hoped Susan would be willing to dream about a better life, but it was a hard thing to ask someone to do before they had created any trust between them. Suddenly she wondered if she should have arranged to meet face-to-face instead.

"Well, I'd like to live in a nice little place where I could have a few of my own things around, and I'd spend a lot more time sewing every day. That's what I really enjoy doing. I'd like the grandkids to visit me, rather than me always being in their house. That's it, really."

"Oh Susan, that sounds wonderful! How can I help you get to this destination?"

"I really can't leave right now. The family is in so much chaos. There's stuff everywhere in the house. If I don't make a proper dinner the kids eat junk food all night. And Lucas needs his soccer gear washed every week—I'm the only one who remembers to do it! And my daughter really needs to stop gallivanting around and spend time at home with her kids. That would solve a lot of problems."

"Do you feel responsible for them?"

"Yes, absolutely!"

"*Are* they your responsibility?"

"Well, no one else is taking care of those kids!"

"I hear you," Carrie answered gently, "but tell me, are they *your* responsibility?"

"I just want them to be OK."

"Sometimes, when we take responsibility for other people's lives we give them an excuse to not be responsible themselves. Do you think this might be happening with you and your daughter?"

"I, well, I don't know. If I don't take care of these things, no one else will."

"You're in a really difficult situation. I can hear it in your voice. And I'm sorry you're going through this. The past years have been hard on you, haven't they?"

"Yes."

"Normally when I'm working with someone I take some time—a few weeks—to get to know them and build some trust. But I sense you need something today to help you survive. Am I getting close to what's going on?"

"Yes, you are. Very close."

"OK. So please take what I'm about to tell you as just information. There's no pressure from me to do one thing or another. That's up to you. It's your life, and however you live your life I won't judge you, OK?"

"OK..."

"When we start to feel responsible for others, a few things happen. If they do well, we build our own self-worth around their success. If they don't do well, we blame ourselves. And when this happens, we shift to trying to make them change their behaviors. We try to control them."

"Now," she quickly added, "it's not intentional, but when your whole focus is your daughter's actions—or lack of—you can't help but try to control her in the things you do. You want to influence her to make the choices you think she should make."

"But she's not your job Susan. Your job is *you*. Regardless of what your daughter chooses to do next, your only responsibility is your own choices. I know you love her and your grandchildren, but they're not your responsibility. No matter what your daughter or your son-in-law tell you."

Carrie heard sniffing on the other end of the phone. "Susan? What do you think of that information?"

"Well, I feel like it goes against everything I believe. My whole life is about how other people are doing."

"Is it possible that you're ignoring what *you* need in the process?"

"I don't want to be selfish."

"I hear that a lot, and I used to feel the same way! But it is *not* selfish to take care of your own needs. It's essential. Of course, it's important not to deny someone else what they need in the process, but you're not doing that at all. Whether they know it or not, your daughter and your grandchildren do not need you to slave for them. In particular, your daughter's responsibilities to her family are not your responsibilities."

"You know, I felt like it was my fault when my husband left."

"And he was happy to let you think that, wasn't he?"

A bitter sound came out. "Oh, yes."

"But all you have power over is what you do today. What happened in the past isn't going to change, is it?"

"No, it's not."

"So, what do you *really* want Susan?"

After a pause, she answered, "I really want my own little place. Oh, Carrie, I really do want that."

Carrie felt something shift in the conversation. She knew that focusing forward rather than to the past would transform Susan's life. "That's really wonderful! Now, if we only focus on you, and nothing else around you, what do you need to do this? Do you need money, a place you like, help moving furniture, that sort of thing?"

"Well, thanks to Jaz I have my own money. I've been sewing for her since last fall and I have enough saved up. I do need a place to go to. And I don't have anything big I need help moving. Everything can fit in my car. Oh! I suppose I'd need some furniture!"

"This is great! You've done a quick analysis of what you have and what you need, which is an excellent place to start! After you pay for the damage deposit and the first month's rent do you have money for furniture?"

"I don't really know. I'd have to double check. I *think* so..."

"How comfortable are you with putting together a budget and planning for future expenses?"

"Well, I always worked with what my husband gave me for things like groceries. I've never been a big spender because I didn't work. So I think I can handle that!"

"OK, I'll give you a name and a phone number. This lady is another friend of mine and Maria's so you're in good company. She does all sorts of financial planning."

"I feel bad asking everyone for help," she admitted.

"When you feel that—and it might happen a few more times—start by reminding yourself of what you really want. And then ask yourself, 'is what I'm asking for taking away someone else's ability to meet their needs'? If the answer's 'no' then you're good to go!"

"You know," Susan's smile showed in her voice, "I thought when I called you we'd talk about my past! You're not, well, it's not what I expected!"

"I know it's not very traditional, but this approach has changed my life. Shifting your thinking towards this focus of meeting your needs and not controlling others is really liberating. I even use it with my kids!"

"How is that possible?"

"I remind myself that their choices are theirs, not mine." She laughed. "Of course, I often tell them what I think the best choice is, but the choice—and the consequence for that choice—is theirs. It takes a lot of pressure off me to bend them into someone they're not."

"I wish I would have heard this when my daughter was little."

"Remember, no matter what happened in the past, you have today. That's *your* choice! So what's next for you now?"

"Well, I'm going to call some places for rent and go see them. I have some time now before the kids get home from school, and tomorrow everyone will be away for a while too, which gives me some more time."

"That sounds like a good plan! I'll add two things to think about. First, call my friend Jenny if you have any money questions. Second, I'm an expert yard sale shopper and I have access to a truck and a garage to put things in for a few days. If you need my help getting set up, I'm available."

"Oh, I suppose that would make a difference. Not suppose. That would really help me out. Thank you!" Susan's voice was lighter now, with a hint of excitement.

"You're welcome! You started this all off by calling me, so enjoy the momentum you're creating!"

"I will, thank you again, Carrie."

"You're welcome. Please keep me updated on what you find!"

Carrie set her phone down and laid her head back on the chair. A realization that had been floating around her head while talking to Susan became clear while she sat there. She had been taking responsibility for the outcome of the girls and women at the center. Despite all her training, she went in there thinking she would change them.

She rubbed her hands across her forehead. Time to take her own advice. One of her favorite sayings was *When you know better, do better.* Now that she knew, she decided to shift her focus. Each of those women needed to know they had a right to meet their own needs in healthy ways. *That* was her job. What they did or didn't choose was *not* her job.

Carrie got up and stretched. She felt a little less tension in her neck and shoulders now. The frames were still drying on the table so she went downstairs to look at her inventory. There were a few paintings from Lauren that needed listing, and a large frame that needed some sanding before she could paint it. She decided to get the paintings listed and then visit a few thrift stores to look for more supplies. That, along with a good yard sale run tomorrow could really help her jump start her plan to get her old debts out of the way.

She smiled to herself as she took pictures of the paintings. The 'old' her was back, and she liked it!

CHAPTER EIGHTEEN

Lisa

Lisa lay in bed trying to figure out what she was feeling. After the excitement yesterday with the camera crew there wasn't much to do today. She *could* stay in bed for a while, but now that she was awake she knew she wouldn't fall back asleep. All her freelance work for the week was done. The Jazzy Clothing Company finances were completely up to date.

Her eyes popped open. Bored! She was bored!

She thrived on having big projects and challenging deadlines. Without it, life just wasn't as fun. With a sigh, she got up to have a shower and start her day.

Sitting at the table with her mom and Jaz, she tried not to let her grumpy mood rub off on them. They were still riding on a high from the TV interview and counting down the days until it was shown.

"Did you see the responses to the email about the fourplex?" Her mom's voice interrupted her thoughts.

"Oh, no, I missed it." She picked up her phone and opened her emails.

This was the problem with nothing to do. She lost track of the few things she should be doing! Scanning through, it seemed there was enough interest to book another viewing with Frank. Lisa felt her spirits lift a little bit. "Let me see if Frank can set-up a viewing for tomorrow afternoon, and I'll invite everyone."

An hour later she had a viewing set up, and Manuel, Carrie, and Jonathan had already confirmed they would come. Now she just had to pass the time until then.

By the afternoon she was ready to tear her hair out. She didn't like reading. She was pretty sure there was nothing on TV on a Saturday afternoon. There weren't even any weeds in the flower beds to take her frustration out on! She decided to take another drive to the duplex and look over the outside.

After checking that her Mom and Jaz didn't need anything and didn't want to come, she set off. Jaz was wrapped up in working on another jean jacket, and her Mom was about to lay down for her afternoon rest. Even Alex was contentedly kicking his feet in the bouncy chair set up in the sewing room.

She parked a few blocks away from the property so she could walk through the neighborhood. It had a nice feel to it. There were a few people out mowing their lawns and washing cars, kids were on bikes and scooters, and in the distance she heard an ice cream truck.

The worst two properties in the area were the fourplex and the house beside it. Already, Lisa was picturing a fresh paint job and some landscaping to brighten up the property. Even the 'For Sale' sign was faded and tired looking. She pulled out her phone and made a note to research trees that were low maintenance. The bare yard needed a few trees.

She started to walk around to the back. The house to the right looked like it belonged to pensioners. It was pristine, with well-tended flower beds and shrubs in the front. Lisa saw through the fence a backyard with a clothesline, raised garden beds, and an adorable shed with eyelet lace curtains visible through the small windows.

The list on her phone was growing. Maybe the new tenants would like to grow some of their own food in raised beds like the neighbors. And then they'd need a shed to store the tools. She smiled to herself. Already she was acting like she owned the place. As she stood back to see whether there was room for a small playset she noticed a strange sound coming from the overgrown yard on the other side.

Carefully, she walked over. Tucked in the overgrown grass was the child she had seen the other day when she first viewed the property. She was on her knees, rocking back and forth, and making a heartbreaking whining sound.

When she was a few feet away from the fence Lisa stopped. "Hey," she said softly, "are you OK?"

The girl didn't acknowledge her, but it seemed like she might be listening. Slowly Lisa walked closer and then sat down on the ground. Through the long grass on the other side, she could see the girl was wearing the same nightgown as the other day. Her hands seemed to be cradling something.

"What do you have?" Lisa whispered. She desperately wanted to reach out and comfort her, but felt she needed to be very careful not to startle her. "It's OK. I can just sit here. You show me if you want to."

The girl began to slow her rocking, and then very gently opened her hands towards Lisa. A bee lay there, clearly dead. Lisa's first thought was that she had been stung, but she couldn't see any sign of a bee sting. And the girl was holding the bee so carefully—like she didn't want to hurt it.

"Oh... Do you like bees?"

The strange sound stopped for a moment and she nodded slowly once. Then she resumed her sounds.

"Me too," Lisa said, just a little louder. "I have lots of flowers at my place, so I have lots of bees. I wish I knew more about them. Are there different kinds?"

Again, a single nod. The slightest connection. "My name's Lisa."

"LEAVE HER ALONE!" The sudden interruption startled Lisa, but the little girl didn't even flinch. An older child came marching across the yard. Her hair was in perfect rows of braids, and she was wearing a Warriors jersey with bony dark legs showing from under ripped jean shorts.

"OK. We were just chatting about bees."

The older girl struck a defensive pose above her sister, standing with her legs apart and her fists on her hips. "She can't talk."

"You don't need to talk to communicate."

"I know that. What are you doing?" Suspicion and anger seemed to ooze out of her pores.

"Well, I was walking around this property and I heard something so I came over to see if your sister was OK. She's holding a bee very gently in her hand, so I asked her about bees." Lisa figured the older girl was ten or eleven. There was something about her that suggested she would do anything to defend her territory. But when she looked down her attitude changed instantly.

She crouched down in the grass, "Oh, Thea, another one?" Her voice was the complete opposite of the one she used with Lisa.

Thea lifted her hands, showing the dead bee.

"I know, I know. Are you ready to let it go?"

There was no response, and Thea went back to her rocking. The older girl glared up at Lisa.

"If you all would quit using weed killer for everything and actually let flowers grow instead of mowing the life out of everything then my sister wouldn't be devastated by finding all these dead bees!" The angry voice was back in full force.

"Take a minute to get to know me before you judge me. I'm kinda new to the whole gardening thing but I don't use weed killer. At all. And

I'm doing my best to grow as many flowers as possible. Is there anything I can do to help you and your sister right now?" She tried to keep her voice soft, but she had no intention of letting this girl decide she knew Lisa just because she was an adult.

"Oh. Uh, no. She'll let the bee go when she's ready. But it will all start again when she finds another one."

"I can sit here for a while. I'm not in a rush."

"No. I'll stay with her. You go." She sat down beside her and Lisa saw that she was careful not to make physical contact with her little sister.

"OK. She's lucky to have a big sister like you looking after her."

"Brother."

"Pardon me?"

"I'm her brother."

"Oh, OK. Well, I'm not sure if I'll have any luck buying this place, but if I do you have my word that I'll plant flowers and never use weed killer." Lisa carefully walked away, the image of the two siblings crouched in the tall grass mourning the loss of a bee seared into her mind.

On impulse, she stopped at the garden center to see if there was a potted flower that attracted bees. While she admired the willingness to leave the lawn wild to attract insects, there hadn't been a flower in sight. She spent almost ten minutes on her phone in the parking lot looking up which flowers bees loved best before deciding what to do.

An hour later Lisa was at home with two plastic flower pots planted. Each of them had yellow and blue snapdragons in the center surrounded by sweet alyssums. She'd deliver them tomorrow when they all went to view the property.

Washing her hands, she went to start supper. The little project helped her feel somewhat productive. All she needed was ten or twenty more of those!

CHAPTER NINETEEN

Maria

"Oh, this is so exciting!" Maria was thrilled at the chance to see a property—even if she could only sit outside in her wheelchair. Lisa had offered to bring the walker so she could navigate through the bottom levels, but Maria was nervous about falling. She assured everyone she was happy to view the outside from her wheelchair.

They left a little early so Lisa could deliver some flowers to the house next door. She had told them over supper about her experience with the unusual kids.

"Lisa, I want to come with you to drop off those pots."

"Yeah, of course. I can plop them on your lap and wheel you up. Saves me carrying them!"

They all watched the neighborhood carefully as they got closer to the property.

"Wow, the school looks old, but what a fantastic playground!" Jaz noted.

"Sometimes that's the sign of an active parent's council," Maria suggested, "Definitely a good thing if the community supports their children."

When Lisa parked in front of the house for sale, they were all quiet for a minute, wondering if this was the property that would make their dream a reality. Lisa got out first to take the wheelchair and flower pots out of the trunk. She got Maria settled in the chair and then balanced both pots on her lap.

"I'm going to walk around," Jaz started while she put Alex into the baby carrier she was starting to use. He loved being against his mommy's chest, but facing the world so he could see everything. "Good luck!"

Lisa parked her mom in front of the two steps that led to the bungalow and walked up to ring the bell. An older child opened it. Maria knew he told Lisa he was a boy, but she would have thought he was a girl if she didn't know better. He looked up at Lisa suspiciously.

"What do *you* want?"

"Hello to you too! I thought some flowers might help attract some live bees for Thea so these are for your family." She gestured to Maria, barely visible behind the flowers. "And that's my mom Maria holding them."

"Don't want them," he answered and started closing the door.

Lisa stuck her foot out and propped open the door, "Really? Because you have some problem with me you won't accept a gift that might make your sister happy and is good for the environment?"

Maria was shocked. She had never heard Lisa directly challenge someone like that, let alone a child.

"Liam, who's at the door?" A deep voice called from inside.

He rolled his eyes and opened his mouth, and then stopped when Lisa gave him a pointed look. With a sigh, he called into the house, "That lady from yesterday thinks Thea needs some flowers."

"Thea *and* the bees." Lisa corrected him.

"Thea *and* the bees," he parroted.

A wild-looking girl appeared behind Liam and then dashed out when she saw the flowers. He reached out to try to grab her, but wasn't fast enough. She stopped in front of Maria and gently touched each of the flowers. Lisa walked back down the stairs and stood about a foot away.

"These are both good for attracting bees," Lisa said quietly. "The ones in the center are snapdragons. I read that bees can't see red but they *are* attracted to yellow and blue. And these flowers along the edge are called sweet alyssums."

After inspecting the flowers she reached out and touched one of the wheels on the wheelchair. "Hi," Maria said, "I'm Maria. And these flowers are getting a little heavy. Where do you think the bees would want them?"

Thea turned towards the backyard and then back to Maria. "In the backyard?" Maria asked.

"Hello there!" The voice came from a kind-looking man walking through the doorway. He was tall and dark with short black hair, rimless glasses, and a smile that made his eyes crinkle at the side.

"Oh, hi! I'm Lisa. I met your son and daughter yesterday and found out some bees have been dying in the neighborhood. So I made up these to help." She gestured towards the pots. "Where can we put them?"

He reached out his hand, "Lisa, I'm Aaron." He shook her hand, and then reached to Maria and took one of the pots from her lap. "This is very thoughtful of you! Thank you!" Setting the pot down, he took the other one, and reached out his free hand to shake Maria's.

"Hello, I'm Maria, Lisa's mom. We might be buying the property next door, so we're looking around today."

"That's wonderful! Been a shame to see it sitting empty for so long." He turned to Thea. "Have you said thank you to these nice ladies?"

Thea faced Maria and touched her hand to her chin before doing the same with Lisa. They both returned the gesture.

"Liam?" Aaron asked.

With obvious reluctance, he thanked them and went inside the house.

"Thea seemed to want these in the backyard, is that OK?" Lisa asked.

"Yes, although I'd rather have them up front. They're really nice. But the backyard is much safer for Thea and I know she'll be watching these to see when the bees find them."

"OK," she turned to Maria, "I'll be back in a minute." She picked up a pot and followed Aaron through the side gate and into the backyard with Thea close beside her.

A minute later they were walking back without Thea.

"You've done the most thoughtful thing today," Aaron said to both of them. "I've left the yard to grow wild for the kids' sake—actually for the bee's sake. Most people just think it's unkempt." He turned to Lisa, "But somehow you understood what's important to them. Thank you again."

"You're welcome," Lisa answered, "But, to be fair to your neighbors you could tidy up the front *a lot*. Especially since there are more flowers in the back for the bees now."

A contagious laugh rippled through Aaron, "You've got quite a way with you! I'll take your advice under consideration."

Liam appeared in the door again, but he looked much less defensive. He walked to the edge of the front porch where Lisa and Aaron were standing. "If you buy that place I know someone who would like to live there. They'd be really good. You know, quiet and clean."

"Thanks, Liam. Would you like me to keep you updated on what we're doing?"

He nodded and then looked up towards the road as two cars pulled up.

"Oh, there's some more of our people!" Lisa looked back at the two of them. "I hope to see you again, maybe with a few happy bees keeping you company!"

"Bye bye." Maria added, and Lisa turned her around and wheeled her towards the sidewalk. Soon everyone was following Frank into the first door of the complex, and Maria was left to her thoughts. She looked over at the house next door and wondered about its owners. Aaron was easy enough to figure out. He was the strong, steady type. Obviously a good dad.

But Liam and Thea were different than any children Maria had met. There was something about Liam that was powerful and vulnerable at the same time. Like he had already fought many battles and proved his strength, but was deeply wounded as well. And Thea, well, she certainly seemed like a wild child. The best way Maria could explain it to herself was that it seemed like Thea might float away if she didn't have her daddy to ground her.

After everyone had carefully inspected the property, they stood in a loose circle in the front yard, discussing their options.

"The neighbor said it's been almost vacant for years," Lisa offered. "One mom and her daughter were the last ones here, and it was a while ago that they were evicted. I'm not sure of the story, but it sounds like really poor management."

"If that's the case, we may have more leverage. I'll try to get more information, but if you all agree we could test the waters with a low offer—maybe in the $525,000 range."

"What kind of work does it need inside?" Maria asked.

Chris answered, "Ideally we'd replace most of the fixtures. The kitchens and bathrooms are pretty dated, and I'd prefer to get new, efficient appliances and quality finishes." He turned and looked at the building. "The windows are OK, but they're hard to slide so it would be nice to replace them. And we definitely need to re-caulk to make them airtight. The roof and the structure look good, but I suspect blowing insulation into the attic will make a difference."

"We were also looking at turning one of the units into two smaller ones," Jonathan added. "We could do a lower accessible unit and a space suitable for one occupant above it."

Maria felt her heart lift when she heard Jonathan's suggestion. If only they could make a safe, accessible unit for someone with a wheelchair! She was sure there were people out there who were making do in places that just weren't suitable.

"That sounds like a lot of work and money," Jenny said, and Maria tried not to get too excited about the idea.

"And how long would it take?" Jaz was gently swaying back and forth with Alex asleep in his carrier.

Chris and Jonathan exchanged smiles, "Oh, we know how to bomb out a project! With lots of help we could have it ready in two months."

"Two months!"

"Plus the time to complete the purchase," Frank reminded her.

Jaz groaned. "Why does everything have to take so long?"

"Well, it'll take even longer if we don't make a decision." Lisa looked around the group. "Who would like to proceed with trying to buy this property?" Everyone raised their hands. "All right then! Let's give it a try! Frank, can you check with Sandra to make sure everything's set up for a pre-approval? And then go ahead with the offer. Hey, the worst that happens is the owner says no, right?"

Slowly the group broke up, with some taking another look around, and others heading off. Lisa pushed Maria around the yard, pointing out the ideas she had for a garden and playground.

"What do you think about Liam's suggestion for a tenant?"

Lisa paused before answering, "I thought about telling him we had certain people in mind, but I have a feeling whoever he was talking about is exactly the type of tenant we want to help. I don't know why.

There's something about him that suggests he really fights for the underdog."

They continued their tour of the yard until they were beside the fence to Aaron's house. Thea was visible sitting beside the new flowers. "I think there's a bee there already," Lisa whispered. Quietly she wheeled her mom away.

CHAPTER TWENTY

Jaz

Jaz leaned back and stretched her arms over her head. She had been sewing for three hours straight after getting Alex to bed. A private request had come in for a set of t-shirts with cut-outs in Greek that said either 'Bride', 'Maid of Honor', or 'Bridesmaid'. The maid of honor was organizing a bachelorette party, and all the girls were big into sororities. It was a large order with twelve shirts and Jaz wondered if all twelve girls were close.

She appreciated the friendships she had with the women in her life, but couldn't imagine knowing eleven people enough to ask them to be part of her wedding. Carrie wasn't even doing bridesmaids, just a simple ceremony that was all about her and Jonathan.

After a few more stretches Jaz got back to work. Lisa and Maria kept trying to get her to take a day off, but she preferred to keep busy. As she sewed, she thought about the fourplex. It was the grungiest place she had ever seen. Everything was old and faded. The floors had linoleum peeling up, the carpets on all the stairs were worn right down, and it didn't smell very nice.

Jaz had lived in the same house from the time she was six, and she barely remembered anything before that. Her parents were definitely 'house proud' and their stylish, professionally decorated house in one of the nicer neighborhoods in the city was extremely important to them. It was a shock for Jaz to see how depressing that housing was, and the contrast between that and her own childhood felt wrong somehow.

But at least everyone else was excited about the 'potential' of the place. Jaz couldn't see it herself, but she knew people like Lisa, Jonathan, and Chris knew what they were talking about. She learned a lot by listening to everyone else. Probably the biggest thing she learned was that she didn't know anything about renovations. Maybe tomorrow evening she'd actually take a break once Alex was in bed and watch one of those home reno shows Lisa and Maria loved so much.

By midnight Jaz had finished the last of the t-shirts. It had taken all of her spare time over the weekend but she thought it was worth it. And anyone willing to pay $600 for twelve t-shirts was definitely her kind of client!

Now she had no choice but to try to get some sleep. Tomorrow evening she was meeting with her dad and Ellison's dad to talk about her business. She tried to pick a time and place when it wouldn't be convenient to bring Alex, but her dad insisted they meet at her parent's place.

"Your mom can take Alex if he gets fussy. And besides, I need to show off my grandson!"

Jaz felt like she had no choice, but she constantly reviewed possible scenarios in her head. Would she be judged for having a baby and not going to university? If Ellison's dad saw the resemblance between Alex and Ellison would he freak out? Accuse Jaz of taking advantage of his son? Turn her parents against her again? There were no scenarios where things turned out fine.

With a sigh, she got into bed and picked up her phone. Scrolling through Instagram she tried to ignore her thoughts until she fell asleep.

The next morning she was definitely out of sorts, and Alex seemed to pick up on it.

"If he's always in a bad mood when I'm in a bad mood we're going to have trouble," she warned Lisa and Maria at the breakfast table.

Lisa snickered, "Jaz, your bad moods are like everyone else's average moods. Trust me, we can live with it."

"You know, a day off would be a nice change for you," Maria suggested. "Actually, we all need a break. Once that TV thing airs we're going to be super busy. And if the fourplex purchase goes through it will be even worse! Let's go to the lake for the afternoon. The kids are still in school this week so it won't be too crowded yet."

Reluctantly Jaz agreed. She'd rather work, but Alex needed fresh air and more variety in his days than what she was giving him right now. Quickly she finished eating so she could get as much work as possible done before they left.

It was a perfect pre-summer day. The weather was warm enough for tank tops and dipping toes in the lake, and there was almost no breeze. Jaz helped Lisa set up a beach umbrella to protect Maria from the sun, and then carried Alex to the edge of the lake. The sand stopped them from wheeling Maria right up and Jaz felt bad she had to miss out.

"Do you have sunscreen for Alex?" Lisa asked.

"Oh, I never thought of that! Yeah, I guess I should. This hat helps, but I'll only let him play in the water a bit and then we'll hang out under the umbrella." She wished she had thought of it earlier. Maybe while he napped she'd look up some mommy blogs about sun protection. Too bad babies didn't come with instructions manuals.

Alex's squeals of delight were loud enough to reach Maria, and she was still chuckling when they made their way back to her. "I think he approves of our afternoon plans."

"Definitely!" Jaz agreed as she arranged herself under the umbrella. She sat him between her legs and gave him some toys to play with. He was getting better at sitting up, but still randomly toppled over. Eventually, he started to rub his eyes, and Jaz put him in his carrier and walked around until he fell asleep.

She laid him on a blanket and then lay down beside him. Shading her eyes, she looked up at Maria.

"What are you reading?"

"It's this book called *Factfulness* all about how the world is better than we think." She held up the book for Jaz to see.

"I thought you only read fiction."

"Well, I'm trying to expand my brain a little bit. That email thing Bill Gates sends out said it was good, and I have to agree. I didn't think it would be interesting, but it's amazing."

Lisa put down the magazine she was flipping through, "You follow Bill Gates?"

"I'm more than just a pretty face!" Maria teased.

Jaz thought about picking up her phone, but the warm sun on her face convinced her to lay down instead. With Alex's little body tucked into her, she felt herself relax. It didn't matter what anyone thought of her, or who Alex's sperm donor was. *I'm good,* she thought, smiling, *I'm good.*

When Alex woke up they started packing everything up.

"You were right Maria. We all needed a break."

The nerves came back as Jaz was walking to her parent's house that evening, but she tried to ignore them and focus on her business. Lisa gave her a folder that showed all the financial transactions for the Jazzy Clothing Company, as well as projections for the next six months. They were pretty impressive, and Jaz hoped she'd make her dad proud.

Alex cooed and grabbed his toes from his place in the stroller and Jaz wondered what kind of baby she had been. It was only after Alex was born that her parents revealed she was her dad's biological child but not her mom's. They hadn't talked about it much, and she wondered if she'd ever get a chance to learn more about why they chose to get married and pretend Jaz was both of theirs.

Before she could ring the doorbell her dad was at the door, "Come in, come in! George should be here any minute!"

"Shouldn't I call him Mr. Chen still?"

"Yes, of course you should!" her mom called from the kitchen.

"Well, let's see what he says," her dad diplomatically replied as he took Alex out of the stroller. "Hello little man! Did you miss pa pa?"

Jaz smiled. At least her son now had a pa pa and a ma ma to spoil him! Well, her mom probably wouldn't spoil him, but at least she accepted him as her grandson now.

When the doorbell rang her dad rushed to the door with Alex. There was much cooing and comments as he introduced his grandson, and then both men joined Jaz at the table.

She stood up, "Hi Mr. Chen. It's nice to see you!" She hoped her smiled looked genuine, and not like the grimace it felt like.

"Jaz, wow, I haven't seen you in so long!" He sat down, and Jaz's mom immediately brought glasses of ice water for the three of them. "So tell me," he started, "Where have you been?"

It was a quick reminder to Jaz that the people she was with were Chinese and would approach things differently than Lisa or Maria, but she easily slipped back into her role. There would be no talk about business until they had covered all the other points of conversation. Jaz knew to give just enough information and then sit quietly. "I do enjoy walking with Alex. The weather has been perfect for it lately! And today I took him to the beach for the first time."

"Did you go to the beach?" her dad asked Alex. He looked up and cooed an answer. "Pa pa and ma ma will have to take you again sometime soon!"

Her dad and Ellison's dad continued to talk, covering golf, the weather, and the gardener. Jaz sat quietly and waited. She wished she had remembered to bring the paperwork from Lisa upstairs. Now she'd have to leave to get it when the talk turned to business.

When Alex started to whine, Jaz's mom quickly came in to get him. "Can I have the diaper bag?" she asked Jaz.

"Of course, just a minute Mom." She was grateful for an excuse to leave, and came back with the bag which she gave to her mom, and the paperwork which she carefully set on the chair beside her.

When talk turned to her business Jaz had to push down a sigh of relief. She carefully answered each question about her business plan, her customers, and where she got the business idea from. Money was the very last thing they talked about.

"What are your sales like?" Mr. Chen asked.

She handed a small folder to each man. "This was prepared by Lisa, who does all the bookkeeping. We are grossing a little over $10,000 a month and Lisa is projecting that this will continue to increase."

"What is your biggest challenge?" her dad asked.

"Well, I can only sell what gets completed in a week so I'm limited by the number of seamstresses I have." She realized that might sound negative, "It's not a big problem though," she added.

"What about that TV interview? How will that change things?"

She was glad her dad had mentioned it, since it was something she was really excited about. Forcing her voice to stay calm, she answered, "I expect the exposure will have a positive impact. I've been preparing by increasing our inventory, and all the seamstresses are working full-out this week."

Mr. Chen set down the folder, "Your balance sheet is strong. What do you plan next?"

Jaz looked at her dad, unsure if she should talk about the housing project or not. Seeing her hesitation he stepped in.

"Jaz is pursuing a very unusual project. She has partnered with some people who want to invest their money in providing affordable housing in the city."

The room became so silent Jaz could hear the clock on the living room fireplace mantel ticking. She tried to breathe evenly and keep her body relaxed, even though her heart was pounding.

Finally, Mr. Chen spoke, "This is a good thing. You are using your success to take care of your community. I wish that more people your age would think about their community and not just about themselves."

Jaz smiled her first genuine smile of the evening, "Thank you."

The outside endorsement of her project impacted her dad, too. She could see him thinking about what he had just heard.

"But you need to have a plan for meeting demand," Mr. Chen continued. "These things don't happen overnight. Without more employees you may run into trouble, and you shouldn't have to do any of the sewing yourself. If I tried to make up for my employee's shortfall there wouldn't be anyone to run the business."

Jaz thought about what he was saying. "I, um, you're right. I do really enjoy the sewing. Next to spending time with Alex, it's my favorite thing to do. But I understand what you mean."

"I've been doing some research on creative businesses like yours," her dad added.

Jaz looked at him, surprised.

He smiled, "Just because I don't agree with your choice doesn't mean I'm not interested. But when it comes to running the business, you need to make decisions as an owner, not as a creator. You're smart Jaz. You can do this."

"Thank you, Daddy," she whispered. She felt her heart beat a little faster as his words sunk in. He thought she could do this!

"Do you have a plan for recruiting more employees?"

Jaz cleared her throat and looked at Mr. Chen, "I don't right now. But I will soon."

"I'd like to check back again in a month, Stanley. Does that work for you?"

The two men set up a follow-up meeting while Jaz sat there quietly. When they stood to go she followed them.

At the door, Mr. Chen reached out his hand to her, "We'll see you in a month."

Jaz shook his hand and thanked him. After he left, she turned to her dad, "Did I do OK?"

"Yes! That was very good. By tomorrow the whole community will be talking about your business and your project. Now, let's go find my grandson!"

They found Alex and her mom in the master bedroom. He was laying on the bed kicking his feet. Jaz's mom was singing to him in Chinese. They stopped at the doorway, taking in the scene. When she finished singing, Jaz walked in.

"I feel like I know that song."

"You should! I sang it to you all the time when you were a baby. I had almost forgotten it."

Jaz sat down and tickled Alex's feet, "You used to sing to me?"

Her mom smiled, "Yes. All the songs my ma ma sang to me."

"Alex will be all ready for Mandarin preschool when it's time," her dad added. "Can I walk you home?"

As they walked, Jaz told him about the fourplex. "I can't imagine living there. Everything was so worn out. It was depressing." She turned to look at her dad. "How can poor people make better lives if everything around them brings them down?"

"I don't know, Jaz. I really haven't ever thought about it. You know, compared to people like the Chen's we really aren't that well off. But, maybe our life is better than I realized."

"We're lucky, aren't we Daddy?"

"Very."

CHAPTER TWENTY-ONE

Carrie

Carrie rested her head back and closed her eyes. Viewing the fourplex raised a lot of emotions for her. While she had gone from subsidized housing to renting a pretty nice bungalow, other people had gone from subsidized housing to something even worse. Living in a place like that would be so depressing.

"What are you thinking about?" Jonathan asked. They were in his car because it now had a permanent booster seat for Katie. Just another little way of slowly becoming a family.

"About how fortunate I was to be able to move to a better place two years ago. It could have been a lot different. We could have ended up somewhere like that."

"I have to admit, it was worse than I expected. I mean, the townhouse you used to live in was worn out, but it felt nice inside anyways." He looked at her sideways, "Maybe I was so blinded by your beauty I didn't see any flaws."

She laughed and gently touched his shoulder before resting her hand on his thigh, "Yep, you were definitely blinded by something. That place was rough!"

The buzzing of her phone interrupted, "Hello?... Susan! How are you?"

"I'm doing OK Carrie. I wanted to call and give you some good news!"

"I'm all ears!"

"Well, I went out yesterday and signed a rental agreement for an apartment!"

There was pride and relief in her voice—along with something else. "That's fantastic! Tell me about it."

"Well, it's just a few blocks from my daughter's house so the grandkids can visit whenever they want. It's got a nice view of the park, one bedroom, and I can move in on Friday."

"Whoa, that was fast. Have you told your family?"

She took a shaky breath, "I did this morning. I'm out for a little walk right now. They're quite upset. *But* what you told me earlier? You're right. I'm not responsible for their lives. So I'm trying to focus on that. I suggested that Janie stay with me after school still."

"It might be nice to have her at your place. And then you don't have to feel obligated to do all the other household chores because you're not in their home."

"Exactly," Susan agreed. "And aside from that, I'm really quite excited!"

"How can I help? Do you need a truck for your things? And what about furniture?"

"I can fit all my belongings into my car, that's not a problem. But I am going to need some furniture."

"I'm busy the first three days of the week, but maybe we can meet for coffee Thursday morning and look through the Buy and Sell site? Then if there isn't much there we can go to yard sales together on Saturday! I have to go out anyways to look for frames, so we can do both at the same time."

"Are you sure? You've got so much going on."

"Are you kidding? This is going to be fun!" She suggested a coffee place near Susan's neighborhood and encouraged her to call if she had any concerns before they met.

"Who was that Mommy?"

"That was Susan, she's a friend of Maria's who's moving into a better place next week."

"Why? Is she in a yucky place right now?"

"The place isn't yucky I don't think. But the people there aren't very nice to her."

"That's mean! We should go tell them to be nice!"

"If only that fixed things Katie-girl."

Carrie wondered if her previous conversation with Susan was just the last grain of sand that tipped the scales towards her taking action. Maria told her Susan had been trying to move into her own place since before Christmas and kept running into resistance from her daughter. It wasn't the same as leaving an abusive partner, but she questioned how emotionally safe Susan would be during her last week at her daughter's.

Jonathan's voice interrupted her thoughts. "Do you need any groceries or anything while we're out?"

"Hmmm? Oh, no thanks. I got a few crockpot meals in the freezer yesterday, and I'll get soup going as soon as we get home."

"Can I go to the park when we get home Mommy?"

Carrie glanced back at Katie, and then Matthew. He was turned towards the window looking outside and she suspected he needed a break from being around people—especially his sister.

"No, you can spend some time downstairs or in the backyard."

"That's boring!" she pouted.

Jonathan turned to Carrie, and she shook her head. Although Katie preferred to always have people doing things with her, it wouldn't hurt to entertain herself for a while. Back at the house, Jonathan sat at the counter with one of Katie's sketchpads while Carrie started making soup. She'd make enough for supper tonight and one more meal during the week. Although her budget left room for more interesting meals, she still wanted to keep costs down as much as possible. Especially now that she was focused on getting out of debt.

"Can I use your laptop to look some things up?" Jonathan asked after starting to sketch something out.

"Yeah, for sure. What are you doing?"

"I'm trying to figure out how we can re-do the layout of the fourplex. I like the idea of converting one of the units into two smaller ones. Just seeing how it might work."

When the soup was simmering, she sat on the stool beside him. "How's it going?"

"It's tricky," he admitted. "There are good choices for smaller spaces, that's not a problem. It's making it small *and* wheelchair accessible that's the problem."

Carrie looked at the picture he had pulled up online. It was a small apartment that looked perfectly designed. Everything fit in such a small space. "Is this what you're thinking of?"

He nodded.

"It's so cute! Having the fridge below the counter will work I think, but you'd need to leave space under the sink for a wheelchair to roll right up. Hey, I wonder—" she started a new tab and typed in a few search terms, "—yep, look. That company that did Maria's accessible bathrooms has a whole section for small bathrooms. Um, the outlets need to be moved up and the light switches changed out so they're easier to use. But we're practically gutting the place anyway so that's not a problem. We need to consult with an accessibility expert though, in case there are important details that we're missing."

"You sound like you're sold on the place."

She smiled, "Yeah, I am. It was too overwhelming at first. Probably because I was so overwhelmed about my practicum. But now that things are settling down a bit I want to be a part of this. You know, I learned a lot from my dad as he adapted our house for Mom over the years."

"Maybe I can speed up the renos to the house so your parents can stay here and your dad can help us work on the fourplex—if we get it, that is."

"Seriously? That's a great idea! The kids would be so excited to have them close by for a bit. Wow, we're really getting sold on this property. Good thing we're not the ones bidding, because I'm all about the feelings now, not the numbers."

"You know, if we can figure out how to convert one of those units into two, why don't we do it with two of them? That would make two accessible units, two single room top floor units, and two two-bedroom units."

"That makes sense. Although it would significantly increase the cost of the renovations. It's funny. At first, I just wanted to make enough money to buy a frozen pizza once a week. Then I wanted to make enough to pay for grad school. But now I want to make enough to help buy a house—or six—for someone else."

"You're not really one to settle for mediocre Carrie."

"Well, I guess I settled for less than mediocre until I left Don, and now I feel like I have a lot of good living to make up for!"

Jonathan leaned over and kissed her temple. "I sure do love you."

That night, Carrie lay in bed thinking about her group therapy session at the center. With so many different women that may or may not show up, she was finding it hard to engage everyone. The same people talked every time, which was OK, but she wondered if the quiet ones were getting anything out of it. If only there was a way to reduce the intensity of everyone facing each other...

Just before she drifted off to sleep, she thought about the box full of frames she found at a yard sale on Saturday. Ugly, beige, and full of potential. What if she gave everyone the chance to work on a frame during the session? She mentally took an inventory. There were enough yogurt containers in the recycling bin that she could wash them and give each person their own container of primer. And newspapers to protect the table. But she'd need more brushes and sandpaper. Maybe baby wipes instead of rags in case there was a spill... OK, so she couldn't pull it off for tomorrow, but she could have it ready for Tuesday.

Monday afternoon she set up the group therapy room with two tables pushed together. In one of the cupboards she found some leftover plastic tablecloths that Donna said she could use, and there were enough aprons in the kitchen to offer them to anyone who wanted one.

She stopped at the hardware store on the way home to pick up enough paintbrushes. She was as ready as she'd ever be.

It was nice to walk in the front door and be ready to spend time with her family. After two years of grad school and always feeling like she needed to be studying, her evenings now felt like holidays. And with Katie needing help with reading and homework every night, she couldn't imagine coping with her own schoolwork too.

The next morning she was at the center early to get everything set up.

"What's this?" Dr. Bradley asked as he walked into the room.

"Oh, hi Dr. Bradley. I haven't seen you in a while." She faced him straight on and waited for him to answer. He was supposed to be supervising her therapy sessions and providing direct feedback. If he wasn't going to show up consistently, she wouldn't wait for his permission to try something new.

"Yes. I have patients to see."

Carrie resisted the very strong temptation to roll her eyes at him. Instead, she turned and finished setting up the frames while she answered his question. "This is a little chance for the women to be creative, and for me to lower the intensity of the session by providing a place for the quieter ones to focus while they're listening to others."

Without another word he took his place in the corner and set up his laptop. Carrie ignored him for the rest of the time. He'd still get her carefully written reports, but since he didn't care about the women, she wouldn't bother with him.

When people started to come in, Carrie sensed a little bit of excitement. "Hi everyone," she started. "I thought we'd try something a little different today. To give you a little background, after I left my husband I was pretty much broke. If I was careful I could pay all my bills and buy the cheapest groceries, but that only left me a few extra dollars for the entire month."

"I was getting desperate, and started taking things out of dumpsters if they looked decent, and then selling them online." Now she had everyone's attention.

"That led to a business I still run now, where I take frames like the ones in front of you, paint them, and either sell them empty in groups, or I frame anything interesting I might find and sell them like that. I made enough money to pay for grad school and keep my kids clothed and fed."

"Didn't you get child support?"

"Not a penny. And my ex tried to blame *me* when he got evicted for not paying the rent on his house. Oh, and I'm still paying off our joint debts, too."

"Asshole," someone whispered.

"Anyways," Carrie continued, "today if you want you can start your own frame while we chat. It's kinda fun, and really there is no way you can mess this up. Next week I'll bring a bunch of different colors and you can finish the frame however you want. I've brought a few samples of finished products."

She pulled some frames out and passed them around. "The sky's the limit. Those ones that are black with a little gold are usually bought in sets of seven or nine, and people use them to make a statement wall. Those glossy colorful ones are sometimes sold in sets of three all the same size and color, or in bigger sets with all the colors."

"Are you going to sell these when we're done?"

"What? No, these are for you to keep."

They got started priming their frames and slowly conversation picked up. Carrie was pleased to see that some of the quieter women began sharing as well. She occasionally directed the conversation to keep the focus on present and future opportunities and not on negativity but for the most part the session progressed naturally.

"I guess it's like a makeover," Char said. She was back to chewing gum loudly now that her injuries had healed. "You know, make it look better on the outside."

"But without the swirls and curves on the frames it wouldn't be as interesting," Carrie added, "It's like bringing out the best of the frame that the nasty beige color was hiding."

Julia looked up from the frame she was finishing, "I grew up in a house with beige everything except gold curtains."

They all started talking about the homes they grew up in, laughing about ugly décor and the common theme of beige. It was the first time Carrie heard any of them talk about their childhoods with a smile.

At the end of the session all the frames were drying, and everyone looked happier. They lingered, comparing how different the frames looked before slowly making their way to the front office. Carrie followed them to sign off on each of their attendance before heading back to clean up.

Char joined her. "Want some help?"

"Yeah, that'd be great! I was going to pour all the primer back into the can and then wipe the containers out with paper towels. If I was at home I'd wash them in my sink but I don't want to wreck anything here."

They worked side by side for a few minutes, "Did you really only have a few dollars left each month?"

"Yeah. It was awful. My son couldn't do any of the school field trips because I didn't have the fees, and they wore thrift store clothes all the time. I know it wasn't my fault exactly, but I felt like a bad mom because I couldn't provide for them."

"You look rich though."

"Well, I'll have to tell you about my clothes sometime—that's a whole other story! But I'm definitely doing a lot better thanks to the business. I can even buy take out on the days when I'm too tired to cook."

"I guess maybe you're more like us than I thought."

"Maybe." They finished cleaning up and Carrie thanked Char for her help. It wasn't until she reached to turn out the lights that Carrie saw Dr. Bradley sitting in his corner. She had forgotten about him.

"They'll still break your heart. Even if you think you've connected with them now, don't expect it to last."

Carrie went back and sat a few chairs away from him, "That's not an issue for me. I'm not here to make them change. I'm here to give them information they can use if they want. And I *am* here to be a friend. These are all good women who have had some really hard knocks in life. Which means they're no different than me."

"You didn't learn this in school."

"What? Believing in your clients?"

He looked a little ashamed, and Carrie mentally cheered. "I'll email you the summaries from yesterday and today. Have a good week Dr. Bradley." She got up and walked away, putting him and his negativity out of her mind.

CHAPTER TWENTY-TWO

Lisa

"Aargh! Why haven't we heard back yet?"

"Lisa, it's only been three days. Be patient."

"How long does it take to say, 'yes you have a deal' or 'no here's our counteroffer'? No wonder the property is run into the ground. Lazy owners!" She took out her frustration on the pot she was scrubbing. Not having control over the sale of the property was getting to her. She was used to seeing what needed to be done and then doing it. Having to wait for a reply on their offer was not part of her plan.

"I know. This doesn't exactly suit you—the waiting part." Maria finished putting the leftover salad away and put the bowl in the dishwasher. Thank goodness the kitchen was big enough for her to still be able to help out a bit. "But there might not be a pot left if you keep scrubbing like that!"

Lisa stopped and took a deep breath, "OK. But what am I going to do in the meantime?" She turned and leaned against the sink. "I'm bored."

"You could register for online dating! I've heard it works really well!"

She rolled her eyes, "Ha ha. I'll find something."

"I'm sure you will."

"Hey! I bet Chris and Carla can use some help on their house! If we're going to be renovating a property eventually anyways it would be good for me to learn how to do things." She quickly started the dishwasher and wiped the counters. "Be right back!"

She missed the thoughtful look on her mom's face as she went downstairs. Chris quickly answered her knock, "Lisa! Come on in!"

Carla was setting the table for supper, and Becky was watching TV.

"Oh, that's OK. I just was wondering if I could help you at all with your house renovations. I need something to keep me busy while we wait for a reply on our offer."

"What did you have in mind?"

"Anything! Please, let me paint a wall, or pick up garbage, or whatever."

"Did you have a wage in mind?"

"No! Definitely not! I'm free—in more ways than one!" she laughed, "I've never had nothing to do before and I'm going to go crazy soon."

"OK, would you like to join me tomorrow?" Chris offered, "I was going to put in a few hours in the morning before going to our other jobs."

"Definitely!"

"Great! I leave at five."

Lisa looked at him carefully before realizing he was serious. "I'll be waiting outside. Enjoy your dinner!"

She went upstairs a little deflated. She liked spending breakfast with her mom, Jaz, and Alex every morning instead of rushing to catch the bus to work like she used to do. Oh well, at least she had something to do now!

The next morning she dragged herself downstairs wearing her grubbiest clothes. Getting a coffee, she tried not to fall back asleep. How did Chris do this every day? Her long hours were nothing compared to this!

It was a ten-minute drive to the house Chris and Carla were fixing up. Lisa had to agree with Carla's assessment that it was the worst house for miles around. The only good thing about it was the beautiful tree in the front yard.

"Are you sure you can turn this into something livable?" It was the typical 8os box house, but with siding hanging down, paint around the windows peeling, and an unfinished extension to one side that looked haunted in the early morning light.

Chris laughed, "Of course! Come on in for the grand tour." He opened the front door and Lisa gasped. It was opened up inside, and even though it was just wall studs and plywood floors, the brand new bank of windows at the back gave a hint about what a show piece the house would become.

"The front windows are coming next week, and then we can really get started with making it look good. This will be the kitchen here, facing the front yard. We switched it around so we could have more windows facing the backyard. It was Carla's idea! It still gives us lots of wall space for cupboards and everything. And we're putting a gas fireplace in here to create a focal point. Plus, it will feel really cozy in the winter."

The rest of the house was in a similar state of demolition and huge potential. "Wow, I can see why you guys worked so hard to get back into the business. This is what you're meant to do!"

"Thanks! Are you ready to get to work?" For the next hour, Lisa pulled off the trim from around the upstairs windows to prepare for replacing them. It felt good to pull something apart and vent her frustrations in a useful way. She hauled everything to the dumpster out front and then went to find Chris. He was putting new wiring in the walls and quickly put her to work as his assistant.

By ten Lisa was dirty, sweaty, and feeling better about everything.

"Carrie should conduct all her counseling sessions while doing renovations! Very cathartic."

"Yeah, it feels really good to be back at it after working on other people's projects for so long. Speaking of other people's projects, I'd better get on to the next place. It was great to have your help!"

"Can I join you tomorrow?"

He laughed, "Boy, you really are bored! Yep, meet me outside at the same time."

Lisa filled the rest of her day with her freelance work and the Jazzy Clothing Company bookkeeping. By ten she was more than ready for bed and she said a silent thank you for having a reason to get up and get going the next morning. She'd miss breakfasts together, but it wouldn't be long before she'd be working on the fourplex. At least that's what she hoped.

For the rest of the week, Lisa spent her mornings helping Chris, and she was more than happy to keep busy. Frank was good about keeping in touch, but he didn't have any news to share every time he called. They agreed that he should continue looking for other properties with promise, but so far nothing else had shown up.

Saturday morning they all gathered in the living room to watch the Go Green morning show. Chris had been out to the property early, and returned to pick up Carla. Maria was going to watch Becky so they could have a day working together, but Carla convinced Chris to wait until the episode aired.

The intro began with a view from the outside that slowly zoomed in to the front door. Lisa hadn't known they would use any shots of the front yard, and she was relieved it looked so good.

After a few bars of music, the host's voice began. "Here in a house that any of your neighbors might live in, a quiet green revolution is starting. Join me for this inspirational story where we see the power of a few good women and a sewing machine."

"Oooohhh, good intro!" Maria exclaimed.

The show was everything they imagined. He portrayed them all exactly how they were—Jaz with her quiet determination and unending creativity, Lisa with her numbers mind and her business experience, and Maria with her loving way of mothering everyone.

When it was over they all cheered. "I love the way they filmed the seamstresses all bringing their work! It made it look like we were a happy little commune or something!"

"Well Mom, you've kind of made it that way. I'm pleased with how well they incorporated the business name and how they highlighted the quality of the work. Now I guess we wait and see what happens."

Jaz had her phone out, "It's happening already. We just got three new orders, and we hardly ever see orders show up this time of the morning!"

"No way! Wow! Carla, you'll be busy on Sunday night!"

"Well, if you want you can leave any orders and shipping labels at the bottom of the stairs, and I'll start tonight. We definitely want these people to have their orders in hand as soon as possible."

Jaz giggled, "At first I thought we should celebrate, but now I think I'd better get sewing!"

"You're ready for this," Lisa reminded her. "There's lots of inventory, and more coming in next Friday." She knew Jaz well enough to offer a compromise that would allow her to work a bit, but not too much. "Why don't you work for the afternoon, and then we'll all go out for supper to celebrate?"

"Can I watch Alex?" Carla offered. "After all, you'll have Becky here for the day."

"How about you two go for dinner *and* a movie?" Maria suggested. "You're too young to spend all your time working and taking care of the rest of us. Go have fun for a change."

"Sewing is fun!" Jaz protested, but the idea of going to a movie was too good to resist.

Lisa warned her as soon as they got in the car to go downtown that it was a work-free dinner. "We're going to chill out and forget about building an empire and saving the world, OK?"

"Yeah, yeah," Jaz answered. "It *is* fun to get out."

Both of them had dressed up for the occasion. Jaz was wearing a short black skirt with an off-the-shoulder white blouse, gold gladiator sandals, and her favorite chunky turquoise earring that were definitely from the eighties.

Lisa was wearing a deep blue jersey wrap dress with tan ballet flats and gold accessories. They both agreed they were overdressed for a movie, but didn't care.

"I think I understand why some pregnant moms are so happy to have something nice to wear. It feels nice not to wear the same old shorts and t-shirts for a change."

"Was that work talk?" Lisa laughed.

They chose a Mediterranean restaurant near the theater and were seated near the front window. Jaz was debating which drink to get when another diner came over to them.

"Excuse me, I'm sorry to interrupt but aren't you the ones from the morning show this morning? The Jazzy clothes?"

Lisa and Jaz exchanged glances, and Lisa could tell Jaz was speechless.

"Yep, that's right. I'm Lisa, and this is Jaz."

"Oh my gosh, it's so neat to meet you! Can I get a picture?"

"Uh, sure?"

She turned and stretched her arm out, and Lisa and Jaz leaned in and smiled. "This is so exciting, thank you! I put in an order right away. Will it come soon?"

"The next shipment goes out Monday morning so I'm sure you'll see your order in a couple of days."

She went back to her table, and Lisa was vaguely aware that she kept looking over. "So Jaz, I guess we didn't prepare for stardom in our plans."

Jaz rubbed her hand over her face, "Do you think there'll be a lot of that?"

"Maybe, but don't worry. I'll cover for you."

"Great. Now I need you to be with me every time I go out in public," she groaned.

"I'm sure it's just a one off," Lisa assured her, but Jaz didn't really relax until the lady left.

CHAPTER TWENTY-THREE

Jaz

Jaz struggled to relax after having a stranger recognize her. She loved spending time with the people she knew and trusted, but apparently strangers stressed her out. And she wasn't completely joking about only going out in public with Lisa. How would she handle it otherwise?

But by the time they ordered dessert, she was back to enjoying the chance to get out. After eating, they both agreed they couldn't do popcorn and snacks too, and they went straight into the theater. It was hard not to talk about work, but Jaz loved to hear about how Lisa had managed on her own when she first came to the city so she kept the conversation there.

"Jaz?" A voice from behind her made her tense up. She turned and felt almost relieved to see one of her old high school friends.

"Anna! Hi!"

"I hope… I don't want to bother you. I heard you were back in town. Did you have a good time in Europe?"

"Actually, I didn't go to Europe. I was here, having a baby."

"Oh, wow. I'm so sorry. I guess I just..." she looked uncomfortable and honestly apologetic.

"It's OK," Jaz assured her. Suddenly she wanted her to feel OK, "I have pictures of him—his name's Alex. Do you want to see?"

Anna took the empty seat beside Jaz. "Oh wow. Jaz, he's beautiful! Wait, is it OK to call him beautiful? I'm sorry!"

"Of course it's OK. Thank you! What have you been doing this year?"

"Oh, well, um, I finished my first year of university—Education. I'm working this summer as an aide to a special needs boy. He's really sweet and I'm super lucky I got the job!"

Someone from behind them called Anna's name, and she looked back and waved. "Sorry, I guess I should go sit with them. It was really nice to see you!"

"Did you want to hang out sometime?" Jaz was shocked the second the words were out of her mouth.

"Really? You're not too busy? I mean, I'd like to. But only if it works for you."

"Yeah, I'd like to. Um, can you send me your number? I might not have it."

"Sure—" a male voice called again and Anna looked annoyed, "—sorry. I'll catch up with you for sure then."

Lisa waited until she was out of earshot, "She seems nice."

"Actually, she does seem nice, doesn't she? Anna was kind of on the outside of our group because she's from a single parent family. Wow. That sounded really snobbish."

"Especially coming from a single mom," Lisa agreed.

Jaz groaned, "I can't even believe myself. Well, as Carrie would say, I know better so now I'll do better."

The lights dimmed, and Lisa and Jaz sat back in their chairs for two hours of mindless entertainment. Afterwards, Jaz saw that Anna had sent her a text. She looked back and waved before leaving with Lisa.

It wasn't until she was home and walking downstairs to get Alex that she realized it was kind of her first time leaving him with a babysitter. Lisa and Maria didn't count because they were like family. But she had left him with Carla and not felt worried at all. She wondered if that made her a bad mom. Should she have missed him? Or texted Carla to ask if everything was OK? That was what moms did in TV shows.

But when Carla opened the door Jaz's worries disappeared. Chris was on the couch holding a peacefully sleeping Alex. He looked more relaxed than Jaz had ever seen him.

"Thanks for sharing your son," he said quietly as he passed him over, "I forgot how nice it was to hang out with a baby."

"He was perfect," Carla assured him. "You have to leave him with us more often, OK?"

Jaz nodded and carried her son up to bed. It wasn't until she was falling asleep that she remembered about bringing the orders down to Carla to get a start on them. *There probably won't be that many more,* she thought as she fell asleep.

The next morning she realized she hadn't plugged in her phone and it was dead. She quickly plugged it in before heading downstairs with Alex. Lisa was making up for her lost mornings away by making omelets for breakfast.

"Hi! How are you this morning?"

"Good," Jaz answered, "And you?"

"Just good?"

"Yeah, why?"

"Have you looked at your sales?" Maria asked.

"No, I forgot to charge my phone last night and it's dead."

"You might want to take a peek."

"Um, OK. I guess I'll do that after breakfast. I'm really hungry considering how much we ate last night! Did Lisa tell you about us being recognized at the restaurant? That was way too weird—" she suddenly realized that both of them had goofy smiles. "What's going on?"

"Can you bring me my laptop?" Maria asked.

"Yeah, for sure." She went and got the laptop from Maria's side table in her bedroom and set it up on the table in front of her.

"Look," Maria said, pointing to the screen.

"I don't understand. Is that... that's not *our* site is it?" The numbers were too high. Thousands more followers than yesterday. And hundreds of notifications.

"I might be a little older than you Jaz, but I think this is what it looks like to go viral."

"No way," Jaz whispered as she sat down. "What about sales?"

"Let's put it this way," she answered, "Sunday is officially off the books as a rest day. We've got a *lot* of orders to fill!"

In the 24 hours since the TV interview had aired, the Jazzy Clothing Company had sold over $3,400 worth of clothing.

"Do we even have that much to sell?"

"We do," Lisa assured her, "but now inventory is running really low. That's OK though! A little bit of a situation where demand is higher than supply can work to our favor."

"We need more seamstresses!"

"A lot more!" Maria agreed.

While they ate, they tried to think of ways to find more seamstresses. Lisa offered to call the community college she had attended for her bookkeeping certificate. "I think they offered casual classes in the evenings. I'm sure I saw something about dressmaking."

"Oh! I could call my old sewing teacher at school! Gosh, I sure wish I had stayed in her classes. I would have learned a lot more useful skills than I learned taking Calculus!"

"Don't bash the math classes!" Lisa warned jokingly. "I'll clean up everything this morning. You focus on the orders, and let me know if you want me to help with Alex."

Jaz thanked her, and went upstairs to get started. After an hour she was desperate for a break. These kinds of things always felt like work to her—not like sewing where she got so caught up in a project she'd forget to eat. Although Lisa offered to take Alex, Jaz didn't mind the break when he started to get fussy. He was easily distracted with the colorful clothes so she alternated between giving him attention and putting together another order or two.

When he was ready for his morning nap she lay on the bed beside his crib watching him fall asleep. So much had changed in a year. Sometimes it felt like the first 18 years of her life were a dull blur, and she only started to really live in the past year. What would have happened if she hadn't had Alex? Would she be happy with her life? She couldn't imagine *not* sewing every day. It was tempting to stay and watch him sleep, but Jaz had work to do.

It took Jaz, Maria, and Carla most of Sunday to get all the orders ready to send out the next day. And when Maria's hands couldn't cope with any more typing, Lisa took over printing shipping labels and carrying everything downstairs. Jaz thanked Lisa repeatedly for insisting they order shipping supplies in bulk to save money. Without that, they wouldn't have been able to get everything packaged!

By early evening everything was ready to go, and Lisa and Maria were relaxing in front of the TV while Jaz played with Alex on the floor.

"I think he's getting bored," Jaz said. "Is there something I can do with him that doesn't need me to hold him while he tries to jump?"

"What about the extra baby stuff we put in the garage?" Lisa asked. "Weren't there some things that Lauren said would be good in a few months?"

"I forgot about that," Jaz admitted.

Minutes later Lisa was back inside with an exersaucer. She wiped it down, and they all forgot the TV while they watched Alex squeal and bounce around.

"This thing is amazing! I'm getting my phone to send my parents some video!" She ran upstairs and came back with her phone. "This will totally help entertain him!"

"I forget about all these baby things. When Lisa was little we had a Jolly Jumper that attached in a doorway and she'd jump in that for hours."

"Sounds dangerous!"

"No, it was perfectly safe. He's too little now, but that might be something else to have in a few months. You should check it out online and see if they still exist!"

After Alex was in bed for the night, Jaz got to work sewing. She was running low on everything—inventory, supplies, and seamstresses. Using the program Lisa had set up for her to track inventory and projects, she started adding 'things to do' and 'things to buy' to an ever-growing list. There was no point looking for more seamstresses if she didn't have anything for them to work on, so tomorrow she needed to hit all the thrift stores first thing. Hopefully, Lisa could watch Alex so she could focus on shopping.

It was after midnight when she realized she was too tired to do any more. She plugged in her phone and collapsed in bed. Alex's voice cut into her sleep far earlier than she was ready for, and for a moment she wanted to roll over and ignore him. But when he started to get upset she forced herself to get going.

They were all quieter than usual at the table, but Jaz didn't mind. More orders had come in overnight, and she was feeling pressured. Her dad and Mr. Chen were right. She needed more help. Between needing to prove she was a success, and wanting to make as much money as possible for the housing project, she had to make this work.

"Lisa, is there some time this morning when you can watch Alex? I need to do a run to all the thrift stores."

"Yep, we have an Airbnb guest coming this morning so I'll be home."

"Thanks. And if I can get enough supplies I'll try to phone my sewing teacher when I get back. No point hiring more people if we don't have anything for them to work with!"

Forgetting about her now-recognizable face, Jaz entered the first thrift store and got lost in the fabrics, colors, and ideas that always seemed to fill her mind when she was shopping for supplies. With more seamstresses, she'd be able to bring more of her ideas to life. There were still so many things she wanted to add to her lines of clothes, and she needed a lot more time to work on the line of accessible clothes, too.

But her excitement dropped when the teller started talking to her.

"I saw you on the TV, and told my husband I knew you! I didn't realize you were running a *business* with all the stuff you were buying. You know, some people just like the deals here, but *you're* using it to make money!"

She chattered on about Jaz selling 'their' clothes, moving slower and slower as she entered in each price. By the time she had totaled everything, there was a line of people behind Jaz waiting, and she was desperate to get out of the store.

Once she was safely in the car, she called Lisa.

"I can't do this! People are recognizing me and it's freaking me out!"

"What do you want to do about it?" Lisa asked calmly.

"I want to quit!"

"You know that's your choice, right? This is *your* business Jaz."

"OK, so I don't actually want to quit. But I can't do this without you. You're so much better at talking to strangers."

"Did you get enough supplies?"

"No," Jaz answered in a quiet voice. "I have two more stores to check out. What am I going to do?"

"I'd offer to go with you, but I think the two of us together would attract even more attention... I know! Disguise yourself! Isn't there a sports shop right near where you are?"

"Yeah, but—"

"—Go buy a ball cap, and maybe a plain t-shirt that you can put over what you're wearing. You look too classy Jaz! Try to neutralize your look and see if that works."

Jaz agreed to give it a try, and walked over to the discount sports store. She found a cap with a wide brim and bought a plain, dark green t-shirt to go with it. The cashier seemed to stare at her, but Jaz kept her eyes down and quickly left with her purchases. Back in the car she put on her 'disguise' and forced herself to go to the next two stores.

When she came back home she had a trunk full of supplies that would hopefully last for more than a week. Even though she hadn't been recognized again, it wasn't anything she wanted to repeat if she could help it.

CHAPTER TWENTY-FOUR

Carrie

Carrie tried to contain her excitement when she picked up Susan in the truck she borrowed from Lauren. She didn't want to overwhelm her, but she was beyond hopeful that everything would work out.

A few hours later Susan had picked out a used bedframe, a mattress, a table and two chairs, and a small couch from a thrift store in the industrial area of the city that carried furniture. Two volunteers helped load everything into the truck and strap it down. Carrie would store it all in Jonathan's garage until Saturday when they'd meet her at her new place and help her move in.

"It's not much," Susan admitted, "but it's mine, and I can hardly wait to have my very own space!"

Jonathan was horrified at the idea of buying a used mattress and sofa, but Carrie insisted it was the best way to get started on a small budget. He reluctantly put everything in the garage, and made the decision that everyone in their future housing project would sleep on brand new mattresses. Carrie just smiled. If they pulled off new mattresses after everything else, she'd be more than happy to support his idea.

She had a babysitter come for the morning on Saturday so she and Jonathan could focus on getting Susan settled. Susan was hoping to surprise Lisa, Maria, and Jaz with a new address when she brought her sewing to them on Friday. It wasn't long before her few belongings were moved in, and Carrie and Jonathan were saying goodbye. The picture of Susan looking exhausted, but peaceful and happy would stay with the two of them forever. If they hadn't been on board with the housing project already, that morning convinced them.

On Monday Carrie woke up truly looking forward to spending the day at the women's center. The frame project the week before had somehow helped almost everyone open up, and she felt like they were beginning to accept her, and she was beginning to understand them. She was continuing her idea of creating something together today, and hoped it would work out.

While she was setting up the room, Donna, the center supervisor, came in.

"I wanted to thank you for the project you did last week. You know, it's easy to focus on funding, compliance, and just keeping the doors open, and forget that these are all women who want more out of life than a bed for the night. Between you and Mary, I saw more smiles last week than I've seen in a while."

It was a good start to the week. Even Dr. Bradley said hello to her when he came in. He took in the tables Carrie had set up with books, glue, and notepaper, but didn't say anything.

"Oh, so it's crafting with Carrie again?" Julia asked sarcastically as she walked in ahead of the others.

"Well, yes and no. You're welcome to sit and relax if you'd rather."

"As long as we don't have to read anything," someone else said.

"Definitely not. Actually, these books are for cutting up." She smiled at a few of the shocked faces, "Oh, come on. You mean you've never hated a book so much you've wanted to rip out the pages?"

"I've never met a book I *didn't* want to rip the pages out of!"

"Then this is perfect. I have a personal question for each of you. But instead of trying to get you all to answer out loud, I thought it might help to write the answer down and tuck it away. Here, this is mine." She held out a miniature envelope made from the page in a book. "You can cut out a page from one of these books, and fold it into an envelope, and then the answer to the question goes on these little pieces of notepaper that you put in the envelope."

"What's the question? Something like 'what's your biggest regret in life'? Or maybe 'bad habits I need to change'?"

"Nope. Nothing like that. The question is, What do you really, really want?"

"That's a stupid question!"

"Thanks, Julia," Carrie answered dryly, but with the hint of a smile. If it wasn't for her, Carrie would spend a lot of the sessions having a one-way conversation with herself. "Just let yourself think about it while we make envelopes. The answer might surprise you."

There was lots of joking while everyone made their envelopes, but when they picked up the notepaper and pens, things got quiet. After they had all closed their envelopes Carrie sensed some excitement and nervousness.

"Alright. My next question—and again, no one has to answer out loud if they don't want to—is, what are you doing to get what you really, really want?"

There was silence for a minute, and then Char answered. "I really, really want to be a preschool teacher. But I can't do anything to get it. I barely graduated."

"That reminds me a little bit of a friend of mine," Carrie started. "Maria is in her late 40s now, but being a preschool teacher was her dream. When she was eighteen, she married a really controlling man who kept her under his thumb until he died a few years ago. Her health isn't that good now, but every afternoon she watches a girl with special needs. The things she's done for Becky are really amazing. It's not *exactly* the same as her dream of teaching preschool, but she's so happy now." She looked around the room, wishing she had some way to encourage them. "My point is that she found a way to make her dream come true, using the skills she had. Char, you might not even know all the things you already have that will make you a great preschool teacher."

Char looked at Carrie for a moment, as if she was trying to decide whether or not to believe her.

"I really, really want to be rich," Liz smirked. "I'm tired of never having any money."

"OK, what are you doing to get rich?"

"I work sometimes."

"Is that getting you closer towards your goal?"

She laughed, "At what they pay me? Never!"

"Sometimes we put a lot of energy into doing the same things we've always done, but it doesn't get us better results. Does anyone feel like what they're doing right now *isn't* getting you closer to your goals?"

The conversation began to pick up momentum, and soon they were all starting to share what they really wanted out of life. There were some harsh responses to things people said they were doing to get what they wanted, but Carrie felt they were all pretty accurate.

"OK, we're almost out of time. One more question: What can you do today, or this week to get what you want? I'm looking for things that will get you closer to your goals without taking away someone else's needs. So, stealing someone's car to get richer would be a no," She smiled when Julia added a 'duh' "but looking for a way to earn more money would be a yes."

Nobody offered an answer, so Carrie encouraged them to think about it. "I'll be around today and tomorrow if anyone wants to chat."

After signing off everyone who attended the session, she came back to the meeting room to tidy up only to see that Char had already done it.

"Hey, thanks! So, what did you think about the stuff we talked about today?"

"You know, when I was little I always talked about what I wanted to be when I grew up. But by the time I was in high school I figured it was just stupid. It's the first time in a long time that anyone's asked me what I want."

"I truly believe that the things we want the most—good things, like being a preschool teacher—are part of what God has made us for. I know it sounds cheesy to say, 'follow your dreams', but when it comes to what you want most in life, go for it!"

"Are you always this… chipper?" Char's disbelief was written all over her face.

"Definitely not. Right now I'm genuinely excited for you and where you're going to go, and I'm pretty happy about my own life too. But there are days when everything sucks. Then I just try and survive, and hope that the next day is a little better."

"Thanks, Carrie."

"Anytime Char."

It occurred to Carrie that the only other thing she needed to make her week perfect was to hear that their offer on the fourplex got accepted, but they were still waiting for any response. Once they had a place, everything would pretty much be under their control. Until then, they couldn't control anything except earning more money to contribute to the project if it ever went anywhere.

CHAPTER TWENTY-FIVE

Maria

"I'm telling you, something's up with Susan," Maria insisted. It was Thursday evening, and they were all sitting on the lower deck with Carla and Chris. Becky was in her playhouse, humming a song that only she knew.

"If she needed help she would have asked, Mom."

"I don't know. She doesn't answer her phone, and when I text her she gives these super short answers. That's not like her."

"Should we give you some time alone when she comes tomorrow?" Jaz asked.

"Please. I'm going to get to the bottom of this!"

"I wish my Mom had a friend like you. She's so lonely most of the time because she has nothing in common with the other people in her complex." Carla's mom lived on the other side of the country in a gated community. Both Chris and Carla were hoping that the suite they were adding to their house would be an incentive for her to move in with them. But if not, they'd rent it out.

"Well, at least when the house is ready she'll have somewhere to stay. Then she won't have any reason not to at least come for a visit! I'm looking forward to meeting her!" If Maria could have one wish, it would be that all grandparents would live close enough to enjoy their grandchildren on a regular basis. She hated loving families being separated by hundreds of miles.

That night as she lay in bed, she said an extra prayer for Susan and for Carla's mom. It was all she could do for now, but as soon as she figured out some practical way to help, she'd be all over it.

When Susan came in the next day, Maria was not prepared for what she saw. "Susan! What on earth? You look... I don't even know what to say. You look spectacular!"

She set a huge bag down and sat down beside Maria, "Well, I have some news." Her smile lit up her entire face. "I have my own place—!"

A chorus of exclamations drowned out her words as everyone started talking at the same time.

"—I took your advice Maria, and I called Carrie. You know, she didn't say anything different than what everyone else has been saying, but this time I *heard* it. I suddenly realized it's not my job to try and make my daughter and her family happy. I still want them to be happy, of course. I'm just not going to make myself responsible for it. After I got off the phone with her, it was like a huge weight lifted off my chest. I went right out and found an apartment and then I told my daughter."

"How did *that* go?"

She smiled and squeezed Maria's hand gently. "It was terrible!"

They all laughed with her. "That bad, huh?"

"Yes, that bad. But I kept reminding myself that I needed to take care of myself, or I wouldn't be up to doing *anything* for *any* of them! Carrie took me out to get some used furniture, and she and Jonathan moved me in on Saturday."

"You! You moved in without me?" Maria didn't know whether to be upset or pleased.

"I did. You have been so supportive and encouraging of me for so long. I wanted to make this happen so I could tell you it's a done deal. And," she looked at Jaz, "I can get a lot more sewing done now! You need to send more stuff with me because I finished everything I had."

"Oh, wow! That is *such* perfect timing! We are crazy short on inventory and I've been freaking out. Can I see?"

Together they admired everything Susan had done. She was by far the most detail-oriented of all the seamstresses, so having her excited about doing more work was a relief for everyone.

"Now that all the business is taken care of, when can we visit you?" Maria was already planning at least a few housewarming gifts to celebrate Susan's newfound freedom.

"Well, I have Janie every day after school until about six. How about tomorrow since it's Saturday? Come for coffee and tea!"

"It's a date!"

Maria felt like she was floating for the rest of the day. Knowing that Susan was safe, happy, and free to do her own thing in her own place was the best news she could have imagined.

CHAPTER TWENTY-SIX

Lisa

Visiting Susan in her new apartment was a blessing and a curse for Lisa. The change in Susan's whole outlook was striking. Even in a humble one-bedroom apartment with nothing decorative and used furniture, she was glowing with happiness.

She exclaimed over the flowers and vase they bought her, and the treats from the bakery that Maria couldn't get enough of. And she proudly served them tea from beautiful china cups—the one thing she had insisted she keep after the divorce.

"I feel like I'm standing on my own feet for the first time in my life! It's amazing! And having Janie here after school is so much easier. I don't feel obligated to clean up and make the kids behave. Here, she's at Grandma's house and we can just have a nice afternoon together." She smiled at Jaz. "And I'm teaching her to sew, so we'll do our best to keep your grandma's memory alive for the next generation."

"Thanks, Susan. I think the two of you would have really gotten along."

But when they left her apartment, Lisa struggled with feelings of helplessness and frustration. She needed to do something! For the past five years, her life had consisted of making plans, following them through, achieving a goal, and then making the next plan. Even when her mom suddenly re-entered her life, it only took a few days to reset and get a new plan.

Now, she had done everything she possibly could. They had a good pre-approved mortgage thanks to Manuel and Betsy contributing to the down payment and co-signing. They had money and hands to do any renovations they needed. They even had a property that would work! And that's where the action stopped.

There was no point driving over to the property again, even though she was tempted. All she could do was wait.

She decided to see if Carrie was going to her church tomorrow. It hadn't really been something she wanted to do before, but she figured it wouldn't hurt. Both her mom and Jaz wanted to stay home and relax on Sunday morning, so Lisa put on a bright sleeveless dress with navy flats and went on her own.

Carrie told her where they usually sat when they went, and Lisa easily found them before the service started. She said her hellos to everyone, and Katie came over to sit beside her.

"Where's Alex?" she demanded.

"He stayed home with Jaz and my mom. They wanted to rest today."

"Oh," she nodded wisely, "sometimes grown-ups get tired."

Lisa enjoyed the energy and happiness she felt around her as they sang songs. She hadn't heard anything like it before, but it was easy to follow along. It was a good thing the music was so loud, and no one could hear her try to sing along!

After the kids left for Sunday School, Carrie motioned for her to shuffle over beside her. "Nice to see you!" she whispered before the sermon started.

The pastor talked about forgiveness, and Lisa found herself nodding in agreement more than once.

"Forgiveness isn't something we feel. It's something we do. Forgiveness isn't saying 'what you did to me was OK'. It's saying, 'I'm not letting a chain connect us in anger'. Forgiveness doesn't require anything from the other person. We're not responsible for them! And when we choose to forgive, we begin a journey of personal freedom. *That's* what God wants for us!"

His enthusiasm made her smile. This pastor really did believe what he preached—and probably practiced it too. She thought back to her own journey of forgiveness. It was easy to forgive her mom. Even before she knew why her mom was so cold to her when she was growing up, she still wanted a relationship with her. Maybe that made it easier to forgive. But it was a lot harder to forgive her dad. He had nearly ruined her life *and* her mom's life. She still got angry when she thought about it.

The pastor's voice interrupted her thoughts. "Unforgiveness is like drinking poison and hoping it kills the other person. Ask God to help you forgive so you can be free to enjoy the good things he has for you." It wasn't something she had ever considered—that *not* forgiving her dad could be harmful to her. She bowed her head when the pastor started praying and said her own little prayer that someday she wouldn't feel so angry when she thought about her dad.

After the service, Lisa chatted with Carrie while Jonathan went to pick up Katie. "They're pretty careful here," she explained. "Because it's a big church and the helpers don't know every parent, you need to register and then bring photo ID to pick up the kids."

Soon Katie was bouncing towards them holding Jonathan's hand. "Daddy Johnny said we can go to McDonald's for lunch Mommy! Can you come too, Lisa?"

"Oh, um, let me see if my Mom and Jaz and Alex want to." She stepped back to call, and agreed to pick them up on the way. "Yep, we'll meet you there, OK?"

"YAY!" Katie shouted, startling a few people around her. Lisa noticed Jonathan trying not to laugh, and Carrie trying to glare at him. They made an adorable family.

Having something to do—even if it was meeting friends at McDonald's —helped to keep Lisa's mind off of all the things that were out of her control. All she needed to do was get through the rest of the day, and tomorrow she'd have new files from her clients to work on, plus any new work she could do for Jaz. *We won't wait forever to hear about the house*, she assured herself.

When she got up the next day, there was a voicemail from Frank. Trying to keep her hopes down, she dialed in to listen: "Hi Lisa, I sure hope this call doesn't bother you, but I didn't want to wait to tell you the news! The owner has finally gotten back to us with a counter offer of $540,000. I don't know anything about them, but it could be the break we've been hoping for."

Lisa looked at her watch. It was 7:15. It was probably too early to call, but not too early to send a group email. She sent a short message with the details and added that she was voting to accept the counter offer. Then she called Frank, hoping he was an early riser.

"I thought that message would get your attention!" Lisa heard Frank's smile through the phone.

"It sure did! As you might see, I just sent off an email to everyone. Do you know anything about when we might get the property if we accept the offer? And should we make it conditional on an inspection?"

"I don't know anything about a possession date. The whole thing is really strange. Such a long delay in replying, and then only the most basic information in the counter offer. But considering everything, it should definitely be contingent on an inspection. We don't want to be moving people into an unsafe building."

Lisa agreed, "I guess it's another waiting game to see what everyone says. But at least I know *these* people, and I will hunt each of them down if they don't reply today!"

"I wish all my clients were as enthusiastic as you! Keep me posted, and have a good day."

"You too, Frank. And thank you!"

Lisa found herself singing part of one of the songs from church while she showered. This *had* to be a sign of good things to come! When she came out of her room, Jaz was just coming out with Alex.

"Well, now I know why you don't walk around the house singing!" Jaz teased.

"Hey! What I lack in talent I make up for in... um... enthusiasm?!" she laughed, "But I do have a good reason to sing. We *finally* got a reply from the owner of the fourplex! He or she or whoever they are countered at $540,000."

Jaz's eyes got big, "But, we can totally do $540,000!"

They both started walking downstairs, "Yep, we totally can! I just sent out an email to everyone with the info. So I guess we have to make sure we all agree. Frank said we should make it contingent on an inspection though."

"What does that mean?"

"It means we would accept that price, but only if an inspection doesn't turn up any major problems. If it does, we can renegotiate. Or at least try to. I don't know how you negotiate with someone who takes weeks to give a single answer."

Maria called to them as they walked past her room and they all went in. "So, I read your email! I won't be ready to get out of bed for a bit yet, but count me as a yes!"

"Are you OK Mom?"

"Well, I'm having a bit of a rougher morning. So I'll have to take my time."

Lisa looked at her carefully. She didn't have the same look of agony she had when her rheumatoid arthritis flared, but she didn't look quite right, either. "Do you want me to bring you a cup of tea?"

"Please. Could you put it in the travel mug with the handle and bring a straw too?"

"Of course. Be right back."

Jaz leaned over and kissed Maria on the forehead. "Feel better soon, kay?"

Lisa and Jaz were subdued as they ate breakfast. It just wasn't a celebration with Maria not feeling well. "You know," Lisa said quietly, "we can't mope around all day. Then she'll pretend she's fine and overdo it. We need to be as normal as possible."

"Sure, you figure out what normal is and I'll follow!"

"Well, you know that we're not normal at all so I guess we'll just be ourselves."

Jaz sat Alex in his bouncy chair. "I don't know if I've said this, but I'm really grateful for everything you're doing for the project," she said as Lisa turned on the kettle. "Without you, nothing would have happened."

"Are you kidding? Working on this has saved my sanity! And it's been really neat to use the things I learned buying this house. I have to admit, this whole buying property thing is kind of addictive."

"I don't know how you did it the first time without knowing anything! And I get to keep doing my sewing thing while you're making it all happen."

"Hey, I think it's something that was meant to be." Lisa smiled at Jaz. The other benefit was sharing this home with people like Jaz, Alex, Chris, and Carla. If only she would have known as a teenager that her life would turn out this good.

It wasn't long before everyone had replied to agree to the counter offer except Amy and Jesse. Lisa decided to call them, but both phones went to voicemail. She left a message on each of them, and got set up for her freelance work. When Amy called back, Lisa was almost done with her first client.

"Hey, I didn't know if you guys were both working early this morning. I hope I didn't bother you!"

"Oh, no, we weren't at work…"

Lisa thought she heard muffled laughing in the background, and then she realized what was going on. "Oh, my gosh. Um, sorry to interrupt *that*. Guess you both took the morning off?" She was laughing now too.

"Yeah, something like that! Anyways, we think you should accept the counter offer. There's still an inspection, right?"

"Yep, we'll add that in for sure."

"OK, Jesse thought he and Chris should be there for the inspection to make sure they can see everything. Is that all right?"

"Yeah, that's a great idea. If everything goes well, we'll have to pick a time when you two aren't so… busy." She hung up to the sounds of more laughter.

Jaz was smiling and blushing, obviously clueing in to what was going on.

"Hey," Lisa said, "At least they're happily married, right? I have to go tell Mom, she'll think it's hilarious."

"Don't forget to tell Frank to accept the offer!"

"Oh, yeah. OK, that first, then Mom."

CHAPTER TWENTY-SEVEN

Jaz

"Hello, Mrs. Morton? Um, this is Jaz. I used to be in your sewing class at Pleasant Hill High School?"

There was a pause on the other end of the line, "Oh, yes, Jaz! One of my star students. How are you?"

"I'm really good, thank you. Um, the reason I'm calling is because I was hoping you could help me out. So, I started this business upcycling clothes—"

"—upcycling? What's that?"

"Well, I buy used clothes from thrift stores and online, and then I re-style them, or change them into something different and then sell them."

"Oh! Like recycling?"

"Yeah, like recycling! Anyways, the business is going really well and I'm having trouble keeping up with everything. I have five ladies sewing for me right now but it's not enough. Do you know of anyone who can sew who might be looking for some work?" She put her hand over her chest and was glad her teacher couldn't see how scared she was to be calling and asking for help.

"I'm not sure... Can you tell me more?"

"Of course. What happens right now is that every Friday the ladies come to the house where I live, and they bring me the pieces they've finished and they get paid, and then I give them more projects for the next week."

"Mmm hmmm?"

"Well, um, the projects vary based on their skills. It can be anything from turning men's flannel shirts into cute little bandana bibs for babies, to doing a sort of reverse applique on t-shirts, to converting men's dress shirts into women's wrap dresses."

"Wow, that sounds like quite the business!"

"Oh, it is!" Jaz found herself talking about all the projects, how happy her clients were, and how she wanted to grow the business even more because she wanted to give back to the community. Suddenly she realized she had been talking for over five minutes straight. "Oh my goodness. I'm so sorry Mrs. Morton. I got carried away there!"

"Don't apologize! I got excited about everything just listening to you! I have to admit, you don't really sound like the quiet little girl who was always hiding at the back of the classroom!"

"Well, a lot's happened since I graduated. I, um, I had a baby. And he's wonderful, and it kind of changed everything for me."

"If you're happy—and it sounds like you are—then I'm happy. Now about some extra help, I do have a few people in mind that might be interested."

"Oh, that's wonderful!"

"How many do you need?"

"Honestly? I could probably keep another six or seven busy. Everything we complete seems to sell before we can get more done. I've been trying to do as much as I can myself, but I don't want to spend too much time away from Alex."

"In that case, would you consider adding me to your list as well?"

"Are you kidding? That would be so cool! Really? You really want to?" She couldn't believe that someone as talented as her teacher would want to work for her.

"It's the summer so I have some free time. And I have to admit, the idea of getting paid to sew is quite appealing!"

They agreed to meet at Jaz's house the next day so Jaz could show her more, and if all went well, send a week's work home with her.

"Lisa! Maria!" she yelled before clapping her hand to her mouth. She stopped and looked into the bedroom where Alex was asleep. Good, she hadn't woken him up. She ran down the stairs to where they were watching TV. "I can't even believe this, but my sewing teacher is going to work for us! She's coming tomorrow!"

"Oh Jaz, I'm so happy for you! Maybe now you can start getting to bed a little earlier?"

"Yeah, I think so. And she said she'll ask some other people who might be interested."

"Do you still want me to call the college? I totally forgot today with all the excitement of the offer on the property."

"Well, let's wait a few days. At least anyone Mrs. Morton recommends we know we can count on. I just had to come tell you. I'm going to go get a bunch of projects ready for her and then I'm going to bed!" She started to leave and then turned around. "Maria? Are you feeling better?"

"I am, thank you. Still really tired and a bit achy, but I hope it's not anything major. I'll just have to take it easy until I get my groove back I guess."

Jaz went upstairs, wishing again that she could find a cure for Maria's illness. She wondered if there were any private treatments that might work. The way her business was going, maybe she could help Maria *and* see the housing project happen.

CHAPTER TWENTY-EIGHT

Carrie

Carrie joined the line of parents waiting to pick up their kids from day camp. With Jonathan away for the week, and school out, it was an ideal solution for childcare—and one she was thrilled to pay for without pinching pennies. Having Matthew and Katie at the same location made it easy to drop them off on her way to the women's center and then pick them up on the way home.

"Mommy! Mommy!" It was easy to find Katie in the crowd of kids. She always seemed to put out more energy than anyone else around her. Carrie signed out both kids and headed for the car with Katie chattering a mile a minute and Matthew patiently waiting his turn to talk.

"OK Katie, let's give Matthew a turn to talk while we're driving." She was glad both kids had had a good time—although Katie would probably be happy anywhere. It made it easier to leave them and go in to work.

Once supper was cleaned up, she got out her laptop. A few orders had come in over the weekend and she needed to get them ready for shipping. Her neighbor had agreed to let her drop off the packages at their house for pick-up in the morning, since Carrie would be gone before the delivery company came around.

Matthew helped her with packaging and carrying everything next door. There were three orders, but one of them was for a set of seven frames so it took both of them to carry it all.

Then she poured herself a glass of wine and finally relaxed. It was still such a relief to not have to fit in studying and writing papers after a full day. And she got all of her reports written for both practicums before she left the center or clinic, which gave her a bit of a mental break at home.

Jonathan managed to FaceTime before the kids went to bed and she was surprised at how much she missed him already. They were both excited about the possibility of closing a deal on the fourplex. Jonathan had talked to Chris about turning two of the units into four, and it sounded like they could make it work.

Both Jonathan and Carrie had a taste of what was possible after helping Susan, and they couldn't wait for more.

"But remember to leave time for a wedding in there!" Carrie teased.

He smiled, "Only 117 days left!"

"You're counting?!"

"Of course, aren't you?"

"Oh, um... Yeah, of course!" She couldn't believe he had actually counted the days until November 2nd. It hadn't even occurred to her with everything else going on.

"Hey, you've got a lot more going on than I do. No worries, OK? I'll do the counting, and you try not to do too much."

"I miss you."

"I miss you too."

Before Carrie went to bed, she sent a group text to Jenny, Lauren, Kara, Lisa, Maria, and Jaz:

Hey ladies! It turns out I'm getting married in 117 days (Jonathan counted)! Any chance we could meet up for coffee so you can help me with planning?

She forced herself to relax and try not to worry but it seemed like there was a lot to do. Reaching over to her phone, she turned on a meditation soundtrack, and slowly started repeating her mantra for relaxing, *I love myself, I love myself.* Before she knew it, her mind wandered to the first time she learned the strategy when Jaz was still living with her and the kids.

They had all learned something that day—that focusing on loving yourself made everything better. With all that was going on she had forgotten the practice for a while, but it was time to get back to making sure she spent five minutes every day saying *I love myself.* Even if those five minutes were at the end of the day. Realizing her mind had been drifting, she started over again.

At the center the next day, Carrie talked about the *I love myself* habit, and how much of a difference it had made for her and her kids. "I can see that you're all skeptical," she laughed. "That's OK, just give it a chance for a week or two before you dismiss it. And I'll bet by then you'll be sold on it."

It was nice that they all trusted her enough now to try things, even if they weren't sure it would help. Establishing authentic friendships had become a priority for Carrie and she felt privileged that they were willing to let her into their lives.

There were little signs that the group was changing for the better. Most of them attended every session, even when they didn't need a bed that night. A few of them were working now, so Carrie added a lunch break option which allowed those close enough to pop in for a chat during their lunch break.

Char continued to open up to Carrie, and was looking at options for becoming a preschool teacher. Together, they talked to Donna about Char's goal, and it sounded possible for Char to start her first college course in September. Carrie was excited to see her feel more confident, and focus on her future. She was still with her boyfriend, but she had brought him to the center to meet Carrie and they all talked together about how to have a healthy relationship that worked for both of them.

The last thing Carrie expected at the women's center was to be counseling a couple, but she enjoyed it. Char's boyfriend seemed genuinely interested in making their relationship work, and had taken Carrie's advice to join an anger management group run by the drop-in center nearby.

She was thinking about whether to offer to stay on as a volunteer after her practicum was finished. If she didn't need full-time paid work, she could manage without it being a paying position. But she planned to wait another month or so before talking to Donna, just in case it ended up not being a good fit.

Even Pamela, the grumpy receptionist was warming up to Carrie. Well, at least she said hi to Carrie in the morning, and knew her name. A few years ago Carrie would have done anything to get someone like Pamela to like her. Now, she knew better than to take it personally, and didn't go out of her way to be nice. Somehow it was working.

The work at the medical clinic was going better too. Although in some ways it was easier to have one-hour appointments instead of spending most of the day with the same people like she did at the women's center, it offered different challenges because the patients had such a variety of problems.

Sometimes she was a friendly face and a listening ear for someone who was lonely. Other times she needed all of her training and Dr. Henshaw's experience to work through complex mental health issues. She was glad to have Thursdays to be at home and working on her business after clinic days. It was a nice balance to have a quiet, creative day after a full day with clients. By the end of the day she always felt recharged and ready for another day of counseling.

CHAPTER TWENTY-NINE

Lisa

Once everyone agreed to accept the counteroffer for the fourplex, Lisa immediately phoned Frank to get the process going, but it wasn't until Thursday that he called back.

"I guess a three-day wait is fast for these people!" he joked.

"Frank! No small talk! What did they say?"

"Well, as long as the inspection goes well you are now the new part-owner of a fourplex!"

"WOOOHOOOO! That is the best news possible! Oh my gosh, I can't believe it!"

"I'm pretty sure you'll believe it when you've got mounds of work to do on it!"

"I can't wait! I have been dying to get started on a big project! What do we have to do now?"

"We'll need to have all three of you, plus Sandra, meet at the office to complete the paperwork. In the meantime, I'll book an inspection. I saw in the emails that Jesse and Chris want to be there for that. And I suppose you will as well?"

"Definitely. If you could work with the guys to pick a time that works for them, I'll be able to be there. EEEEK! I'm so excited!"

She hung up after setting a time that afternoon to sign the paperwork and laughed at the look on her mom and Jaz's face. They were both holding their breath.

"OK, breathe you two! We got the house!"

They both cheered, and Alex clapped his hands together.

"I don't know if I can concentrate enough to write an email to everyone!"

"Why don't I do it for you?" Maria offered. "Is there anything specific to say?"

"Well, just that we'll sign everything this afternoon, but we still have to wait for the inspection. I wish I had a date to give everyone so they could start working their schedules around the renos. Hopefully that will come this afternoon. The important thing is that we're *finally* getting close enough to make this happen!"

"You know, with the extra seamstresses working, I'll have some extra time. Do you think there's anything I'll be able to help with?" Jaz asked.

"I'm sure there will be! Have you ever painted before?"

Jaz gave Lisa a look that had them all laughing, "Do I *look* like the type of person who was raised doing manual labor?"

"Hmmm, good point. We'll have to break you in slowly! Did you even imagine a year ago that you'd be asking to learn manual labor?"

"Never," Jaz admitted, "but hey, if you all can start strange new lives with zero experience then so can I!"

"That's my girl!" Maria said with a proud smile.

There was a knock at the door from the basement, and Chris came up with Becky to join the celebration. "This is perfect timing! We'll be winding down work on our own house so there's more time to work on the new property!"

"Oh, but that means you'll be moving out soon." Maria reached out to Becky, who leaned against her for a moment before pulling back and asking for a cookie. "Who's going to ask me for cookies when you're gone, Becky?" Becky repeated the sign for 'cookie' and Maria, laughing, told her "Only one!"

"I guess we'll have to all hang out at the property!" Chris answered. "Bring the cookies, and Becky will happily stick around!"

When it was time for Lisa, Jaz, Manuel, and Betsy to sign the purchase papers, Lisa tried to pay attention to everything so she could remember the moment. She thought she had big dreams as a 19-year-old trying to get her bookkeeper's certificate and maybe one day buy a house. Now, to be buying a property that would give multiple families a safe place to live felt unreal.

Her eyes started to feel hot, and she blinked quickly. Here she was, about to be part of something that could really change someone's life. She had been so focused on survival when she was younger that helping others never crossed her mind. This felt like a dream—but one she hadn't known she wanted. One paper at a time, she added her name to the project.

"So, when can we get into the place again?" she asked as soon as all the documentation was complete.

"The next chance will be the inspection next Wednesday afternoon."

"Another case of hurry up and wait?"

"I'm afraid so. But I'm fairly certain these few more days won't really matter in the long run."

They thanked Frank and Sandra, and headed out of the office. Lisa noticed that Sandra seemed to be hanging back with Frank. Maybe more than one good thing would come out of this project!

Manuel, Betsy, Jaz, and Lisa all stood outside, enjoying the warm sun and chatting about the property. Betsy had immediately asked to hold Alex for Jaz, and she was reluctant to let go.

"It's been too long since I've held a baby! Although he's growing so fast. You know, I won't be much help with the renovations, so maybe you want to drop him off at our place sometimes so you can go work with the others?" she asked Jaz.

"Well, I'm not sure how much help I'll be either. But I'll give it a try and see. Maria would love to watch him, but it's too hard for her to pick him up now."

"Oh, the poor thing. That must be so hard on her!"

She reluctantly handed him back, and Lisa and Jaz headed back to the car. "When we get home, do you have time to go over the numbers with me so I know how much Jazzy Clothing can contribute to the renovations for the property?"

Lisa gently bumped Jaz's shoulder, "You've got to be joking with the whole 'do I have time' thing! Of course I do! I have sooooo much time."

"We'll try to fix that for you next week! Oh, in the meantime, we do get to go to Carrie's tonight to talk wedding stuff!"

"That's true. Although I'm not really a wedding person myself, I'm happy to help if someone gives me a job to do. Have you told her about the dress?"

Jaz had found the perfect starting point for Carrie's wedding dress during one of her recent thrift store runs. It was a white dress with cap sleeves, a fitted bodice with delicate embroidery, and a mermaid fit. Jaz planned to convert the top to an off-the-shoulder style with silky soft chiffon sleeves and take off the mermaid bottom. Then she'd add a long slit along the center at the back and overlay the skirt with gathered chiffon.

"Not yet. I know it's risky to do the whole design without checking with her, but if she doesn't like it I can do any changes she wants. I want to see if my idea works before I show her. I've never done anything like this before so if I screw up the first time I'll just give it another try."

Lisa was the only one of their friends reluctant to help with the wedding, but she wanted to be there for Carrie. While marriage wasn't for her, it was definitely perfect for Jonathan and Carrie.

As soon as Lisa, Jaz, and Alex got to Carrie's that evening, Matthew took over entertaining Alex. Katie was at Jonathan's, who was also watching Angela so Jenny could join the ladies. Lauren and Kara were the last to join them.

Once they were all set with either wine or coffee and a cheesecake Maria insisted on sending along, Carrie got started.

"I have to admit, I don't know what I want. Jonathan's proposal was such a surprise I hadn't spent any time dreaming about a wedding! And I haven't really had any time since to think about it, either."

"Bet you're thinking about the honeymoon!" Kara quipped.

"Oh yeah..." Carrie said with a huge smile and a wink. "But I'll try to focus on the task at hand. So, what do I do?"

Lisa found herself getting excited for Carrie as everyone threw out ideas and recommendations. When they had a general plan, Carrie FaceTimed her mom and sister Jessica so they could have their say.

Jenny had suggested they look through Carrie's Pinterest boards to see what she liked. They all agreed Carrie didn't need a 'theme' or a 'color' since she clearly loved anything colorful and happy. Instead, she'd carry a bouquet of brightly colored roses, and keep decorations to a minimum—only a vase of colorful flowers on each table at the reception.

A restaurant that Carrie, Jenny, and Kara had gone to the first time they went out as friends was available for an early-afternoon reception, and its eclectic décor would go perfect with Carrie's personality. The manager had even invited Carrie and Jonathan for a tasting dinner on the evening of their choice to choose their menu.

They'd have the ceremony at one in the afternoon in the church Carrie attended. The main area where the services were held was too big for their low-key wedding, but there was a fireside room that seated up to seventy-five people and would be perfect.

Carrie wasn't having bridesmaids, insisting that "I'd have to have all of you in my wedding party, and then there'd be nobody sitting in the chairs!"

Jaz asked if Carrie wanted her to create outfits for Katie and Matthew too. Jenny and Carrie shared a glance and then both burst out laughing. "Jenny told me to ask you, but I thought doing my wedding dress was more than enough! Yes, I'd love it if you'd dress all of us! What about Jonathan?"

"Won't he want to get a tux?"

"Actually, I have no idea! I'll ask him and get back to you!"

The rest of the evening was full of laughter and plans. When they left, Lisa realized all of her feelings of frustration at the delays over the property were gone. "Do you feel, I don't know, weirdly happy after tonight?" she asked Jaz.

"Yeah. It's not like it changed anything for us, but hanging out with everyone and helping Carrie made me feel like I'm the one with all the reasons to celebrate."

"Is that what it's like to have girlfriends?"

"What do you mean?"

"Well, I never really had girlfriends to hang out with in high school, so I don't know what it's supposed to be like. I feel really happy right now, and I feel really lame for saying that."

"I think it's the way it's supposed to be. But after I hung out with my friends in high school, I didn't feel like this. Actually, I sometimes even felt relieved when I had an excuse to go home. So yeah, let's call this weird—but good weird."

CHAPTER THIRTY

Maria

When Maria heard the front door open, she quietly called out to the girls to come and see her. Jaz went to put Alex to bed, and then they both came and sat on her bed. These times were some of the highlights of Maria's week—having her two 'daughters' sit and visit. She would put up with any pain and problems in her life if she had the gentle conversation of people she loved to lift her spirits.

"So, tell me all about the wedding plans!"

They took turns telling her everything they had talked about, and updating Maria on everyone's news. With their circle of friends growing, it took more time to keep up with it all, and Maria didn't want to miss anything.

When they left, she forced herself to get up one more time to use the bathroom before trying to fall asleep. It was too much of a struggle to get up in the middle of the night, so she was learning to stop drinking anything after supper, and plan her bathroom visits when it was easier to get up.

Last summer she was still feeling well enough to watch Becky, but it was too much for her now. At least Carla had found a special needs daycare that would take Becky on the days they needed care, and it was working out, but it was also a reminder to Maria that her disease was progressing faster than she wanted to admit.

Settling into bed she thought back over her conversation with Jaz and Lisa. It seemed like Lisa was a little warmer to the idea that a wedding could be a good thing. While she knew that it was still unlikely Lisa would ever agree to try dating, the whole thing gave Maria a tiny glimmer of hope that Lisa would find someone to spend the rest of her life with.

There were times when Maria felt overwhelmed with anger at her husband and herself for how their actions changed Lisa's future. She tried to imagine how things could have been different. She should have stood up to Robert and insisted she get a job when Lisa went back to school. Or refused to cave to his bullying when he got angry about how close Lisa was to her mom when she was little.

She sighed. The problem was that he had scared her. His anger was like a slow burn, always threatening to explode. And no matter what, it was always someone else's fault. He never acknowledged that Lisa avoided him because he scared her, too. Or that their financial problems were because of his shopping and gambling problems.

The shock of finding out she was buried in debt was greater than the shock of Robert dying. And without Lisa there to figure everything out, talk to the bank, help Maria find the one small life insurance policy, sell the house, pay off the debts, and bring Maria to the city to live with her, Maria knew she'd be just as bad off—or worse—than the people she was trying to help.

And Lisa didn't seem to realize that she had already saved her mom's life. Not just saved her, but gave her a fresh start. Getting proper medical treatment, new clothes, and this beautiful house that Maria loved so much. Gone were the days where Maria sat at a living room window, watching the world go by and dreading the moment her husband would walk in the door from work.

The biggest challenge Maria faced now was enjoying her life no matter how many freedoms rheumatoid arthritis took away. She tried not to let herself think about how unfair it was to have her health stolen from her just when she was starting to live again.

At least now she knew that Lisa was surrounded by good people, and loved the work she was doing. If the housing project worked out, then she would have more than enough fulfilling work to keep her busy. Maybe that would make Maria's deteriorating health easier for her to handle.

CHAPTER THIRTY-ONE

Lisa

"Do you think they'll find any big problems?" Lisa asked Chris. Her heart was beating faster and her palms were sweaty as she watched the inspector go through the fourplex. They had been following him around for two hours already.

"Wow! You're really committed to this place aren't you?"

Lisa nodded, "I don't know what I'll do if this doesn't work out. Go back to work or something? But I can't imagine doing a job that fills someone else's pockets without doing any actual good."

"You could always take nursing training with Amy!" Jesse suggested.

"Very funny. You know I'm a numbers girl! So, when is Amy done?"

He beamed, "December! And then we're taking two weeks off to go to Mexico! It's my first time leaving the country!"

"That was my first time too, when I went with Mom for Christmas a few years ago. You're going to love it!"

The inspector walked over to them. "There's just the roof left to inspect and then we'll call it a day."

Lisa wanted it to be done so they could find out if there were any major problems. With a regular real estate transaction that would mean more negotiating, but she wasn't sure the current owner would budge on the price, even if anything was found.

"I'm going to wander down the street, guys." Maybe a little walk would help. Again, she was impressed with the nice feeling the neighborhood had. They'd probably all appreciate it if the fourplex was fixed up and occupied. Nobody liked an abandoned building on their street.

As she was walking back she saw Liam and Thea's dad getting out of a nice-looking car. He saw her right away and waited while she walked over. He was wearing a white short-sleeved shirt with a colorful tie and light grey dress pants and was carrying an elegant black briefcase.

"Lisa, right?"

"Right! Hi Aaron. How are the kids?"

"They're doing alright. Thea spends hours watching the bees at those flowers. I can't thank you enough for your gift."

"You're welcome! It's neat that Thea appreciates bees. Most girls would run screaming."

"Well, Thea is not like most girls." The sound of the ladder clinking loudly as the inspector brought it down caught his attention. "Does that have anything to do with you?"

"Me, and a few good friends. Hopefully we're you're new neighbors—in a manner of speaking. Our offer's been accepted on the property, subject to this inspection."

He looked at her carefully, and Lisa found herself caught by his kind, dark eyes. She opened her mouth to say something more, but didn't know what to say. When a smile broke across his face she couldn't help but smile back.

"Any chance I could convince you to leave the property as it is?"

"What do you mean?"

"I'm sure you know it's zoned for twelve units. But that would be quite the eyesore to our community. And all the construction would be upsetting to Thea."

"And the bees, I'm sure!"

He laughed gently. "Yes, the bees too."

"Well, there's a group invested in this property, and any decisions are made by all of us. But we only had plans to convert two of the units to four, so we could have two accessible, ground floor apartments to rent. I really don't think turning the building into something more than double the size is appropriate. But, like I say, it's not just up to me."

The front door opened, and Liam walked down the walkway to join them. His dad reached out and hugged him. "Hey you, how's it goin'?"

"Good Dad." He turned to Lisa, "Hey."

"Hey Liam."

"Lisa was just telling me that her and some others are hoping to buy the property next door."

"Can my friend and her mom come back?" He looked at Lisa with such hope in his eyes she didn't want to let him down.

"I don't know. Can you tell me a little about—" She was interrupted by Chris calling her over. "—sorry, I guess I have to go. But I'd like to hear about your friend."

"I'm always home from work by 5:30. Come on over if you're in the area."

Lisa paused for a second. She wanted to get to know this family more. "I'll do that. Bye!" She jogged over to the three men who were now waiting for her.

"Seems strange for a black family to be in this neighborhood," the inspector said.

"Seems strange to think that skin color dictates where someone should live," Lisa shot back.

He looked a little ashamed. "Uh... well... about the property. I really can't see much wrong except for the things that are so dated. Furnaces, hot water tanks, and windows all need to be replaced. But that's to be expected since nothing's been updated in decades. Foundation, structure, plumbing, and roof are all fairly good. I'll put it all in my report."

They thanked him and watched as he loaded the last of his things on his van and drove away.

"So, what do you guys think?" Lisa asked as they watched the inspector drive away.

"Actually," Chris started, "I was wondering what the neighbor said. Does he think it's a good neighborhood?"

"Yeah, he seems to. He was concerned that we might tear it down and build something bigger. Apparently it's zoned for twelve units."

"Twelve! That would be quite the contrast to the rest of the neighborhood!"

"Exactly what he said. Well, he used the word 'eyesore'." She made a face as she pictured how terrible a bigger housing unit would look in this older neighborhood.

"Personally I'd rather work with what we have here now. We're not in this to get rich and destroy a community."

Jesse nodded, "I'm with you. I like the idea of converting two units into four, but that's it."

"Well, this is it then!" Lisa found herself getting excited. "I'll send out a group email to everyone tonight. Guys! We're going to do this!"

"Looks like you won't have to get that job after all, hey? Well, I'd better get going. It's going to be crazy traffic leaving the city."

"Thanks for coming Jesse. Say hi to Amy!"

"Oh, I'll do more than say hi to her!" He winked and Lisa rolled her eyes.

"Newlyweds." She turned to Chris, "I'm going to go chat with the neighbor for a minute so I'll catch you later."

Looking at her watch, she hurried over. She really needed to get home and get dinner going so her mom didn't have to wait too long to eat. But she wanted to let Aaron know what was going on. As she walked up to the front door, she took a minute to appreciate the changes he had made. Now, the grass was neatly mowed, and the front yard blended in with the neighborhood.

When he opened the door, he was wearing a fitted t-shirt and denim shorts with a 'Kiss the Cook' apron over it. The smells coming from the house were mouthwatering.

"Oh! I had something to tell you, but those smells have taken over my brain!"

"I can honestly tell you I'm the *best* cook this house has ever seen. Come on in!" He stood back to let her in, but she shook her head.

"Sorry, I've got my own family to get home and start dinner for. I wanted to let you know that we're going ahead with buying the property next door. And we won't be expanding it beyond the current size."

"That's a lot of good news for us. Thanks for letting me know." He stepped forward and lowered his voice, "Were you serious about Liam's friend's family?"

"Definitely. I wouldn't offer if I wasn't. I *will* pop over in the next few days to talk with him if that's OK."

"I'll look forward to that. If you time it right, you can join us for dinner!"

Lisa laughed, "Very tempting. I'll see you soon! Oh, and the yard looks miles better!" It wasn't until she was driving home that it occurred to her how natural it felt to think of going to a strange man's house and eating dinner with him and his kids! This whole property thing was changing her.

CHAPTER THIRTY-TWO

Jaz

"So we're going to fix up the place really nice, make two of the apartments into four smaller ones, and then rent them out at really good rates to the people that need them most!" Jaz was in a coffee shop with Anna. They had been messaging back and forth for a few weeks, but this was the first time meeting up. It was Friday night and the excitement about buying the fourplex still had Jaz buzzing.

"Holy cow Jaz, that's amazing! You know, when my dad stopped paying child support my mom had a really hard time with everything. I remember watching her try to do the budget one night when I was supposed to be studying. She kept on scratching out the numbers for groceries and gas, trying to fit it all in. Having a decent apartment with lower rent would have made our lives so much better."

"How's everything now?"

"It's a lot better. I mean, I know I'll have huge student loans when I graduate, but at least I'll have a good job. And now that I'm working full time for the summer I'm helping her out."

"Yeah, you're really busy!"

"Well, I do babysitting in the evenings and on the weekends whenever I can. That one time I saw you at the theater was the first night I had off for the summer! And this is the second!"

Jaz paused, "I feel like I wasn't very nice to you in school. I judged you because you had a single mom and didn't have money to do all the stuff the rest of us did. I'm really sorry."

"It's OK. I did really want to fit in with that group... Funny how things change. Now I couldn't care less."

"Me too. But it took having a baby to wake me up."

"Look at you now, though! Did you even know anything about housing and poverty a year ago?"

Jaz smiled. "It was my first introduction to it. My parents kicked me out when they found out I was pregnant, and I ended up homeless. Well, sort of. A lady at the clinic where I got the pregnancy test took me to another lady who just let me live at her place! It was crazy!"

"Jaz! Why didn't you call me? Mom and I would have totally helped!"

"I was so ashamed about getting pregnant I didn't want any of you to know. But if I would have taken the time to know you better, I would've known you wouldn't judge me."

"Definitely not. But look at you now! Things have totally worked out!"

Jaz agreed. And now she had a friend her own age who accepted her just as she was, and wasn't trying to use their friendship to get something for herself. She felt pretty lucky. Her former teacher and Susan were both her top seamstresses now, and Jaz was confidently sending them more complicated projects. That, along with the other six women doing sewing gave her the chance to slow down a bit. Having time to visit with a friend was one of the perks.

"So, are you dating anyone?" Anna's question surprised Jaz so much she burst out laughing.

"Seriously? The one time I slept with a guy I got pregnant. And I didn't actually even get a date out of the deal. I think I'm done before I even start. How about you?"

"Wait. You got pregnant the first time?" Jaz nodded, "Wow. I mean, I know it's possible, but still. Wow. Me? I did go on quite a few dates at university. It's a lot easier without my mom breathing down my neck. But I really can't afford to get distracted. The only way I'm going to make it is to graduate in the shortest amount of time, get a job teaching, and keep working on the side too. So any future guys need to be nice, patient, and preferably very, very rich."

"I'll keep my eyes out for one of those!" Jaz joked. It was fun to have someone to laugh with about dating.

The next morning she was up early for another business meeting with her dad and Mr. Chen. Lisa had offered to watch Alex since Jaz's mom was playing tennis with friends and wouldn't be there.

This time she felt more confident talking about her plans. She had enough seamstresses lined up to more than meet demand, and she was slowly building up some inventory so they weren't always running low. Plus, with the extra help, she had time now to focus on the accessible clothing line. That was what she wanted to talk about the most, but she still had to wait for the men to chat about everything and anything, then cover where she was in the business right now.

"And is there anything else you have planned?" Mr. Chen finally asked.

"Yes. Now that the upcycling portion of the business is doing so well, I want to start a line of accessible clothing for people with disabilities. From what I can tell, this will need to be all new clothes. There are too many specific requirements to try to work with existing clothes." She paused, knowing the next statement could change everything about how her business was run. "I'm wondering if this needs to be something we outsource to another country."

The silence stretched on as both men considered her suggestion. Jaz knew they would speak when they were ready, and forced herself to breathe slowly and keep her body relaxed.

"It's a good idea. But it will take time. This isn't something you can start today and sell next week."

"I agree. And I'll need a full website, and maybe some professional marketing. I have quite a few rough designs already, so I know the direction I want to take, but actually producing it is a different story."

"How much can you invest in this?" her dad asked. "You've made quite a commitment to the housing project. And this new line won't come cheap."

"I don't know," she admitted. "I wanted to talk to you both first. I'll sit down with Lisa and see where we're at. Sales are doing really well now that we have more inventory, but I'm not sure of the exact numbers."

"You should always know exactly where you stand," admonished Mr. Chen. "If you're going to run this business like a professional, be confident with your information. Don't rely on someone else, even if you trust them. This is *your* business, not Lisa's."

His words stung, and Jaz had to fight not to let her feelings show, "OK, I'll do that from now on."

"That's good. I'll talk to some of my contacts about manufacturing clothes. Although it would be nice to take advantage of the Chinese market, you may need to look at somewhere less expensive."

"Thank you, George. I don't really work on the manufacturing end anymore. It's good that you have some contacts. Now, we have our tee time booked for 11, so that's all we have time for. When should we meet next?"

They set a date in a month, and Jaz was relieved she'd have time to put together some formal suggestions for the clothing line. She wanted to come across as a legitimate business owner, not some brainless teen.

As she walked home, she tried to shake off the hurt feelings from Mr. Chen's lecture. Popping in an earbud, she turned to her meditation playlist and focused on her '*I love myself*' mantra until she was home. When she walked in the door, she felt much better.

"So, how did it go?" Lisa was duck walking through the main floor holding a very proud Alex by his hands as he waddled slightly in front of her. He loved trying to walk, although he was still quite wobbly. He squealed when he saw his mom, but didn't slow his pace. Jaz walked beside them.

"It was good, but Mr. Chen gave me a lecture about not knowing my numbers. I guess I rely on you too much, and I need to try harder to always know where the business is at."

"What do you need?"

"I need to know what I can invest towards developing the accessible line. I want to do what you suggested, and build them new, which will probably require using another country for manufacturing. Mr. Chen asked me how much money I could invest since I'm already committed to the housing project, and I didn't have an answer for him."

"That's not a problem. We can look it over when Alex goes for his nap. Don't worry Jaz. You're learning a ton of stuff every day and running a very successful business. Whatever you don't know right now you can learn!"

"Thanks, Lisa. You always make me feel better."

CHAPTER THIRTY-THREE

Lisa

Everything suddenly got very busy for Lisa—just the way she liked it. She set up a joint bank account with Manuel and Jaz that allowed all three of them to deposit and withdraw funds for work on the property. It always gave her a thrill to go do what needed to be done, rather than waiting for someone else's approval. There was a lot of trust being shared within the group, but everyone seemed to be fine with it.

The day they got the keys, Lisa booked an industrial-sized dumpster to be parked in the yard. Everyone agreed they needed to keep the work off the street as much as possible, in consideration of the neighbors. One of the last parts of the project would be some landscaping to boost the curb appeal and give the new residents a home they would feel proud of.

Because most people were only available to work in the evenings, it was only Lisa and Manuel working on the first day. Together they began removing cupboards, fixtures, and appliances from the first unit that would be converted into an accessible suite. Manuel was very careful to set aside anything recyclable or reusable, and had already arranged for a charity to pick up the first load on the weekend. It was nice to know they could still do a bit to help other organizations.

By late afternoon the suite was stripped to the studs, and Lisa was exhausted. She left to make supper for her little family, and then they'd all be back that evening to get some more demolition done.

When she got home, her mom had surprised her by ordering in supper. "You'll have enough to do these next few weeks without having to cook for us too," she insisted. "Jaz will take care of lunches, and I'll order in suppers and pay for it."

Grateful, Lisa ran upstairs for a quick shower before joining them for supper. Between talking about the renos, Jaz's work on her new clothing line, and all the daily details of the Jazzy Clothing Company, conversation was fast and furious. Finally, Alex screamed in frustration when all his attempts to get everyone's attention failed.

Jaz turned to him, "No no Alex. You can wait your turn." She finished what she was saying to Lisa and Maria, before turning back to him and lifting him out of his highchair. "I think I just channeled my mom there for a minute. Weird."

Soon they were all headed back to the property after dropping off Alex at his grandparents. A few people were already there, and Chris had taken over supervision of the demolition. They were careful not to do too much until the drawings for the new units were approved by the city. Carla was taking care of that, and assured everyone it shouldn't take too long.

Maria parked her wheelchair where she could keep an eye on everything and everyone, and quickly found herself the designated contact person for all the neighbors who wanted to know what was happening. They were all relieved to hear the footprint of the building wouldn't change. She was in the middle of talking to an older mom who was complaining about the former tenants when the woman visibly stiffened.

"Here comes a problem," she muttered. "That kid is disgusting."

Maria turned in surprise and saw Liam walking towards her, "Who, Liam? Oh, he's lovely!" she waved her arm, "Hi Liam!" The woman stormed off.

"Hi. I guess everything worked out with the sale."

"It sure did! We're so excited to get started!" She briefly wondered what the other woman's problem was.

"So, when can I talk to Lisa about my friend?" Seeing her confusion he added, "The one who used to live here with her mom."

"Oh, well as soon as she comes out we can call her over. She really should take a break. She's been working all day already. In the meantime, why don't you tell me about yourself? After all, we're kind of neighbors now."

"Well, I'm going into eight grade now. I like all kinds of sports, you know, just stuff I play with my dad. And I like to play guitar."

"Are you on any teams?"

"No, they don't like my kind."

Before Maria could ask what he meant, Lisa came out the door with an entire bathroom counter in her arms. Liam ran over to help her carry it to the dumpster.

"Thanks!" she said as she walked over to Maria. "That thing got heavier as I carried it down the stairs! Are you doing all right Mom?"

"I'm fine, thanks. Liam here was wondering when he could talk to you about his friend." She looked pointedly at the dumpster Lisa had been filling. "Don't you think now might a good time for a break?"

"Oh! Well, sure. Where's a good place, Liam?"

"How about on my porch steps?"

"OK." She followed him over and they sat down. Lisa tried to stretch out her neck and back. "I'm so not used to this hard labor! So, tell me about your friend."

"Well, her name's Cherish and her mom's name is Nancy. They were doing OK here, but then the landlord raised the rent and they couldn't afford it. They stayed until they were evicted. It was really bad. I wanted them to live with us but my dad said it would create more problems for everyone. He gave them money for a hotel, but then after that her mom wouldn't take any more. When social services found out they were living on the streets they made Cherish go into a foster home."

He stopped to look at her carefully, almost as if he was deciding how much to say, "She keeps running away and getting into trouble. I told her to stay there. It's not too bad. But she thinks if it looks like she likes it there then they'll try and stop her from seeing her mom."

"Will they?" Lisa didn't know anything about the foster care system.

"Not according to their guidelines." He looked at her. "I read everything I could about it. But I guess sometimes social workers just do their own thing. So maybe? But if they came back and lived here again, then everything would be fine."

"Does her mom have a job?"

"Yeah, she's a care aid. It's really hard work. Especially when she doesn't have a place to stay and she sleeps in her car."

"Holy cow. That's rough." She turned to face him. "What makes you so sensitive to their situation? I thought boys your age were just interested in video games."

"I'm different than everyone else. It's fine. I guess it's made me notice stuff."

"What do you mean, you're different?"

"I'm trans."

How should she respond to that? "What does that mean for you?"

"People see me as a girl, but I'm a boy."

"Oh," Lisa paused. "That sounds like a hard thing to live with. But you don't seem upset by it…"

He shrugged, "It's just who I am. I'm lucky. My dad is cool with it. Most other kids like me, but their parents are pretty harsh."

"Well, having a supportive dad probably makes all the difference in the world. My dad hated me."

"That's stupid. Why?"

"Why did he hate me?"

"Yeah."

"I'll never know. He died a few years ago. I didn't even talk to my mom much until after he died. Then I found out he was really bad to her too. It nearly destroyed both of us, but now we're fantastic."

"That's good. Why's she in a wheelchair?"

"She has something called rheumatoid arthritis. It's where her body attacks itself, especially her joints. She *can* walk, but it's painful and she can fall and hurt herself."

"So you take care of her?"

Lisa smiled at her new friend. "Yep, that's my most important job."

"I take care of my sister. She's autistic."

"Ohhh, yeah I noticed you were pretty protective of her."

"Sorry if I was rude to you that day. I guess you're OK."

"You guess? At this point in our friendship, I expect to hear that I'm the most amazing person in your life—next to your dad of course."

Liam laughed. "Nice try!"

"Well, I should go back and get working some more. Can you see if Nancy and Cherish would pop over some evening so we can meet them? I'd definitely like to try and get them set up somewhere that they can live together."

"Really? You'd really do that?"

"I'll try!"

"Thanks! I'm going to go tell my dad right now that I'm going over to talk to her!" He got up and ran into the house and Lisa started walking back to all the activity at their property. A minute later Liam tore off on his bike, hollering something unintelligible to her as he went past.

She made sure everyone knew that a mom and daughter might be popping over one evening, and to see what they could do to help. It seemed unreal that things might actually work out, and she tried to shift her thinking from getting the project off the ground to having real people living there. She didn't realize she was smiling as she went back to pulling apart the old bathroom fixtures in the unit they were working on.

CHAPTER THIRTY-FOUR

Carrie

Carrie was working on removing carpet from the stairs of one of the units. She thought back to the worn, stained carpet of the townhouse she used to live in with the kids. It would have been very cathartic to pull it out! Oh well, she'd just have to live vicariously through this place!

The bathroom fixtures had already been removed, and Lisa was taking off the trim from the bedrooms upstairs. It was a good feeling to have everyone together working towards a common goal. Matthew was somewhere working alongside Jonathan, and Carrie had insisted Katie stay home with a babysitter. With all her chatter no one would get anything done, and Katie was excited to get the teenager's attention all to herself for the evening.

While she pulled away carpet and watched for staples, her mind wandered. Thanks to the brainstorming session with her friends, all the wedding plans were starting to come together. The church and restaurant were booked, Jaz was taking care of all their outfits, and decorations were all planned.

For favors for the wedding guests, Carrie was making a small hand-painted frame for each person with different quotes or sayings in each one. She was enjoying finding the right one for each guest.

And the honeymoon—Jonathan asked if he could surprise her, and she was relieved to have one less thing to plan. She knew it wouldn't be too far away, since it was only three days, but Jonathan hinted that it would be nice. Her parents and kids would be the first to try out the 'new' house, thanks to ongoing renovations to make it completely wheelchair accessible on the first and second floors.

Then they'd be coming back to pick up the kids and go to Disneyland for five days! Whenever Carrie got too caught up thinking about the honeymoon, she focused her attention on traveling with the kids instead. It was hard to believe they would finally go on a vacation together—something that was just a dream only a few years ago. Most days it felt too good to be true.

"Earth to Carrie!" Lisa called from the top of the stairs.

Carrie looked up to see her standing there with her arms full of trim, "Oh my gosh, sorry, didn't see you there." She stood up and moved the carpet out of the way so Lisa could get by. Definitely time for less dreaming and more paying attention!

The group agreed to finish up by nine, so they wouldn't disturb the neighbors. It was an incredible, satisfying feeling to see the worn-out, outdated items filling the dumpster and to know they would soon have things ready for new tenants.

Lisa was talking to a man at the house next door, so Carrie, Jonathan, and Matthew went over to meet the neighbor and say goodbye to Lisa.

"Oh, hi guys. This is Aaron. Aaron, my good friends Carrie and Jonathan, and their son Matthew. Hey! Matthew's the same age as Liam!"

Aaron said hello and shook their hands before sticking his head in the door and quietly calling Liam. Carrie decided there was something about these two that she liked right away. Liam came out and started talking to Matthew while the adults talked about their plans for the fourplex.

"Hey Mom? Liam was wondering if he could help with renos too when we come back."

"Oh!" Carrie turned to Liam "It's a volunteer position, but more capable hands would be a good thing. If your dad's OK with it."

Aaron smiled at his son, "You want to spend some time getting your hands dirty then?"

"Yeah!"

"Fine by me!" He looked at Carrie and Jonathan, "Lisa tells me this is a charitable project without it being a charity?"

"It is!" Carrie answered, "Some of us have very recent memories of struggling to keep a roof over our heads, so it's quite exciting to be part of something where we can help others with the same challenges."

"I'd love to help, but I need to stay close to the house for my daughter's sake. How about if I cook dinner for all of you and your families on Saturday? Lisa said there's about thirty of you including kids?"

"Uh, well, are you sure?"

"More than sure. Just have everyone bring some lawn chairs. That's about the only thing I don't have enough of!"

"Wow! Now we're guaranteed to have a full work crew on Saturday!" Jonathan reached out to shake his hand again, "Thanks! I'll happily work for food!"

They left Lisa still chatting, and Matthew said goodbye to his new friend. Back at home Carrie paid the babysitter and went to check on Katie who was in bed, but still wide awake. After an excited summary of everything she had done that evening, Carrie said goodnight and went back downstairs where Jonathan and Matthew were on the couch talking.

She felt like pinching herself to see if this was real. Never in her wildest dreams had she imagined a time when she'd be finished school, enjoying practicum, living in a nice house, not worrying about money, *and* getting ready to share her life with the kindest, smartest, best-looking man she had ever met. How did this happen to plain old her?

CHAPTER THIRTY-FIVE

Maria

"What kind of man offers to cook for a bunch of strangers?" Maria wondered out loud. "And what was going on with that neighbor who was so hateful to Liam? Is it because he's black?"

"I don't know much about Aaron but he seems like a nice guy. Those *do* exist Mom." Lisa pulled up to Jaz's parent's house, and Jaz got out to go get Alex.

"I know, I know. But he seems more than the usual nice."

Lisa agreed. "And as for Liam, he told me when we were chatting that he's transgender. Like, he has a female body, but he's a male."

"Oh, the poor boy."

"He seems fine with it. And he said his dad's really supportive. But what's this about the neighbor?"

"Well, when Liam started walking over the neighbor said he was disgusting and stormed off."

Lisa breathed out, "Wow. Just when one person shows how nice they are, another person shows what an ass they are."

Jaz came back carrying a sleepy Alex, with her dad behind carrying the diaper bag. "Did you ladies get a lot done this evening?" he asked through Maria's open window.

"We did! Well, I stayed in the yard and visited with people, but they made a lot of progress. You'll have to come by sometime and take a look!"

"I might do that. All right, then. Good night."

"What were you guys talking about when I came out? You looked so serious."

"I found out that Liam's transgender and Mom was telling me how one of the neighbors wasn't very nice to him."

"Oh, that's really bad. We had a transgender person at our school, and one day a group of people just attacked her. They had to call an ambulance. I didn't see her again."

They were all silent for the rest of the ride. It was hard to compare the little good they were trying to do with the huge amount of evil some people had to face every day.

On Saturday morning Lisa was gone early to work on the property. Jaz and Maria would join her later in the afternoon. They both had a day of work to do, keeping up with all the demands of the Jazzy Clothing Company. Besides managing all the listings, orders, and seamstresses, both of them were spending a lot of time researching accessible clothing. Between Maria's focus on practicality and Jaz's focus on style, they always had a lot to work through together.

Jaz had ordered a variety of fabrics that would cause the least amount of irritation to sensitive skin, and often used Maria as a guinea pig to see how practical her designs were when it came to actually wearing them.

And in the middle of everything, Alex was getting busier and more demanding. He was starting to crawl, and trying to pull himself up— although he hadn't managed that yet. When he couldn't do what he wanted he resorted to screaming, and Jaz ended up searching for parenting advice, on top of all her research for accessible clothes.

At ten Chris came back from working on their own house, and Carla brought Becky upstairs for Jaz and Maria to watch while Chris and Carla went to the new property to lend a hand. Having Becky around gave Alex someone to focus on, and Jaz made progress on all the things she needed to get done. She hoped it wasn't too much of a bother to bring Alex with her to the property later that afternoon. Her parents were going out with friends and weren't available to babysit.

Maria had her own priorities. She had been trying to get a hold of Martin—a friend she had met at the library—for weeks. Although she didn't know his whole story, she knew he lived with his kids and grandkids, and it was a rough situation for him. All she had was the house phone number for where he lived, but no matter how many messages she left, she hadn't heard back.

Before she broke her ankle, she could manage the five-minute walk to the library to try to find him. But now she really couldn't. The one thing that left her the most frustrated about her physical condition was when she needed to disrupt her girls' plans to help her out. Lisa and Jaz had enough going on without taking care of her, but there was no way she'd get to the library without help.

She had a feeling that she needed to find Martin *today*. The solution was easier than she expected. By the afternoon Alex still hadn't gone for his nap, and Becky had lost interest in trying to entertain him.

"I need to clear my head so I'm taking Alex for a walk. Hopefully, he'll fall asleep at the same time."

"Oh, could you do me a favor then?"

"Yeah, of course!"

"Well, remember that man Martin who I thought needed a better place to live?"

"Yeah—library guy!"

"I have this feeling I need to try to find him today. I've been calling the house where he lives with no luck. Can you pop into the library and see if he might be there? And if he is, have him come over for a cup of tea?"

"So you want me to go to every elderly man in the library asking if they're Martin, and if I find one I'm supposed to bring him home?"

Maria beamed, "Yes! Now he's quite thin, with white hair and glasses. That should help narrow it down!"

"Maria, I wouldn't do this for all the money in the world. But I *will* do it for you!"

"Oh, thank you, Jaz! Becky and I will watch TV together and wait for you to come home." She wheeled herself into the living room, where Becky was more than happy to turn on the TV.

Less than an hour later, Jaz was back with Martin. Maria wheeled to the front door, and was surprised at how much older he looked.

"Martin! You're a tough man to find! Come in, come in! Would you like tea or coffee?"

He cleared his throat nervously, "Well, coffee if you have it. But a glass of water is fine too."

"Of course! Come on in and have a seat at the table while I get things ready." She kept up a stream of small talk and simple questions until everything was ready. "Do you mind bringing the mugs to the table? I haven't quite mastered that in a wheelchair yet."

When they were sitting, she got right to the point. "How are things going at your place?"

"Fine, just fine."

"Fine enough to hide at the library every day?"

"Well, I don't want to complain. They're doing the best they can, and it isn't easy having an old man like me to trip over."

"Would you like to live in your own place?"

"I'm afraid my little pension has ruled that out." He put on a brave smile, "but at least I have a place to set my head at night. I'm very grateful for that."

"Excellent! I have the perfect solution then." She explained a bit about her own history, and their vision for creating accessible, affordable housing. "And someone kind and thoughtful like you will make a wonderful neighbor to the other people who'll be moving in."

The tears in his eyes surprised Maria, and she had to pause for a moment to keep control over her own emotions. "Would you please consider being one of our first tenants?"

"I don't know what to say. You really..." the tears were flowing freely now, and Maria quickly wheeled to the sideboard and brought the Kleenex box over. After a moment he continued, "I decided that this was the last day I would be a burden to my kids. I was trying to get up the courage to end it all."

"No!" Maria gasped, "You *matter* Martin! The world needs you! And so do your kids, even if they don't realize it right now."

"It's like you were sent to rescue me just in time. I don't want to die. I just... I'm so tired of being a burden. My daughter's expecting her fourth child, and with me taking up one of the bedrooms they have no space for another little one. The other three share a room as it is. I thought, if I go now then my life insurance and small pension could help them out and they'd have enough room for their family."

"Well, let's stop those thoughts right now and not entertain them again!" Maria forced herself to be firm and positive, but inside she wanted to collapse in tears. How could someone feel like they were such a burden that they would kill themselves?

He wiped his eyes and blew his nose loudly, "How can I ever thank you for finding me today?"

"Well, my daughter Lisa always tells people to pay it forward when she helps them. In fact, this whole project started when Jaz—that's the girl who found you today—decided it was time to pay things forward. I'm telling you, there's a whole lot of good out there to do. We just have to find it."

The door opened, and Lisa called that she was home.

"Come on in here Lisa, there's someone I want you to meet!"

Lisa walked in, and Maria saw her take a fraction of a second to compose herself in front of the man who had obviously been crying. She gave him her brilliant smile and reached out her hand, "Hi, I'm Lisa!"

He shook her hand, "Martin. Nice to meet you."

"So," Maria started, "Martin is living with a family who's running out of room, and needs a new place to live very soon!"

"That's perfect! Have you agreed to join our little project then?"

"Well, if you'll have me. I can't even say how grateful I am."

"Why don't you join us there for supper? The neighbor offered to cook for all of us and the smells coming from the house are to die for! I just need a few minutes to freshen up."

"Great idea!" Maria agreed, "And then you can see where you'll be staying. Did you need to call your kids to tell them where you are?"

"Oh, I always stay away until the evening if the weather's good, so I won't bother them. Are you sure?"

"Very," she said in a voice that left no chance for questions. "Like Lisa, I need a few minutes to freshen up and then we'll head over. What perfect timing for you to come over today!"

In the privacy of her bathroom, Maria let herself have a little cry. That had been too close! What if she hadn't found Martin today? She felt like forcing him to stay within her sight until she knew he would be OK!

Ten minutes later they were on their way back to the property with a full car. Alex gazed at Martin, who spent the entire drive making faces at him. Maria was so proud of her girls for the way they accepted him without questions.

When they arrived, he jumped out and helped Lisa take out the wheel-chair and lawn chairs, and then helped Maria get settled. "You're very good at this!"

His smile was a bit sad, "I did my best to take care of my wife. Lots of practice getting in and out of the car and the chair."

"You'll have to tell me all about it sometime. In the meantime, if you can wheel me over near that table, I'll introduce you to everyone."

Maria loved the way everyone welcomed Martin. Right away, Jonathan offered to give him a tour. As they walked away, she heard him say, "I'll show you your place first. It's not much to look at right now..."

Aaron came over carrying a huge pot. "There you are! How was your day?"

Maria found herself tearing up, and he quickly set the pot down on the table and knelt beside her. "Tell me," he said gently.

She leaned towards him and lowered her voice, "Well, that man Martin. He was feeling like such a burden to his family he was going to end his life. Today! And I had such a strong feeling that I needed to find him. I'd been calling his home for over a week with no answer. So I sent Jaz to the library today and she found him and brought him back." She wiped the tears away. "I just can't believe it."

Lisa came over and crouched on the other side of her. "What's up Mom?"

Maria repeated her story, and Lisa blew out a huge breath. "Thank goodness you found him in time. I'm so proud of you Mom." She reached up and hugged her.

"So this is what you've been up to. I'm really honored to know people doing such a good thing! I'm going to leave you two ladies here and get the rest of supper out." He smiled at them, "I didn't know this morning that I'd be cooking for angels."

By the time Martin joined them again, Maria was composed. He seemed to fit perfectly into their group, talking with everyone and offering to help. When it came up that he was a retired electrician, they all cheered.

Manuel placed a hand on his shoulder, "Teach me everything! I cannot manage to fix anything electrical to save my life."

"Don't teach him anything!" Betsy shouted, "That man and electricity do *not* mix!"

When Aaron came back with the rest of the food, and a clearly reluctant Thea trailing behind him, they all started eating. For the adults he had made jambalaya, and there were hot dogs for the kids if they preferred.

Maria was pleased to see Matthew and Liam sitting and eating together, and once Aaron checked that everyone had what they needed, he sat near Chris and Carla. She couldn't hear what they were saying, but it made her happy to know they could support each other with their special needs children.

She knew the day could have ended up much differently for Martin and his family. No matter whether they found him a 'bother' or not, losing him in such a tragic way would have been devastating.

CHAPTER THIRTY-SIX

Lisa

"Oh. My. Gosh. That was the best jambalaya I've ever had." Lisa stretched her legs out in front of her with a sigh. "And I'm pretty sure I undid any physical work I did today with how much I ate."

Jaz was struggling to eat, with Alex trying to grab her spoon with every bite.

"Here, give him to me." Alex immediately complained about losing access to his mom's moving spoon, so Lisa got up and started walking around with him. Easily distracted, he was soon jabbering back to her in the endearing way babies had.

"Who's this?" Aaron asked, getting up when she walked by.

"This is Alex. He's sort of an honorary nephew. His mom Jaz is over there," she pointed, "and it's her business earnings that will be carrying the monthly costs of this place once it's up and running."

"What? You guys aren't going to even break even?"

"That's not the point. The point is, a few of us have done really well with our jobs, and we want to use our excess income to give other people access to affordable housing."

"If you don't mind me asking, what's your contribution?"

"Well, besides gracing these people with my riveting personality," she laughed, "I used $100,000 in equity in my house to go towards the down payment for this property."

He stopped. "How old are you?"

"I'm 24. But, I guess I had a head start at the whole life thing. Long story, but I admit, it's an amazing place to be."

"What do you do for a job?"

"I'm a bookkeeper. I used to be the head of accounts receivable/payable at Golden Lion Investments, but now I freelance, and take care of the finances for Jaz's company."

"No way! I'm a CFO at a company just down the street from Golden Lion. I remember going out for a business breakfast a few years ago with their CFO and he was bragging about how their new accounting system was going to save them millions."

"Uh, the system I implemented where they started actually paying all their invoices on time and took the money they saved on fees and interest and invested it? Or the system where they started following up when lease payments were late instead of letting them languish for months?"

She laughed at his shocked face, "Like I said, I got an early start. And I had a really good mentor. So you're a numbers guy too, huh? That's pretty neat!"

"Sorry, I'm still stuck back where you saved the company and your CFO took the credit for it."

She shrugged. "It was pretty obvious how to improve things. But after that, the work got boring. I'm hoping this new project keeps me busy."

She shifted Alex to her other arm. He had been watching the new face intently.

"Can I hold him?" Aaron reached out his arms, and Alex leaned forward. "Wow. I miss the baby stage. Hard to remember my kids were once this little."

"You've got a lot going on with your kids. Liam told me a bit."

"He trusts you. And he likes you. Those are big deals for my boy."

"The neighbors... they're not all nice to him, are they?"

"It's kind of a double whammy for them. Maybe a triple. We're the only black family for a few blocks, Liam's transgender, and Thea's autistic. It's not so bad now, but before Thea was diagnosed and started therapy she spent a lot of her day screaming. Some people just couldn't understand that. They even called child welfare on us. Fortunately, Thea's diagnosis happened around the same time, so we had the professionals to back us up."

"Wow, that sounds rough. So she's a lot better now?"

"Well, you weren't here earlier when I was doing her hair. But we've got that down to about ten minutes of screaming, so I'm making progress!"

"And you're doing it on your own, right?"

"I am. I hoped for a long time that my wife would realize she made a mistake and come back to us. But now I can accept that this is my job and I'll do my best at it on my own. And in a lot of ways it's easier, because the kids aren't subject to us arguing about everything anymore." He stopped suddenly and looked at her apologetically. "Sorry, that was more information than you needed. Here, I'll pass this little guy back to you and start cleaning up the food." He smiled as he passed Alex back. "It was very nice to talk with you."

She watched him walk away and ask Liam and Matthew to help him clean up. The both jumped up right away. He was the complete opposite of her dad. Kind, thoughtful, completely accepting his kids just the way they were. She was glad the tenants in the fourplex would have such a nice neighbor beside them. And wow, that man could cook!

July passed quickly as the fourplex took shape. Lisa met Cherish and Nancy one night, and showed them around the first unit that was almost ready. Although it was the same one they had lived in previously, they hardly recognized it.

The cork flooring on the main floor made everything feel warm and look clean. Jenny was the one who had sourced the flooring, and it was a top of the line, sustainably produced flooring that would last for a long time. They chose a wider trim than was typically used in affordable housing to finish things off, and Lisa thought it made the whole place look better.

In the kitchen there were grey lower cupboards and cream upper cabinets with a durable dark grey countertop. The appliances were all top of the line and energy efficient, and each unit would have a stackable washer dryer unit—also sourced by Jenny to work well on minimal water and electricity.

Upstairs were two rooms with light grey carpet, and closets with build-in organizers. There was also a linen cupboard, and a spa like bathroom. Lisa and Jaz had spent a fun day visiting all the bathroom wholesalers in the area and competing with each other to see who negotiated the best deal. They ended up getting the bathrooms at close to cost so they splurged and added towel warmers to the orders for each bathroom.

Nancy was quiet as they toured the house, touching everything but not really saying much. Cherish, on the other hand, was enthusiastic about everything. "Mom! This is, like, a thousand times better than any place we've ever lived! Even the hotel Aaron got for us! This is going to be so *awesome!*"

When Liam called up the stairs, Cherish dashed down to see him, and then called up to say she'd be at his house. Once the kids were out of sight, Nancy turned to Lisa. "Look, this is a beautiful place, and someone's going to be really happy here, but it's not going to work for us."

"Nancy, I didn't work my butt off to get to this place and have a fantastic person like you with a wonderful daughter pretend you don't want to live here."

"Pardon me?"

"I'm no expert, but I know that you and Cherish will love living here. The only things we ask of you are one, understand that none of us is in it for the money. We ask you to pay a fair rent for your circumstances. Nothing more. And two, when you're in a position to, pay it forward. Help someone else in whatever way you can." She held up her hand before Nancy could interrupt. "If you can do both those things—and I already know you can—then you're the right person to live here."

"Why?"

She didn't say more, but Lisa knew what she meant. "Because we believe in second chances. All of us have had life things happen that were totally unfair. *And* we've all had some amazing opportunities that came by regardless of whether we deserved them or not. That's reason enough to do this, and hopefully to do a lot more."

"But I can only afford $500 a month. I don't know if you know this, but I was actually evicted from this house a year ago because I couldn't pay the rent. And it was nowhere near as nice as it is now."

"In that case the rent for this place is $400 a month. No damage deposit. And if life happens and you can't pay the rent, talk to me. I handle all of that personally. No matter what, we can figure things out so you and your daughter have a safe, nice place to stay for a long time. Please say yes."

For the first time, a smile crossed Nancy's face, "You're very determined, aren't you?"

"Determined, stubborn, thick-headed, definitely one of those! So, do we have a deal?" She stuck out her hand, and Nancy shook it.

"Yes ma'am, we have a deal."

"Great! The next step is getting you set up with furniture. That's

Carrie and Jonathan's area. Can I have your phone number to pass on to them?"

"I'm so sorry Lisa. I won't have any extra money for furniture."

"Yeah, it's not a money thing. Carrie and Jonathan will take care of all the costs. So, your phone number, please? And if you can meet me here again tomorrow evening we'll sign the lease and I'll give you the keys." She sensed another protest coming. "The lease will clearly state the terms we've just talked about, *and* it will give you a chance to build your credit. We're going to do everything by the books, but in a way that will help you out for a long time."

As they walked out the door, Liam and Cherish came over, both holding a paper plate with a cinnamon bun.

"Are those your dad's Liam?" Nancy asked.

"Yep, just cool enough for icing. Here, one for each of you."

"I have missed these cinnamon buns!"

Lisa took a bite and almost swooned. How did that man make things that tasted so heavenly every time? She savored every bite, and didn't say a word until she was done. "Wow! This makes me want to seriously consider moving here myself! Amazing!"

Liam grinned, "So can Cherish and Nancy live here?"

"Yep, we just finished working everything out. You two are going to be neighbors again!"

"SWEET!" Cherish shouted, "I get to live with my mom again!" She grabbed Lisa and took her breath away with a huge hug. "THANK YOU THANK YOU THANK YOU!"

Lisa hugged her back, "You're very welcome. We're lucky to have such great people here! And soon you'll meet Martin. He's moving into one of the upper units."

"He's super nice!" Liam agreed. "He's going to build some gardens at the back and plant wildflowers for Thea's bees."

"Hey!" Lisa protested, "I get credit for that idea too!" It had been fun to make plans with Martin about all the things they could do in the yard. His interest in gardening was another bonus for their project. She suddenly had an idea. "Now if it's OK, I'd like to take a picture of the two of you in front of your new house."

They happily obliged, and Lisa left them to look through the house again on their own while she went to find Chris and Manuel who were finishing painting Martin's place.

"Hey guys! Wow, this looks fantastic!" The suite had a bedroom in the back, beside a full bathroom. The rest of the area was an open plan living, eating, and cooking area with a big front window that gave a great view of the backyard. It had taken special planning permission to increase the size of the windows at the back and Lisa was glad they had pushed for the change. Martin could sit in his armchair enjoying the view of the backyard that he was so keen to get working on.

Carrie and Jonathan were out with him right now, visiting their favorite second-hand furniture shop to get everything he'd need. Martin's family was relieved that he had found a place to stay, and he was hoping his older grandchildren would visit on the weekends. Jenny had been looking out for a playground set that would fit along the side of the property, and give all the kids in the area a safe place to play.

"So, how did it go with the new mom?" Manuel asked.

"Well, it took some convincing, but she's agreed to move in with her daughter. I'll formalize everything tomorrow evening and give her the keys."

"I cannot imagine anyone successfully saying no to you!" Manuel said, and Chris agreed.

"You remember that!" Lisa said as she headed back out. She was excited about the people moving in and wondered where the rest of their tenants would come from. The group had agreed not to advertise at first, but keep their eyes open for the right people to help. So far it was working out!

CHAPTER THIRTY-SEVEN

Jaz

As soon as she heard Lisa come up the stairs, Jaz stuck her head out of her sewing room and called her over. "How did it go?"

"Good! She'll get the keys tomorrow. I had to really push for her to say yes though. She said she could only afford $500 per month, thinking that would put me off. Thank goodness we already agreed to charge everyone 20% less than what they said they could afford. I fired right back with $400 and she couldn't argue about *that*."

"I'll bet Liam was excited."

"He was, but not as excited as Cherish. She's like a 12-year-old version of Katie. Very enthusiastic, and the opposite of her quiet mom."

"Give her mom some time to settle in and she'll probably come out of her shell."

"When did you get so wise?"

She shrugged her shoulders and grinned, "Just talking from experience, I guess. Hey, can we go over numbers again tomorrow morning sometime? I have my meeting with Dad and Mr. Chen tomorrow night and I want to make sure I can answer all their questions this time."

"Of course. Let's do it after breakfast. I'm going to watch TV for a while with Mom. Want to join us?"

"No thanks. I've got some more things to look up and I'm watching some eBay bids on big lots of clothes."

"Don't work too hard!"

Jaz made sure Lisa saw her roll her eyes. She might be wise, but she still loved acting like a teenager.

She was nervous and excited about her meeting tomorrow. With a lot of trial and error, she now had a line of 12 basic accessible pieces that all worked together. It included a short-sleeve blouse, a long-sleeve blouse, a cape/jacket, one skirt, one pair of dress pants, one pair of stretchy pants that looked like denim, five t-shirts, and a scarf.

All the pieces could be easily put on and taken off by people with mobility issues, and for those who needed help getting dressed. One of Jaz's biggest challenges was finding fabrics that were easy-care, soft on sensitive skin, and durable. With things like Velcro, elastic, and easy-snap closures, the fabrics had to hold up to lots of pulling and still keep the shape of the fabric.

Plus, everything needed to look good! With Maria's help, Jaz picked patterned fabrics for the tops, and kept the pants and skirt in neutral colors that matched everything in the line. The scarf was a brilliant, multi-colored pattern that gave a pop to everything it was paired with. Jaz had ordered enough fabric to produce 300 scarves.

Her teacher recommended a girl with Down's syndrome Jaz could work with to make the scarves. The girl loved sewing and having a job she could do from home. Already she had produced 20 scarves that Jaz paid her a good price for. She didn't mind not making a profit on one item, and it was nice to know she wouldn't have to worry about quality control. Every scarf came back perfect.

Once Jaz proved there was a market for her clothes, she would expand to include men's and children's lines. She had some experience designing clothes that Becky would wear, and she was confident she could use what already worked to make an entire line for special needs kids.

And then there was Carrie's dress. It was beautiful. Mrs. Morton had agreed to help her with fitting it when the time came, but Jaz wouldn't do that part until a week or so before the wedding, so they knew it would fit. She had watched enough wedding dress shows on TV to know a bride's body could change in the months before her wedding.

Katie's dress used some of the same white chiffon as her mom's dress, but with a bright pink base. The chiffon would create a soft neckline and overlay the sleeves and the skirt. In her mind Jaz thought of is as 'Disney princess costume meets formal wear'. Jonathan and Matthew were both buying grey suits, and Jaz had already made matching dark blue bow ties for each of them.

Jaz was also working on a mother-of-the-bride outfit for Carrie's mom using everything she had learned researching accessible clothing. She had a beautiful dress with a watercolor of blues and greens across it that she was altering to be easy to put on and comfortable to wear.

Two hours later, the eBay auctions were over and Jaz was ready for bed. She won one lot of clothes for an excellent price, even with shipping combined. But the price for the other one ended up going higher than her budget. It was ironic that the girl she used to be didn't ever wonder how much things cost. The girl she was now ran her business—and her life—according to dollars and cents.

The next morning she surprised herself by sleeping until Alex woke her up. Often she tried to get an hour of work in before that. But it felt like she was caught up on sleep for a change.

After breakfast she mentally shifted to numbers. She wanted to be completely prepared for the meeting tonight.

"OK, you ready?"

Jaz nodded. She was sitting at the table with Lisa and her laptop. Beside them Alex was jumping around in his exersaucer, apparently trying to see how noisy he could be while his mom tried to concentrate.

"As you know, that Go Green episode you were featured on really sent the business into a different realm. Before you were clearing about $5,000 per month. Now it's averaging $3,000 per *week*. You're a successful businesswoman and designer in every sense of the word Jaz."

Jaz knew those numbers and wasn't surprised by them. "OK, but how do we use that to plan for the expansion?" She suspected starting the accessible line would cost a lot of money to start up, and would take time before showing a profit.

"Let's take a step back. I know you had committed up to $5,000 per month for the housing project. But with the way everyone's pitching in to help, the money from Manuel and Betsy, and Jenny's knack for sourcing ridiculously good deals, *plus* the fact that we already have two tenants who are contributing, I recommend we decrease your commitment to $3,000 per month."

"Is that enough?"

"Yes. That's enough to handle any maintenance issues that might come up, and to build a buffer in the account to cover the mortgage in case someone isn't able to pay their rent for a few months. And the $10,000 you gave when we purchased it? There's still about $3,000 left, so there's a month's start already."

"OK. That's good. Where are we for the new line then?"

"You've got $8,000 ready for start-up costs. And an additional $1,000 every week. You *could* apply for a business loan at this stage. I don't know too much about that end of things, but your dad and Mr. Chen might have some thoughts."

"It depends on how much it will cost to get the first line made. We have to pay in full for all the fabric, supplies, and labor. I really wish we could do it all from here, but I'm worried it will make the cost of the clothes too high."

"Plus you need the consistency that a factory offers. This is a whole new ball game you're playing."

"*We're* playing," Jaz corrected her. "I wouldn't be here without you, and your mom, and all the people working with us."

Lisa smiled. No chance of all the success going to Jaz's head. She was too grounded for that. "I'm going to print up the exact numbers for you to bring tonight, along with the projections you've made about how long it will take the line to start showing a profit and everything that goes along with that."

"Oh, and Jonathan confirmed last night that his friend from Singapore can take care of the new website. It will cost about $1,100, and then I'd like to find someone who can maintain it for us. We'll only need to update it when we add a line, and for each new season of clothes so it's not a daily thing like we have now with Instagram. But it needs to be perfect. We also need a professional photographer when the time comes."

"You have all that on your list of tasks?"

Jaz nodded.

"OK, next question that we've all been trying to ignore: What are we going to do when Chris and Carla move out at the end of the month?" Carla was still taking care of all the shipping for the Jazzy Clothing Company, which had turned into a part-time job. When they moved, she wouldn't have time anymore. Even if she had time, they needed someone close by. Sales were big enough that shipping needed to be done on a daily basis.

Jaz lowered her voice, "And what will your mom do without watching Becky when school starts again?"

Lisa sighed, "I don't know. But let's face one problem at a time. Actually, it's three. Who will do the shipping, how are we going to manage our increased inventory, and are you moving to the downstairs suite when they move out?"

"Is business always like this?" Jaz wanted to change the topic to something other than moving to the downstairs suite. It would be time to decide soon, but she wasn't ready for it now.

"What do you mean?"

"Well, you have a problem, you figure it out, you get more sales, and then that creates another problem you have to figure out."

"I guess it is like that, but most people love the constant challenge. I know you'd rather just design clothes and sew, and not worry about the rest of this. But it's important for you to be engaged in every decision. It gives you power and control over your destiny, and a lot of people never get that in their working lives. Remember, at the end of the day it's your name on the business. Literally."

"You're right. OK, so we have the money figured out, but we still need to figure out how to handle the shipping and the inventory."

"And all the details about the new line."

"Yeah, and that. No biggie, right?"

"Jaz, you can do this! Just make sure you're keeping track of everything you need to do, and only focus on one thing at a time. Sometimes looking at the big picture is too overwhelming, but if you tackle one small step at a time, it'll all get done."

"*Now* who's the wise one?" Jaz teased.

"Wise enough to know your son's about to hit the roof if you don't give him some attention." Alex was getting louder and louder, and Jaz knew Lisa was right.

"Alright you, is it time for a change in scenery?" She lifted him out of the exersaucer and he kicked his feet in delight. "Ooof. Geez buddy. Go easy on Mommy!"

CHAPTER THIRTY-EIGHT

Carrie

"So," Carrie tried to act casual as she walked beside Jonathan, "I paid off that credit card balance this morning."

He stopped, grabbed her by the waist and swung her around. "Carrie! That's amazing!"

She laughed and waited for him to put her down, "I thought you might like that! Sales were higher than I planned this past week so I finally paid it off! I swear, it feels like I've lost weight doing it. It was bothering me more than I realized."

"I'm so proud of you!" he leaned over and kissed her before opening the driver's door to her car. They were driving to Lauren and Dustin's to get their truck, and then going to pick up Nancy and Cherish for some furniture shopping. The kids were staying with Katie's favorite babysitter again, but Carrie had promised Matthew that when he started eighth grade in September, he'd be old enough to take over babysitting duties.

"And I'll have my student loans paid off before the wedding," she promised.

"How are you pulling this all off? I mean, you're gone three days a week as it is! And you've taken over getting everyone set up with furniture as they move in."

"Yeah, but I still have three days left in the week to work on frames, and Matthew's been really diligent about helping out."

"He'll have enough saved to buy a truck when he turns 16!"

"Probably by the time he turns 14 the way he's going!"

"He seemed to get along really well with Liam last week. That was neat."

Carrie agreed, "Sometimes I worry that he's too content to just stay at home and hang out with us. That will *not* be the problem when Katie's 12!"

"By then Katie will have a few little siblings to keep her busy."

"I hope so..."

He reached out and gently stroked her hand, "We'll figure it out. Don't worry." Carrie wasn't so sure. She had wanted another baby when Matthew was little, but eventually gave up hoping. Katie's arrival was a happy surprise in the middle of a terrible marriage but Carrie always wondered if there was a reason she didn't get pregnant easily. She'd love to have more kids, but she wasn't sure they'd come from her this time around.

After parking in front of the house, she turned to him, "I'll try not to. I love you." She leaned over and kissed him.

A pounding on her window made them both jump.

"Get a room you two!" Lauren yelled, "This is a family friendly neighborhood!"

Carrie got out of the car and didn't even try to hide her blush. She wrapped her arms around Lauren. "Hey you! How's today?"

"Today's not bad. Well, except for the old couple making out in my front yard! Hey Jonathan!"

"Hey Lauren! You've got the beast all ready for me?"

"Well, here's the thing about that..." she held up her hand and clicked a remote. A shiny red truck across the street beeped twice. "The beast can live at your place now. I got me a brand new baby!"

"Holy cow Lauren! Congratulations! Oh my gosh, you didn't even tell me you were getting a new truck!"

"I couldn't believe it until I signed the papers. Actually, I still can't believe it. This piece of white trash is moving up in the world!"

Old labels were hard to lose, especially in Lauren's case. She was a talented artist who spent her days turning cast-off paintings into brand new works of art. But she still saw herself as the broke girl from the shelter.

"You know the facts really don't support this idea that you're white trash," Carrie reminded her.

"I gotta say, I almost agree with you when I'm driving my new baby! OK you two, try not to gross out that mom and her daughter when you're in public, hey? Nobody needs to see you groping each other when they're trying to start a new life."

"I'll keep that in mind," Jonathan said dryly, "but you can't blame me for not keeping my hands to myself. Not around her," he nodded his head towards Carrie.

"Oh my gosh you two. Let's get going!" Carrie said. She started walking to the old truck and then paused. "Wait a minute... you said this truck could live at our place?"

"Yep! It's our contribution to the cause. I'll keep the insurance going on it, but use it for whatever you need to help the new people out. Or to haul stuff from the property. Whatever, babe!"

Carrie walked over for one more hug. "You are amazing, you know that?"

"Yeah, yeah. Get going now!"

As they were driving away, Carrie said, "Did you notice?"

"I did. Not a single swear word. When did that start?"

"No idea. Maybe with Brittany chattering a mile a minute, Lauren couldn't get away with it anymore! And wow, buying a new truck? That is so cool!"

"Well, she couldn't do it without you selling her pictures for her."

"Maybe not, but the point is that she's making enough money to do things like that. I can't wait to see what she does next!"

The rest of the day Carrie felt like she was floating. She would never see another piece of mail come into the house with Don's name on it— those credit card statements were now a thing of the past. Lauren was feeling better about herself and had a shiny new truck to remind her of her success. And shopping for furniture with Nancy and Cherish was a lot of fun.

After finding all the basics at the thrift store, Jonathan insisted they go to Ikea for some accessories. True to his promise, he had ordered new mattresses online that would get delivered to the new house later that day. Cherish was chattering a mile a minute to him while she tried to pick out a lamp for her bedside table.

Carrie walked with Nancy a few steps behind them, "You'll have to give me some advice on parenting an enthusiastic 12-year-old! My daughter's a lot like Cherish and she's only seven!"

Nancy laughed, "If it wasn't for her, I'd be lost. She keeps the life in me whenever I've run out."

"It's been a rough year for you."

"Very. I don't know how we made it. At least we have a good social worker now. He came and visited me at the new place this morning—

even though it's a Saturday—and said she could stay the weekend with me and he'll officially close the file on Monday."

"So, you don't have to deal with any follow-up visits or anything?"

"Nothing! Since there was never any concern about abuse or neglect, we can put that all behind us now. I feel so blessed to be able to give my daughter a home again. I can't thank you all enough."

"I have a feeling you two will do some amazing things for that neighborhood. They're lucky to have you back!"

When they got to the apartment with a truckload of furniture and accessories, Martin came out to meet them.

"Welcome! I'm so glad I'm not on my own here anymore!"

Cherish ran up and hugged him. "Hi Mr. Martin! Wanna see my new stuff? I have everything for my bedroom!"

"I sure do! You fill my arms and tell me where to go and I'll help you move everything in."

It wasn't long before the mother and daughter were happily settled in their new place.

"Oh, I almost forgot one thing! Cherish come give me a hand, please." She got up and followed Martin out of their home.

A minute later they walked back to the apartment carrying armloads of overflowing grocery bags. "This came for you a little while ago! Courtesy of Maria. It's her thing—I got a kitchen full of groceries too when I moved in!"

"Mommy! Mommy! There's chips and cookies and *everything* in here!"

Carrie and Jonathan said a quick good-bye and slipped out so Cherish and Nancy could enjoy unpacking the bags together.

"Wow, the whole day has been amazing, hasn't it?" Jonathan asked as they drove back to Lauren's to get Carrie's car.

"Very. I'm going to need some time to let it all sink in. And we still have room for four more tenants to move in!"

"Any leads on the next people?"

"Not yet. Maria's convinced that the right people will show up at the right time. That woman has enough faith for all of us."

"Have you heard from Susan? Is she doing OK in that new place?"

"More than OK. Maria was talking with her on Saturday and said she's so happy. She gets to spend her days sewing, and doing whatever she wants without slaving for her daughter. They tried to get her to agree to watch the kids for the summer and Susan said no. So the son-in-law decided to take all the holidays he's been banking and stay home himself. Sounds like it will be really good for the whole family."

"That's good to hear. I'll bet he'll have a new appreciation for how hard she was working for them! Now, how about we celebrate your successful day and take the kids out to dinner?"

"Again? We went out for dinner last week!"

"Are you saying you'd rather go home and cook dinner and do the dishes when you could spend it relaxing with me and the kids?"

"Well, when you put it that way..."

CHAPTER THIRTY-NINE

Maria

"Are you sure about this?" Maria asked. "I mean, I'm so happy that you're building relationships with your parents, and getting advice from your dad, but this is a big step. And there may be times when you have to stand your ground."

"If it were Mr. Chen offering to help run the business, that would definitely be a problem. But Dad really respects me, and I'm not afraid to tell him that we're going to do things my way."

"Well, as long as you're sure, then I'm sure. Having your dad to help with all the negotiations and business demands could be really good for you."

"I had no idea expanding would be this much work. And apparently he's been wanting to retire from his current job for a while, but he didn't want to suddenly be at home all day with nothing to do. So I'm pretty sure it's a win-win for both of us. He still gets to do what he loves, but without the pressure of a full-time job. And I can get back to designing and sewing and you can get back to being an Executive Assistant instead of the vice-president of the company!"

"You know I'm happy to help with whatever you need, right?"

Jaz leaned over and hugged Maria, "I know. And I'm really thankful for all the extra stuff you've been doing these past months. But now your only jobs are booking client visits and keeping the seamstresses on track, ok?"

"Yes ma'am! Now, you go off and have a good day with Anna!"

"I will! Thanks again!"

Maria smiled as Jaz left with Alex. She was stopping at her parents' to drop off Alex before going to hang out with Anna for the afternoon. It was good that Jaz finally had a friend her own age to spend time with sometimes. Becoming a mom made her grow up, but she was still young and needed times to relax.

Now that her dad would be helping out with the business, Maria hoped Jaz would relax even more. She tried not to worry about things —that never helped anything. But Jaz was such a hard worker that sometimes it seemed like she would push herself too hard. If Stanley was really joining the team to help Jaz, then Maria would recruit him to help his daughter enjoy life instead of working all the time.

With Lisa away at the new property for the day working with Martin on the landscaping, Maria found herself home alone. Even Chris, Carla, and Becky were gone. Probably putting finishing touches on their new house. Soon they'd be moving out, and many things would change again.

It was the first time she could remember that being home alone felt good. She loved all the energy and excitement that the girls and their projects brought to the house, but the last two months had really been over the top. All she wanted to do was get settled in her recliner with a book that she had been trying to read for over a week.

Her phone ringing an hour later created an unpleasant interruption, and she was tempted to ignore it. On the last ring before it went to voicemail, she answered.

"Hello?"

"Maria? It's Mark Naylor here, the host from the Go Green segment?"

"Yes, of course. How are you, Mark?"

"I'm doing well, thank you. And you?"

"Oh, quite good."

"The reason I'm calling is a little unusual, but I thought you might be able to help. I'm not sure if you ever watch 'Five on Your Side', but it's where individuals who have an issue with a company can get our investigative reporter to help them out."

"Well, I'm afraid I don't watch much news, but I know what you're talking about. Go on."

"Our reporter is trying to help a lady right now who's been evicted for damaging an apartment. The thing is, the landlord has been doing renovations, and it's restricted her ability to get her wheelchair through the hallway to her entrance, so it's been rubbing against the wall. It's full out discrimination, but right now she's living in a hotel room and quickly running out of money. Did that housing project you ladies were working on ever get off the ground?"

Maria smiled to herself. OK, so she wouldn't be getting much rest this afternoon after all. But this phone call was meant to be. "Oh, we more than got it off the ground Mark. We have a completely accessible suite just waiting for a tenant."

There was a pause at the other end of the line. "Are you serious?"

"Completely. Let's get this lady into a home where she'll be welcome, shall we?"

"I can't... I don't... wow! Um, she's going to get a settlement eventually. But she's really low on resources right now. What's the—"

"Mark. Money isn't a problem. Lisa can explain it better than I can, but we don't charge a damage deposit, and rent is a portion of whatever each person can afford. No matter what her situation is right now, she's welcome. I am going to need a few things from you though. Can you send me an email right away with her name and her phone number? Is it OK for us to call her directly or do you want us to go through you to start? Let me see, it's three right now, so we could arrange for her to come look at the place still today. Lisa's over there right now—"

"—Are you even for real? Maria, this is amazing! You know, we really try not to get emotionally involved in these stories, but this one really got to me for some reason. I'm going to hang up and go get my colleague, and then we'll call you right back OK?"

After Maria hung up, she called Lisa to pass on the news. Lisa promised to email everyone right away to let them know about the potential new tenant and find out who was available to help her move in.

"Well," she said to the empty living room, "that's what I get for thinking I'd have a quiet day!" She laid her head back and closed her eyes, breathing slowly while she waited for her phone to ring again. When it rang she was almost falling asleep.

"Hello?"

"Maria, sorry for the delay there. The lady's name is Nicole Sanderson —I'll email this as soon as we've talked. She's having a hard time believing someone will just offer her an accessible suite without a down payment, but I've assured her you're completely legitimate. She saw our episode where we featured the Jazzy Clothing Company, and she's quite the fan. She's happy to have you call her, and then everything's up to you!"

"That's perfect, Mark. Now, we actually have two accessible suites. They're pretty much brand new, and I've checked everything out personally. If you know of someone else in need, please call me, OK?"

"Yes, wow. I don't know where it would fit in, but I'd love to do another feature where we talk about this housing project—"

"—stop right there. This project is not to be featured anywhere. Do you hear me?"

"Well, the publicity could be really good for you!"

"We don't want publicity, and we certainly don't want to use our tenants to promote any sort of agenda. That's off the table. You can call me personally, but nothing of this goes public, OK?"

"Alright. I don't understand it, but I'll respect it. And in the meantime, thank you so much for helping Nicole out."

"You're welcome. Now send me the email so we can get that woman home."

The conversation between Maria and Nicole mainly involved Nicole not believing someone had a home for her, and Maria assuring her they did. But when she agreed to drive over to the property and look at the suite, Maria knew she'd want to stay.

When Lisa came home with takeout for dinner after showing Nicole the place, she gave Maria all the details.

"First of all, we need to get the city over to the property as soon as possible to set up a wheelchair parking space and change the curb. We forgot about that when we looked at the property initially. Nicole's really resourceful. She parked near the end of the street where there's a smooth access onto the sidewalk, but that's not a good long-term solution."

"Does she have some mobility then? How did she get in and out of the car?"

"She's got a Drive From Wheelchair van. I don't know her story, but she seems really determined to handle everything herself. Anyways, once she was on the sidewalk, everything worked really well. She said the suite is miles better than where she was staying, and she even seemed a bit excited when she left."

"So everything's set for her to move tomorrow?"

"Yep. She said she can get help at the hotel to move her things into the van, and we'll be waiting at the other end to move in. Martin gave her his number and told her he's always around to help out. I guess her biggest problem will be getting the rest of her things from the old place because they changed the locks. But the news reporter is going to take care of all that."

"Mark wanted to do another piece on us and the project, but I was adamant when I said no. I hope he listens."

"Can you imagine? Publicity is the *opposite* of what we're looking for!"

"Does Nicole work?"

"Not at the moment. She had a job at a call center, but when she was evicted she missed a few days of work so they fired her. She was pretty worried about paying the rent without a job. But I'm sure she'll find something once she's settled. The former landlords were actually threatening to sue *her* for damages so the whole thing was pretty stressful."

"Sue her? What were they planning on getting from her?"

"Apparently the van she drives is worth a lot of money. They were claiming it was an asset and that she should sell it."

"And lose her ability to go anywhere? To work? Horrible people!"

"I agree. So now she has a safe place to live, and she can still get to and from work. When she gets another job."

"So she doesn't have any issues with her arms or hands?"

"Nope. At least not that I know of."

"Would she be interested in working for us? We still need someone to do all the shipping."

"How would that work? She can't be hauling stuff everywhere."

"Let me think about it. And she might not even be interested. But Mark said she really liked watching the episode he did about the company..."

Just as Maria was falling asleep that night, the solution came to her.

She sent herself a voice memo on her phone, and lay back for a good night's sleep.

The next day Nicole Sanderson officially became the head of shipping for the Jazzy Clothing Company. Six days a week she drove her van over in the morning to pick up all the orders. Back at the property, Martin helped her bring it all into her suite, and she took care of printing the labels and packaging everything. The delivery company came every afternoon at two to pick everything up.

As the self-designated handyman of the property, Martin built Nicole a special storage unit for all the packing supplies that also had a fold-down table so she could have a big surface to work on. That part exceeded Maria's plans, but it was a satisfying feeling to know that Nicole had access to a job where she didn't have to worry about losing it if her circumstances changed. They'd make sure she could do her job for as long as she wanted.

The days were still fulfilling for Maria, even as things slowed down a bit. But the nights were getting harder. That was when she really paid the price for her activity during the day. Often she lay in bed watching the minutes change on the clock into the early hours of the morning before exhaustion would overrule the pain. She wondered if she'd soon be relegated to only doing things from her phone or computer. At least she had played a part in helping Nicole. She decided that after Carrie's wedding she'd finally let her doctor know that she wasn't doing so well.

CHAPTER FORTY

Lisa

Lisa sat in the car for a moment, watching the scene across the street. Aaron was in the front yard with Liam, tossing a football back and forth. She couldn't tear her eyes away. Aaron's kindness and love seemed to float around him, whatever he did. He always came over to chat with Lisa when he saw her at the property, and he already knew all the tenants.

But Lisa was realizing there was more. At least for her there was. It was a strange feeling, but she found herself looking for him, even on days when she knew he was at work. And when he came over she wished she knew how to flirt, or somehow delay things so she could spend more time with him.

Suddenly he noticed her in the car and waved. "Get it together Lisa," she muttered before getting out. She popped the trunk and started to unload the plants she bought for Martin's raised garden.

Aaron jogged over, "Need some help?" he asked before reaching in and grabbing a tray of flowers. His arm brushed Lisa's and she nearly jumped. *Focus! Focus!*

"Uh, yeah. Thanks!"

"You are definitely going to be on Thea's favorites list with all these flowers!"

"Well, um, that's great!"

He paused and looked at her. Lisa found herself trapped by his gaze. In the back of her mind, she was grateful her hands were full so she couldn't reach out and touch him.

"Are you OK?" he asked gently.

"What, me? I'm fine! Yeah, great, actually." She reached her elbow up to try to close the trunk, but Aaron leaned over and did it for her. There was a waft of cologne or something, and Lisa bit down on her tongue to stop from saying anything really stupid. What was wrong with her?

"OK, well lead on. I'd offer to help you plant these, but I'm pretty sure they'd die if I touched them."

You could touch me, she thought. *What the heck Lisa? He's too old for you, and he's got two kids, and he probably wouldn't even be interested in a white girl.*

She tried not to stare as he squatted to carefully put the tray of flowers down. When did he get so irresistible? She'd been spending time with him and the kids all summer and hadn't felt anything different. Why now?

"Are you sure you're OK? Did you need to lay down at my place or something?"

Her eyes nearly popped out of her head. The last thing she needed right now was to be in closer proximity to him. "No, sorry. Thanks, I'm fine. Hey, do you want to see if Thea will come over and plant these with me?" It was the only thing she could think of to get some space from Aaron and catch her breath.

"That's a great idea! I'll go see." He jogged away and Lisa didn't even try to stop herself from staring at him.

"Oh, you got it bad!"

She spun around, "Martin! How long have you been here?"

"Long enough to see that you've fallen quite hard for our good neighbor."

Groaning, she put down the tray of flowers and covered her face, "This cannot be happening to me! I've never liked a guy *ever*! What do I do? How do I stop it?"

He chuckled, "Oh, there's no stopping it my dear. Love's tricky like that."

"I'm not... I don't... Oh boy." She looked up to see Aaron walking back towards her, with Thea beside him holding his hand. *I've got this. Just focus on Thea.*

"Hi Thea! We have some more flowers for your bees here. Can you help me?"

Lisa sat down on the rounded edge of the garden border. Thea let go of her dad's hand, and sat right beside her. The closeness of the little girl grounded Lisa, and she gave her full attention to Thea.

"Here, let's make a nice little home for the first plant." She gently moved the soil away and Thea reached out to do the same thing. "Perfect! Now we need to give this plant a little squeeze so it pops out."

Thea squealed when the plant really did pop out, and Lisa laughed. "You got it! Wow, the bees will be so happy to see these flowers here. Maybe they'll tell their friends to come visit!"

Lisa tried to forget about Aaron, and focus on Thea. Sometimes it seemed like she was really connecting with her, but other times Thea looked right through Lisa. Today was a connection day.

When they finished planting all the flowers along one edge of the garden, they walked over to the hose to wash their hands. Thea shook her head 'no' but let Lisa hold her hands under the water until the dirt was all washed off. "There! Nice and clean. Let's go find Daddy."

She was thrilled when Thea put her hand in Lisa's. Something about that quiet trust made her feel like she was walking on air. Aaron was sitting on the front porch with his laptop. His smile made Lisa's heart do strange things.

"Well, here she is. The newest master gardener in the neighborhood," she said proudly.

"That was fun, Thea, wasn't it?" Aaron asked.

Thea tapped Lisa on her leg. When Lisa looked down, she signed 'thank you'.

"You're welcome! We'll have to do some more gardening soon, OK?"

"Did you have time to stay for a drink?" Aaron asked.

"Ah, no thanks. I promised Mom we'd spend the afternoon doing some shopping. I've been neglecting her a bit with all the stuff going on with the property here."

"You do an amazing job taking care of everything, Lisa. With Thea, too. Thank you."

"You're welcome! I guess I'll see you around then. Bye Thea." She tried to walk away without looking back, but she couldn't help it. He was still sitting there, watching Lisa with a strange look on his face. She smiled and waved before forcing herself to get in the car and drive away.

CHAPTER FORTY-ONE

Carrie

"So, next week you'll be on your own. Although you've been ready for a while." Dr. Henshaw looked at Carrie with a kind smile. The last client of the day had just left, after thanking Carrie profusely for all her help. For the next two months Carrie would see clients on her own, but still keep in contact with her supervisor.

"It's going to feel strange to be here in the office without you. I really appreciate all your advice and support these past few months."

"I'm always just an email or a phone call away. And I'll be interested to read your summaries when you send them to me every week. By the way, you're doing really well with all the paperwork. Keep up with that!"

"I will. Thanks again, Dr. Henshaw!"

"You're welcome, Carrie. You take care now."

Carrie stayed in the office after he left so she could get her notes typed up and sent off. It was always easier to do it before she went home. There was a nice feeling in the clinic today. Sometimes it felt like everyone was just hanging on by a thread, but today everything was running smoothly.

There was a quiet knock at the door, and then Kara stepped in. "Hey you! How did today go?"

"Really good! Give me a second to finish this and send it to Dr. Henshaw... All done!" She closed her laptop and looked up at Kara. "How are you?"

Kara collapsed onto the seat across from her, and Carrie moved around to the same side of the desk and sat down. "I'm exhausted! But good! I'm sorry I haven't had a chance to check out the property recently. How's everything going?"

Carrie updated her on the tenants they already had, and how much everyone was enjoying their new homes.

"So, still three to fill, huh?"

"Yeah. I was actually wondering if we could Airbnb the two-bedroom unit for a while. I know the finances are doing really well, but wouldn't it be great if we could raise the money for the next place?"

"Wow! You've really come around!"

"What do you mean?"

"Carrie, it was pretty obvious you weren't exactly excited about the idea when they first talked to you."

"Yeah. I was in such a rough place then, trying to connect with the women at the center, and feeling totally intimidated about counseling people here."

"But now?"

Carrie smiled, "So much has changed with me! I'm pretty sure Lisa, Jaz, and Maria haven't changed at all. It's just that I'm back to believing we can really make a difference for other people. At the time I wasn't so sure."

"I'm glad you're back to your optimistic self! Why don't you bring up the Airbnb idea with Lisa?"

"You know, I think I will! Although I'll have to drag her away from the property to do it. It seems like she's there every day, working on the yard, and checking in on everybody. You'll have to go by with Magnus sometime. They've got a playground and a playhouse installed along the side, and the back has raised gardens and two sheds—one for gardening supplies and one for kids' gear. It's pretty impressive!"

"And how are things on the celibate-until-marriage front?"

"Kara!" Carrie blushed, "it's fine, thanks for asking!"

"Sure you don't want us to take the kids for a weekend?"

"Yes, I'm sure. It's just over eight weeks now, and we're so busy with everything we hardly have time to get our hands on each other!"

Lisa laughed, "I'm betting you don't even see the light of day on your honeymoon."

"I'm betting you're right!"

"You know, I've been waiting for you to make an appointment to get birth control. Unless you've found someone else you like more?"

Carrie reached out and grabbed Kara's hand, "There's no one I trust more than you, and no one I like more, either! But, we're going to leave that part up to nature."

"Are you sure? There's nothing wrong with taking a year to enjoy life."

"We're sure. I don't want the kids' ages to be too spread apart. And Jonathan's so ready to grow his family."

"You deserve this, you know? You deserve everything good that's happening to you, and all the good things that are still to come."

Carrie let go of Kara's hand, and dabbed at the tears threatening to spill down her cheeks, "It's crazy, isn't it? The business, graduating,

Jonathan, the housing project. And it feels like we're only getting started. How can that be?"

"Well Carrie, sometimes the world gets it right and the good people really do get what they deserve."

Read on for a sneak preview to Book 6:

PART 1:

"Oh Jaz. It's magical!" Carrie slowly turned to one side and then the other, as if moving too fast would break the spell that she was under. Her wedding dress—custom designed by Jasmine Lee, owner and designer of the Jazzy Clothing Company—was beyond perfect.

The bodice fit her perfectly without any room to spare, and yet it felt like she could do anything in it. Over the shimmering white satin, the softest chiffon Carrie had ever felt wrapped around the off-the-shoulder neckline and around her arms in a narrow band.

The chiffon was also somehow overlayed on top of the fitted skirt as well, so it clung to the skirt and floated at the same time. If there was ever a time to channel a princess, this was it. Carrie continued to slowly turn around until she could see the long slit at the back of the skirt.

"Whoa! That's quite the slit!"

"It is OK? I can change anything you want!" Jaz was standing behind Carrie in tailored black dress pants with a white long-sleeved blouse that had an asymmetrical collar. She looked nervously at Carrie.

"Hey, if I can't look stunning on my wedding day, I give up! No, don't change a thing. This dress, I mean, wow! It's nothing like I could have imagined, but wearing it makes me feel like the luckiest bride in the world." She reached over and hugged her friend. "Thank you!" she whispered.

"Oh good! I'm so glad you like it! Holy cow, you're getting married in two weeks! Can you even believe it?"

"Sometimes it feels like Jonathan and I have always been together. And then other times I have trouble believing that any of this is true!"

A little voice called from another room.

"That's Alex done with his nap! Here, let me unzip you and then I'll let you get dressed on your own. Just put the dress on the chair here."

Carrie paused for a minute as Jaz walked out and closed the door behind her. She couldn't help feeling a bit of motherly pride for the teenager who had come so far since showing up on her doorstep, homeless and pregnant last year.

Just as she was pulling a cable knit sweater over her t-shirt, her phone rang. Seeing Kara's name pop up, she quickly answered. Why would Kara be calling her while she was working at the clinic?

"Hey Kara!"

"Carrie, we've had a crisis with one of your clients. I know it's outside your contract, but could you possibly come to the clinic right away? I tried to get a hold of Dr. Henshaw, but there's no answer. It's urgent."

"Yes, of course. I can be there in 10 minutes." She quickly put her phone back in her purse, checked that she was dressed and hadn't forgotten anything, then popped her head into Jaz's bedroom. "Something's come up with one of my clients and I need to rush to the clinic. I'll catch up later."...

PART 2:

"Hi Lisa!"

Lisa took a big breath and turned around. Today was the day. She *needed* to talk to Aaron. No matter what.

"Hey, how are you?"

"Good! Very good! Here, let me help you." He reached past her and took the three snow shovels, and a bucket of eco-friendly rock salt out of her trunk. It was probably overkill, but she wanted to make sure the tenants had what they needed when the snow came.

"Thanks!"

"Guess you're all set for the snow then," he said as they walked towards the tool shed at the back of the property. Lisa was responsible for managing the property that her and some friends had invested in five months ago. It was set-up to provide accessible, affordable housing and was the biggest project Lisa had ever participated in.

Aaron lived next door, and seemed to always be available to help. He had become a good friend, but Lisa was long past thinking of him as just a friend. After unlocking the shed and carefully storing the supplies, Lisa locked it up and turned to Aaron. He was gorgeous.

He was a good five inches taller than Lisa, with short black hair, perfect dark skin, and glasses in front of dark brown eyes that were perpetually crinkled at the corners from laughing. Aaron had a laugh that was like water dancing over rocks on a mountain stream—delightful and soothing all at once.

Lisa refused to let her vision travel down his body, but this single dad of two was in very good shape. She had no idea how he managed it, because he was always offering her baking or inviting her over for a mouth-watering meal.

"Um, where are the kids?"

"Liam and Cherish are out getting their bike-riding in before the snow comes. And Thea's still at daycare."

"Oh, ok. Um..." Lisa was never afraid to speak her mind. Except today. Today she could feel herself shaking inside. She *had* to tell him about her feelings for him. There was a tiny chance he felt the same way. After all, they managed to spend time together every week. But even if he did feel the same way, would he even want to do anything about it?

His ex-wife left when Aaron refused to 'fix' the kids. With a trans-gender son and an autistic daughter, they weren't exactly typical. But Lisa loved both kids exactly the way they were. Even though it had taken months for Thea to accept her as one of the safe adults in her life.

She knew Aaron's entire focus was on his kids. He lived for them, and he was the best dad she had ever met. Maybe that was all he wanted in life. Not to mention Lisa was white. Adding a biracial relationship into the mix might be too much—even for someone as big-hearted as Aaron.

He put his arm gently on Lisa's arm, and she felt heat flow all the way through her body. "Hey, is everything OK?"

She took a big breath, "Do you, um, can we walk?"

"Of course!"

They fell into step naturally and Lisa tried to organize her thoughts. Aaron seemed in no rush to make her speak. The air had that crisp feeling to it that came before the first snow of the year. Lisa was glad for the way it hit her burning cheeks. She tried to breathe deep and calm her pounding heart.

"So, here's the thing..." She looked up at him. No matter what he said, she'd never stop loving him. He was everything she didn't even know she wanted until they met. "I don't know how you'll feel about this. I mean, it's really unexpected and I've never imagined this could happen to me. Trust me on that. Um, the thing is...I've got feelings for you. Strong feelings. I'm so sorry. It's not what I planned at all. But I had to tell you." ...

A NOTE FROM THE AUTHOR

Thank you for taking the time to read *A Roof Over Their Heads*! If you enjoyed it, please consider telling your friends or posting a short review. Word of mouth is an author's best friend and much appreciated!

To be one of the first to hear when my next book comes out, and for a chance to win bookish prizes, sign-up for my newsletter:

www.carmenklassen.com

And please 'like' my Facebook author page:

fb.me/CarmenKlassen.Author

May all your days be full of good books, nice people, and happy endings.

Sincerely,

Carmen

ALSO BY CARMEN KLASSEN

SUCCESS ON HER TERMS SERIES

———

NON-FICTION TITLES

51212359R00163

Made in the USA
Lexington, KY
01 September 2019